A Lot To Die For

Alex Robert

This is a work of fiction. Any similarities to real people, past or present, places, actual events or situations are purely coincidental. This book should not be copied, forwarded, resold or given away in any form or means without the express permission of the author.

Copyright © 2025 by Alex Robert

All rights reserved.

BY ALEX ROBERT

DETECTIVE JACK HUSKER CRIME THRILLERS

Death Sketches
The Dead Don't Talk
A Dish Served Cold
Time To Die
The Killing Game
A Lot To Die For

Fear became his closest friend.

Chapter 1

The room was filled with animosity. Spiteful looks were being exchanged by three men sitting in opposite corners. Not one of them would get any closer to his enemies or offer anything but ill-intent. They had been in the confined space for nearly three hours and would remain unmoved until the end. This was a cut-throat business where there could only be one winner.

At the front of the room, a man was staring at them. His smiling expression was masked by facial hair. Chestnut brown, he would describe it as. To anyone else, his ginger hints were his defining feature. Throughout the three hours, he had done well to control those before him. He was now facing his biggest test.

"Ladies and gentlemen, this is the final item of the day. Lot two-three-nine is a beautiful Chinese lacquered trunk, believed to date from the late Qing period. I will draw prospective bidders to the condition report, which notes the trunk as being locked and without a key. Other than that, the trunk is in remarkable condition for its age. Who will start the bidding at four hundred pounds?"

The auctioneer's eyes flicked around the room. He knew where the bids would come from. Anyone else offering their hand would only be a brief participant. There was real anger amongst the protagonists, which would send the bidding skywards. The only question was who would blink first.

"If it helps, I will start at three hundred pounds."

Three men waited for someone else to make their move. Each could feel their fingers tingling. A narrowing of the eyes from the man sitting at the front was followed by a forceful raise of his hand.

"Thank you, Charles. That is three hundred pounds. Who will give me three-twenty?"

"Thank you...three-twenty...three-fifty...three-eighty...four hundred. I am at four hundred pounds."

The room fell silent.

"Four-twenty...four-fifty...four-eighty...five hundred..."

The action took place between two men in opposite corners of the room. With each bid offered, the hatred between them grew. Neither would be backing down and certainly not to the other. They continued until long after the guide price had been exceeded.

When the bidding reached eight hundred and fifty pounds, the man at the back smiled. His work was done. Charles Rickton had paid the full price and would go home feeling sore. He didn't want the item. He just wanted his adversary to suffer.

"We are at eight hundred and fifty pounds at the front of the room. If there are no other bidders, I will sell at eight hundred and fifty. Going once...going twice..."

"Nine hundred!" barked a voice, the tone filled with fury. Nobody needed an introduction to know where the sound had come from. The only surprise was that it had taken so long for his silence to be broken.

"Henry, stay out of this," growled Charles. "Nine-fifty and that is it."

His words were met by an impassive stare from the auctioneer. His job was to get the best price for the seller. He was not going to intervene in a private feud. Why would he? It was their money and his commission at stake.

"The bidding stands at nine hundred and fifty pounds. I am looking for one thousand."

"Why not?" smiled Henry Davenport, with an over-elaborate wave of his hand.

Charles Rickton's reddening face stared at him. The advice of his doctor had been forgotten. His blood pressure was rising; forced by a man who deserved nothing but contempt. There would be no backing down. The trunk was coming home with him.

"One thousand one hundred," stated the auctioneer in response to Charles's nod.

Another signal took the bidding up by another one hundred pounds. Charles never blinked and fought back, sending the price into orbit. They went back and forth until it reached eighteen hundred. The bid sat with Henry. Charles performed a quick calculation to add the buyer's premium and then shook his head. If he was lucky, he would get half his money back. The trunk was not worth it. With a defeated expression, he watched the auctioneer's hammer come down while a smug-looking Henry Davenport stared directly at him.

"You cretin," he mouthed towards his adversary, the insult doing nothing to dampen Henry's spirits. The battle had been lost. It would not stop Charles from winning the war.

As the room emptied, the enemies came together in the doorway. A jostle of shoulders suggested a confrontation was coming. Two of the auction staff moved closer, their presence preventing any reaction. It did nothing to quell the hatred that was bouncing between the men.

"One of these days you are going to get your comeuppance," warned Charles Rickton with an angry stare.

"Face it," grinned Henry. "The better man won, as he always does."

"Only by overpaying. That trunk is not worth half of what you paid for it."

"Or what you were prepared to pay for it," offered the third man as he walked briskly away from the older men.

Charles turned back towards Henry, their respective bodies puffed up like peacocks. Neither would offer a backward step when there was an argument to be won. It would lay down a marker for their next skirmish, which would be upon them within a week. Charles would not allow Henry to win that one. If he got his way, he would never win another auction lot again.

A LOT TO DIE FOR

***

Henry Davenport could not wipe the smile off his face. His adversary had lost and he was travelling back to his workshop with a van containing Charles Rickton's Chinese trunk. The price did not matter. It had been a profitable day. With Charles vanquished, he would dine out on the memory until he saw the detestable man again.

His driver sat silently beside him. He knew when to leave his paymaster to be alone with his thoughts. Robbie had worked for Henry for eight years. He had accompanied Henry to the auctions for most of them.

As they worked their way through the city's streets, they eased along in the mid-day traffic. A few shoppers were out though nothing like the levels expected at the weekend. That was when the trunk would take pride of place in Henry's shop window. Its prominent display would be perfect to antagonise his rivals.

When they turned in behind the shop, the yard opened up. Henry had done well to acquire the remaining buildings at an auction two years ago. It allowed him the space to expand. He now had two storage barns alongside his workshop. It made him the largest city centre dealer, something else that could only irritate his rivals.

Robbie parked the van outside the workshop. His eyes were on his boss, awaiting his instructions. He had not yet offered a word. Nor would he until they were out of the van. That was when a flurry of barked orders would come. They had bought eight lots in total. Half of it would be up for sale within days.

Henry got out and made his way to the back of the van. Robbie turned off the engine and caught up with Henry just as he was opening the door. The eagerness of Henry was obvious. The sooner his purchases were inside, the sooner he could assess what he had bought.

"I want the trunk to go straight into the workshop. That has to be ready for the shop window by the weekend."

"What about the rest?"

"The two paintings need checking over. The chest of drawers can follow the trunk into the workshop. Everything else can go into storage until we have space."

"I'll get the lads on it."

"Make sure they are careful with that trunk. One dint on the lacquer and we'll halve the value of it."

"I'll move that one with Graham."

"Make sure you come and get me when you open it. I want to be there to watch. You'll have to pick the lock. I'm not having it forced open."

"Don't worry; we're not about to do anything stupid."

Henry smiled. That was the reason why he used Robbie and Graham on such jobs. They both knew when to get on with their work. Better still, they knew when to stop. Too many so-called restorers took a gung-ho approach when a touch of subtlety was required. No matter how many times he told them, their answer was always a hammer and a chisel.

Henry left the trunk in Robbie's capable hands and headed into the shop. He went straight to the counter where Margaret was staring downwards. Her head was in the ledgers, her sharpened pencil making notes. Her meticulous records were something she was proud of.

A glance around the shop offered no notable omissions. A pang of disappointment rippled through Henry. After his spending spree, the last thing he needed was a blank day.

"Any sales today, Margaret?"

Margaret jolted upright, a look of shock etched across her face. Henry smiled. He often wondered whether the woman might one day have a heart attack in his shop. She was only in her sixties and yet offered the appearance of someone twenty years older. There were times when it felt like she was older than most of what he was selling.

"Don't do that, Henry. You startled me," she said as she peered over the glasses perched on her nose.

"Sorry, Margaret," he offered in a rare moment of compassion. "I was just wondering whether there were any sales today."

"Sales…hmmm…I would have to check," she purred softly. Her eyes went back down to the ledgers.

Henry shook his head at his assistant. She had been in the shop all day and could not remember whether she had sold anything. Maybe it was time to upgrade her to someone who had a pulse.

"Sales…let me see…"

"Any time this decade would be fine," growled Henry.

"I'm sure I recorded something."

"Still waiting…"

"Yes, there we are. We sold a silver thimble."

"Is that it?"

"I would have to check. Just give me a moment."

Henry's blood was beginning to boil. The level of inactivity was beyond his comprehension. She would have to go under the guise of an ill-health retirement. That was his rather than hers, the doctor having advised him to remain calm. How could he when Margaret moved at the speed of a lethargic snail?

He was rescued by Robbie coming into the shop behind him. The lad was a breath of fresh air. He was lively and keen to get the job done. That automatically ranked him above Margaret.

"Do you want all the sales or just what has come through the shop?"

"Is there a difference?"

"Yes, we get some over the phone as well."

"Just give me everything," demanded Henry.

"Everything, you say. Just give me a moment…"

"The trunk is ready to be opened," confirmed Robbie.

"I'm on my way. Hopefully, Margaret will either have an answer or will have died of old age by the time I return."

Henry followed Robbie out of the back of the shop. He left Margaret with her head down, oblivious to the absence of her boss. Once inside the adjoining building, Henry saw the trunk on the workbench. He smiled as he gazed at the painted exterior. There was no shortage of pride inside him.

"What's the plan to get it open?" asked Henry.

"I think I can pick it," offered Graham. "The lock doesn't look that sophisticated. How old did they say the trunk was?"

"The catalogue reckoned eighteen-eighties."

"In that case, I think the lock has been replaced. It isn't that old."

"Buggar," snarled Henry. "Is it obvious?"

"Not unless you look inside it. The appearance holds up."

"Then pretend you haven't noticed. If we can make a key for it, we'll treat it as an original. The type of idiot who buys this piece won't know the difference anyway. Just get the bloody thing open without damaging it."

Graham went to work on the lock, displaying the dexterity of a burglar. He picked away at the mechanism carefully. With a light shining from his forehead and a spare tool held in his mouth, his hands moved quickly. He offered a series of noises while around him there was silence. Each of the men knew better than to interrupt a master of his craft.

The lock did not give up easily. Henry's patience was tested to the limit. Graham held up a hand to signal that he was listening. Under his guidance, they waited for the breakthrough to come. When it did, a loud click echoed around the workshop. Graham backed away with a grin etched across his face.

"Have you done it?" asked Henry.

"It's all yours. I thought you might want the honour of opening it."

Henry Davenport rushed forward. He fumbled to get the latch open. It was his moment to savour the glory of his victory. With a nod and a broad grin, he forced the lid open. He reached up and was hit by a rotting smell which sent his eyes downwards.

It took a moment to focus. When his eyes fixed on the inside of the trunk, fear became his closest friend.

Chapter 2

DI Jack Husker and DS Lisa Ramsey walked into the station together. There was no attempt to keep their distance or offer the illusion of separation. They had long since passed the point where they pretended not to be a couple. Now they were spending more time together than apart. It meant Jack's house was often empty, particularly as they approached the winter months. There was a lot to be said for the allure of a modern characterless flat when it came with effective heating.

At Lisa's insistence, they walked up the stairs, leaving Jack to grumble about the perfectly functioning lift. Both clutching a coffee, they were hoping for a quiet day. They had already spoken about some lunch options and whether they could sneak off early. Since the Castle Howard Lake case had been solved, York had been devoid of a major crime.

Lisa liked it that way though Jack hated things to be quiet. Without a complex case to sink his teeth into, there was too much time to think. That came with more opportunities for drinking, which brought out the worst in him. For Lisa's benefit, he was trying to reduce their trips to The Cellars. It was for the best when the hangovers were doing neither of them any good.

Jack followed Lisa into the main office. A glance across offered a hint of calm. Others were enjoying their moment of peace just as much as Lisa. When they turned, they saw DCI Louth, his smug face as punchable as ever.

"My office, two minutes," he barked.

"Why two minutes?" frowned Jack.

"Nature calls."

"When you've finished playing David Attenborough, we'll be waiting for you."

"Excuse me?"

"Nothing, sir. See you in two minutes," smiled Jack.

They headed to Louth's office and settled down on two of the chairs opposite his desk. Lisa puffed out her cheeks and looked at Jack who seemed lost in his own world. At times, it was hard to know what was going on in his head.

"What do you think he wants?" she sighed.

"A good slap?" queried Jack.

"That's what you want to give him."

"Is it? I get so confused at my age. I guess he's about to volunteer us for something dreadful."

"Don't be so cynical, Jack. It might not be that bad."

"A pint says it is. Loser buys the first in The Cellars tonight."

"I thought you were trying to be good."

"That was before I had winnings to collect."

"In that case, mine's a pint of wine."

"Just one of your normal measures," he laughed.

"Hey, I'm not that bad."

Jack knew better than to respond. He sipped his coffee and waited for the DCI to return. Whatever Louth wanted, it was likely to ruin his day.

Louth marched in with enough energy to make Jack groan. His slightly reddened face suggested he might have run. Instinctively, Lisa sat upright while Jack did not move a muscle. They both watched Louth close the door and settle behind his desk.

"Did you see any butterflies, sir?" asked Jack.

"Jack, whatever is in your head, empty it, please. I haven't got time for this. What have you got on today? If you tell me you don't know because you've emptied your head, you'll be on a charge."

"We've got a couple of older investigations to close off," noted Lisa. "It's nothing that can't wait."

"Excellent. I have a new priority for you both. I want one of you to go and see a man called Henry Davenport."

"As in the antique dealer?" queried Lisa.

"That's him," confirmed Louth. "Do you know him?"

"I met him when he reported a shoplifter six months ago."

"In that case, you can go over there. He's just bought an old trunk at an auction, which…"

"Did he get a free elephant with it?" interrupted Jack.

"I will ignore that," growled Louth. "The trunk in question has got body parts in it."

"What sort of body parts?" asked Lisa.

"I don't know. I'm not a surgeon. Take one of the younger DCs with you and find out."

"I'll take Nathan Lewis. He's due some excitement."

"Is that wise? He threw up all over the last gruesome scene he saw. He'll be stuck with that 'Chucky' moniker for the rest of his career."

"He reckons he's toughened up, so let's find out."

"What about me?" asked Jack.

"I want you to go over to the auction house. Find out where that trunk came from and who was selling it. I would start with the auctioneer."

"We're on it, sir," nodded Lisa.

"And try to keep some focus."

"What do you mean?" asked Lisa.

"Well, since you two became a couple, it's been like watching an old romcom without the romance or the comedy," grinned Louth.

"That's better than it being a horror movie," laughed Lisa.

"That was Jack's first two marriages. They came with an eighteen certificate."

"Hey, you do realise I'm still in the room," complained Jack.

"Yes," said Louth and Lisa in unison.

***

Nathan 'Chucky' Lewis was pleased to be asked to go with Lisa. On a quiet day in the station, his main task would be fetching coffee. Still too new to say no to an older officer, there were plenty taking advantage. It was better than fighting back and being the butt of their jokes. He had been there before and had not found it a pleasant experience.

Lisa seemed upbeat when she came over. There was none of the tetchiness he had witnessed when she was put under pressure. Things had to be going well with Jack. Nathan was quick to jump to his feet and follow Lisa out of the station.

They drove in Lisa's car to an antiques shop on Colliergate. Nathan spent most of the time staring out of the window. A briefing from Lisa was the only conversation they shared. Nathan's heart skipped a beat when Lisa told him about the contents of the trunk.

"You are going to be alright, aren't you?"

"I'll be fine," he offered hurriedly, in the hope that he might convince himself.

"If you need to step out, then do so. Or stay back from the trunk."

Nathan could not help but reflect on his incident. The suicide scene had been the most humiliating day of his life. To be sick in such a high-profile place was something that would blight his entire career. There had been a few sympathetic words offered. Most preferred to take delight in his shame.

Lisa pulled her car into the yard at the back of the shop. Parking next to a van, they were met by a middle-aged man coming out of the neighbouring building. Maybe forty-five years of age, he was of average build with slightly greying hair. Dressed in jeans and a scruffy black polo shirt, his appearance was that of an unremarkable man.

Lisa got out and walked straight over to him. Nathan followed obediently, like a well-trained puppy that was not allowed off its lead. There were no words exchanged between them before she addressed the man.

"Hi, I'm DS Lisa Ramsey and this is DC Nathan Lewis. We were called by Henry Davenport. Is he in?" Lisa flashed her warrant card, forcing Nathan to do the same.

"I'm Graham Dexter. I take it you're here about the trunk."

"That's right," confirmed Lisa. "Do you work for him?"

"Yes, I was the one who opened it, Actually, strictly speaking, that isn't true. I unlocked it. Henry was the one to lift the lid."

"That's fine. Shall we go inside?"

"Follow me. Henry is in his office."

Lisa and Nathan followed Graham through the back door of one of the buildings. It took them into a rabbit warren of corridors that ended when they came to an office in the corner. A single knock saw Graham enter. Behind him, the detectives remained close.

"Henry, the police are here."

"The police?"

"About the trunk."

"Oh yes. Tell them I will be out as soon as I can. I shouldn't be longer than twenty minutes. Make it thirty. I have some customer calls to make."

"Mr Davenport, we are here now," interrupted Lisa as she forced her way into the room.

"Can't this wait?" he barked with irritation. "I do have a business to run."

"I'm afraid we don't offer an appointment service," she smiled. "We can't get criminals to stick to pre-agreed times. I'm DS Lisa Ramsey and this is DC Nathan Lewis. I think we've met before."

"Yes, we have," growled Henry. "Fine, I'll come now."

"If you're busy, I could take the detectives through to see the trunk," offered Graham.

"I'm on my way," huffed Henry.

Henry made an exaggerated effort when he forced himself up from his chair. He pushed on the arms and used it to ease his overweight body upwards. The physical exertion of the act left him red-faced. Everything about the man screamed of someone who had enjoyed a little too much of the good life.

Lisa kept a straight face throughout the performance. A small part of her was taking great delight in causing the pompous man discomfort. His manner during the previous shoplifting incident was politely described as rude. The impolite option would have been far more appropriate.

"Will this take long?" growled Henry as he made his way to the door.

"I can't answer that at this stage," said Lisa. "Why don't you show us the trunk and then we can give you a clearer view?"

Henry marched them back through the building. Lisa followed behind, with Graham allowing Nathan to go before him. They emerged into the yard and turned into what looked like a workshop. When the light was switched on, they saw the ornate trunk on the bench.

"That's a nice piece of furniture," nodded Lisa.

"It's a little cracker," smiled Henry. "It will be in my window on Saturday and sold by the end of the weekend."

"Let's not get ahead of ourselves, Mr Davenport. If the contents are as you have described them, this workshop will become a crime scene."

"Don't be bloody stupid," he growled. "All that has happened in here is the trunk has been opened. You are welcome to take the contents with you."

"There will still be a forensic investigation to undertake."

"Not in my workshop, there won't."

"Mr Davenport, will you please open the trunk?"

"Graham, can you oblige?"

Graham Dexter stepped forward and lifted the lid slowly. He turned away to avoid staring down at the contents. Once opened, he eased away and shrugged towards the detectives.

Lisa did not need to look into the trunk to know what she was facing. The smell hit her as soon as the lid was lifted. She grimaced and forced her stomach to retain control. A glance at Nathan saw him ease backwards out of the room.

Nervously, she took a couple of steps towards it. When she peered down, she saw the gruesome contents. There was a severed head and what looked like pieces of limbs. They had been cut off at the elbows and knees to enable them to fit inside the trunk. Already, Lisa had seen enough. She requested that the lid be closed.

"Who else has been in contact with the trunk?"

"Just myself, Graham and Robbie," replied Henry.

"Who's Robbie?"

"Robbie Cartwright. He's my driver. He accompanies me to all the auctions."

"Anyone else?" questioned Lisa, aware that she was now alone. A glance towards the door told her that Nathan had retreated out of the building.

"No, just the three of us."

"We'll require statements from all three of you, plus we'll need to seal off the workshop."

"You can't!" insisted Henry. "I need to get the trunk ready for Saturday."

"Mr Davenport, that trunk is going nowhere. I'm sure you don't need me to tell you that a major crime has been committed."

"Not in my workshop, it hasn't. Graham, move that bloody trunk into one of the other sheds so we can get on."

"Mr Davenport, I'm warning you. If you touch that trunk, I will arrest you for hindering a police enquiry. Will you please step out of the workshop and return to your office? We will take the statements in there."

"And who's going to do that?" sneered Henry. "I think your pet has gone for a walk."

Lisa looked across at Nathan. He was leaning up against one of the buildings. She shook her head in despair. At least he hadn't redecorated the brickwork.

***

It took Jack most of the day to track down the auctioneer. Simon Hayton was not at the auction house and neither was he answering his mobile. Jack feared that something might have happened to him. His thoughts turned to who was in the trunk. It would be difficult to imagine how Simon could have ended up in it. And yet stranger things had happened in his career.

At five-thirty, Jack's messages were finally returned. An agitated Simon called back. Jack answered just as he was leaving the station. He diverted into the meeting room beside the reception desk and allowed the auctioneer to speak.

"Is that Detective Husker?"

"Speaking," confirmed Jack.

"It's Simon Hayton from the auction house. You were trying to get hold of me, I believe."

"That's right, Mr Hayton. I need to see you."

"Call me Simon, please. Could we do this over the phone? I'm at home."

"I would prefer to speak to you in person. Can I come over?"

"I'm in Fulford. I'll send you the address. Does it matter that my partner is at home with me?"

"Not at all. I'll get there as quickly as I can."

Jack collected the keys to one of the station's vehicles. He regretted not having Lisa's car close by. It would have given him an excuse to drive straight over to her flat when he was finished.

A loan car meant he risked being called back in by Louth when he returned it.

He groaned as soon as he got into the car park. The large black estate car was one which everybody tried to avoid. Resembling a hearse, it rocked like a boat, thanks to its over-soft suspension. Jack contemplated going back inside to see what else was on offer. There was little point when he only needed the vehicle to get him to Fulford.

That decision was regretted when the car hit the first street of speed humps. Each one sent a resonating wave through the chassis. Jack felt his stomach turn over. He forced himself to stare out to the horizon as if he was navigating a force-nine gale.

It was approaching six o'clock by the time he pulled up outside Simon Hayton's house. The large detached property was built on an exclusive new development. With as few as ten houses, it was not large enough to be called an estate. It was a high-end offering, with Simon's house the smallest that had been built.

Jack got out of the car feeling queasy. He was pleased to feel the fresh air on his face as he took a moment to survey the buildings. Each of them had been built to look slightly different. The only commonality was their size and the sprawling drives they came with. Most of them displayed expensive cars, to signify that wealthy owners were at home.

As Jack walked up the drive, he wondered whether Simon had the money to back up the location. Was he doing his best to fit in with a crowd that he aspired to be in? It was hard to know what an auctioneer earned. If it was his business, he might be living comfortably within his means.

A ring of the bell saw the door answered by a man with a beard. Jack smiled and offered up his warrant card while performing his normal introduction. Simon Hayton shook Jack's hand and invited him into the house. Jack was taken through to the kitchen where an expensive island unit sat proudly in the middle of the large space.

"I'm sorry to disturb you at home, Mr Hayton."

"Simon, please. I take it something serious has happened."

"Unfortunately, it has," offered Jack, whose attention was taken by a loud crashing sound upstairs.

"Don't worry about that," smiled Simon. "My girlfriend is having a shower. She normally sounds like she is knocking walls through with the noise she makes."

Jack smiled. He could remember a former girlfriend he would say exactly the same about.

"I wanted to talk to you about one of the auction lots you sold earlier today."

"Was something wrong with it?"

"You could say that."

"It wasn't stolen, was it?" asked Simon with alarm. "We do our best to do some due diligence on every lot. We really do."

"It wasn't stolen," confirmed Jack.

"That's a relief. I do have a reputation to maintain."

"I wouldn't count your blessings just yet. It's a bit more serious than that."

The look of shock on Simon Hayton's face when Jack told him about the contents of the trunk appeared genuine. There was no attempt to distance himself from it or pretend that it had not gone through the auction. Simon confirmed that it was the final lot of the day and had attracted some fierce bidding. It was one of many things that had been sold for well above its catalogue price.

"I'll need the full details of the seller," insisted Jack.

"Of course. I'll get them for you first thing in the morning."

"I'll also need statements from anyone who has been in contact with that trunk."

"Absolutely. I can ask all the auction staff to be on standby. When do you need them to be available?"

"Shall we say nine o'clock?"

"That's fine. Rest assured, DI Husker, we will do everything we can to assist you."

Jack studied the mannerisms of the man in front of him. Over-eager to help, he looked like a rabbit caught in the headlights. It would be easy to be fooled by what could be an elaborate piece of acting. For now, Jack would keep an open mind. Maybe he was an innocent party and had been caught up in a macabre event he was never intended to be involved in.

"One final question if I may. Can you think of any reason why someone would want to put a trunk full of body parts through one of your auctions?"

"I think you know the answer to that, DI Husker. For the record, no, I cannot."

Jack nodded. It was a formality that he had to ask.

"Thank you. I will see you at the auction house in the morning."

Jack turned to leave the kitchen. He managed one pace and was stopped by a woman in the doorway. She was dressed in just a towel, having stepped out of the shower. Jack's eyes fought to avoid staring as he looked at her in horror. In front of him was a colleague he knew only too well.

"Cathy!"

"Bloody hell, Jack! What are you doing here?"

Cathy Duggan looked at Jack as if she had seen a ghost. As two former lovers, it was not a confrontation either of them wanted to have. A lot of time had passed since they were a couple. And yet Cathy's presence in just a towel still felt like an act of betrayal to both their current partners. As one of York's pathologists, their paths had already crossed too many times for their liking.

"I...I...I...was just going," mumbled Jack.

Before Cathy Duggan could interrogate him, Jack ran to the door. He had never been so eager to get into such an uncomfortable car. He dived into it and floored the accelerator, hoping for an immediate reaction. With Cathy watching from the doorway, it moved off like a cruise liner that was heading out to sea.

***

Lisa was waiting for Jack when he got to The Cellars. His journey back to the station had been as painful as he expected. It was made worse by his scrambled thoughts about Cathy Duggan and what she was doing in Simon Hayton's house. After a few minutes, the story had come together. He remembered what

Cathy had told him. She had bought the place in Fulford with her new partner.

A walk from the station to The Cellars had been exactly what Jack needed. Though he had no interest in dating Cathy Duggan, it still felt strange to see her with somebody else. That somebody was a man she felt comfortable with, making her happy to walk through the house in just a towel. Jack could remember a time when Cathy felt the same way about him.

Both of them had since moved on for the better. Cathy would be happier without the constant rows a relationship with Jack had brought. Jack now had Lisa and was feeling relaxed as a couple for the first time in his life. It still felt odd. The memories of Cathy Duggan only increased those thoughts.

"I was wondering whether you had stood me up," smiled Lisa. She eased off the bar stool and kissed Jack on the cheek. "I was just about to start chatting up Alf."

"Be my guest," smiled Jack. "I won't stop you."

"I know you won't. You could pretend it bothers you though; just for me."

"If you like. Alf, when you've finished being chatted up by my girlfriend, I'll have a pint."

"Is this on the ever-growing slate or are you paying by cash?"

"Is the slate that bad?"

"Let's just say the Flintstones are having to quarry some more to keep up with your debts."

Jack smiled and handed forty pounds across to Alf. It would not clear his arrears but it showed some willingness to do so.

"Grab one for yourself as well, Alf."

"No, thanks. I don't want to increase your debts with my bad habits."

"Fair enough. I'll leave you to continue being chatted up by Lisa. I need to sit down."

Jack took the pint from Alf and walked away. Lisa declined his offer of another glass of wine. The one in her hand was still over half-full and would get replenished when Jack went for his next pint. That was likely to be in a matter of minutes.

She followed him over to his favourite corner. A frown towards a young lad removed any suggestion that the youngster might sit there. It was Jack's place and the lad had been warned off the space. The kid scowled and then made his way over to the opposite side of the bar. He was not looking for the trouble that Jack's expression made it obvious he could provide.

"How was your day?" asked Jack as Lisa settled in alongside him.

"Fine, if you can ignore a trunk full of body parts."

"What was in there?"

"I didn't do a full count but it looked like a head, two arms and two legs. They were only half-limbs. I don't think much else would have fitted."

"So it wasn't a full body then?"

"No," confirmed Lisa. "The limbs were the bottom halves. The head was...well, it was a head."

"Male or female?"

"It looked like it was probably a young man. To be honest, I didn't get that close."

"How was Nathan? Did he disgrace himself again?"

"He wasn't sick, which was the only positive. He was about as much use as a chocolate teapot."

"What did he do?"

"The smell was too much for him. He went outside and spent most of the time leaning up against a building. The stench was pretty bad in there."

"He's going to find the job difficult if he can't get over that."

"I think he's just worked that out. He doesn't have to like it. He just needs to be able to function in that environment. Anyway, how was your day?"

Jack went quiet. He disappeared behind a thoughtful expression. It was as if he had stepped into a world where he was alone. Lisa frowned and looked across to where Jack was staring. His line of sight was aimed directly at the wall.

"Jack...Jack...are you still with me?"

"Yes, what is it?"

"How was your day?"

"It was okay, I guess."

"Did you track down the auctioneer?"

"Yes, I went to see him. He was fine, if a little shocked."

"You would be too."

"I guess."

"So what's the problem?"

Jack thought for a moment and then forced the words from his lips.

"Cathy was there."

"Who's Cathy?"

"Cathy Duggan."

"What was she doing there?"

"Do you remember me telling you that she was buying a place in Fulford with her boyfriend?"

"Yes."

"I think I've just met her boyfriend."

"Are you sure?"

"I hope so," laughed Jack. "He's either her boyfriend or she goes walking around stranger's houses wearing just a towel."

"You saw Cathy Duggan in just a towel?"

Jack blushed bright red and nodded.

"I didn't go looking for her," he insisted. "I was talking to Simon Hayton and she walked in."

"That must have been a shock."

"It was...for both of us. I don't know who was more surprised."

"What did she say?"

"Not a lot. I wasn't there for long. Like a good detective, I made my excuses and left."

"Was that before or after you checked it was her for the tenth time?" frowned Lisa.

"I only have eyes for you," grinned Jack.

"And don't tell me; hands for everyone else," she muttered under her breath.

Chapter 3

Jack got up early. He left Lisa asleep in bed. It was half an hour before the alarm was due to go off. Jack sneaked out of the flat, leaving a hand-scribbled note in the kitchen. His untidy scrawl told her to meet him at the station. They would go to the auction house together to interview those who had come into contact with the trunk.

On his way down the stairs, he was passed by a young lad with unkempt hair. The lad looked like he had slept in his clothes from the night before. They were going out clothes, with his jeans and a shirt offering a stain from a spilled drink. Jack smiled and watched the way the lad blushed. It was obvious he was in a place he was not supposed to be.

"Morning," grinned Jack.

"Is it?" groaned the lad. He puffed out his cheeks to offer the sense that it had been a long night.

At the bottom of the stairwell, the lad struggled to get out. He pushed at the door and was helpless until Jack pressed the switch to release the lock. Jack stepped aside to allow him to leave first. A forced smile appeared to be a monumental effort.

"That's the problem with these ladies," grinned Jack. "They lock us in to stop us escaping."

"It feels that way." The lad's expression offered more of the story than Jack wanted to know. "I might be regretting this one for a while."

Jack watched him walk off. It was hard to feel any sympathy. Whoever he had come back with, he had done so willingly. Now, with his beer goggles no longer working, he would have a very different view of the previous night.

The lad disappeared out of sight by the time Jack reached Monk Bar. It left him alone in the early morning chilly air. Jack had not intended to leave quite so early though his discipline in keeping to three pints had served him well. Needing fresh clothes and being wide awake had driven his decision. It also allowed him to eat a proper breakfast. Lisa had promised him fruit and yoghurt in the morning. That alone was a good reason to make a break for freedom.

He walked through the city until he reached a cafe just off Parliament Street. It was one of the smaller ones hidden away in the back streets. Used mainly by locals, the tourists rarely saw its frontage. That made it one of Jack's favourites. The large fry-ups were a bonus.

Jack nodded to the owner on his way in. She was a tall lady, with her hair tied back in a ponytail. She was always in there, leaving him wondering whether she ever took any time off. He ordered a full breakfast at the counter and asked for a large cup of filter coffee to go with it.

"Take a seat wherever you want, love," she smiled in return.

Jack wandered over to the corner seat by the window. It gave him a view into the alleyway outside. Across from him, there was one other customer. An old man was clutching a cup of something hot and was filling in the crossword in a newspaper. Jack wondered whether it was today's edition or whether the man had been there since yesterday.

His attention was directed away from the man when the owner approached him with his coffee. She brought it with a small jug of milk and put both in front of him. Jack thanked her and then glanced at his phone. Lisa would still be asleep. If she wasn't, she would be asking why he had done a runner. Jack thought through his playbook of excuses. The need for a change of clothes was a better option than telling her the threat of yoghurt had scared him away.

He picked up a discarded newspaper from the table to his side. He skimmed through it while waiting for his breakfast to arrive. The crossword had been filled in as had the Sudoku. Someone had a lot of time to waste, with the chief suspect being the old man across the cafe.

Jack read most of the tabloid rag in the time it took for his food to arrive. When the lady approached with his plate, he pushed the paper to one side and smiled. The breakfast looked every bit as good as any she had served before. That consistency along with the lack of tourists never failed to please him.

He set about the plateful with relish. Folding a slice of toast around some bacon, he sunk his teeth in eagerly. A sausage accompanied it, leaving the non-meaty offerings dominating the plate. They would be enjoyed with the remaining rasher and sausage. Nothing would be wasted. A full breakfast was something to savour.

Jack was busy cutting up the last of the bacon when the cafe door opened. He barely needed to glance up to know who was approaching. The shadow the entourage cast was enough to provide fair warning. Jack puffed out his cheeks and watched a smartly dressed man come into view. He was flanked by two oversized ogres.

"Still aiming for that heart attack, I see," smiled the man.

"Good morning, Gregor. I see the zoo is allowing the animals out to exercise."

Gregor Banks narrowed his eyes and then relaxed when he realised that Jack was referring to the two men who were accompanying him.

"These two are pets rather than wild animals."

"They still eat raw meat."

"I prefer cooked meat," growled the larger of the two who caught Jack by surprise. He sprung forward and grabbed the remaining sausage off the plate. He took great delight in biting off one end.

"Do you mind?"

"Not at all," grinned the oversized man.

"Well, I do. I'm trying to enjoy my breakfast," complained Jack.

"Don't let me stop you," offered Gregor.

"Do you want to tell your pets that?"

"There's no need. You've only got veggie stuff left. They won't touch that."

Jack gazed down at the beans, tomatoes and mushrooms on his plate and felt a pang of disappointment go through him.

"I take it you want something," sighed Jack.

"Just a quick chat."

"Fine," nodded Jack. "Do me a favour and send your monkeys for a walk. That one blocks out the light."

"How about I sit them down with a cake and some juice? Lads, off you go."

The two ogres moved to the other side of the cafe. They took a seat on either side of the old man and stared across at his crossword. When he saw them, he leapt to his feet and ran for the door. A chuckle from the larger man ended when he picked up the newspaper. He stared at it and frowned.

"You might need to help him with the big words," grinned Jack.

"There's no point," sighed Gregor. "He'll need help with the little words as well."

Gregor Banks sat down on the opposite seat to Jack. He called over the waitress and ordered a coffee for himself. He then sent her across to the table where the thugs were sitting and told her to add whatever they wanted.

Jack finished his breakfast while the lady fulfilled Gregor's order. He did not bother to ask Gregor what he wanted. The gangster would offer it up when he was ready. It was too early to play games. Gregor would either start the conversation or Jack would get up and leave.

The impasse lasted until Gregor had his coffee in front of him. The two goons both ordered bacon sandwiches to go with a cup of tea. It felt unusually sophisticated for the thugs Gregor normally associated with. Jack placed his cutlery on his plate and washed down the final remnants of his breakfast with the remainder of his coffee.

"I thought we might have a little chat," said Gregor unexpectedly.

"Sure, go ahead," shrugged Jack.

"It's a matter you might be interested in," continued Gregor.

"I'll let you know when I've heard it. What's on your mind?"

"There's plenty on my mind. Unlike you, Jack, I can think about many things at once."

"So can I."

"Yes, beer, whisky and plates of grease."

"That's good enough for me," laughed Jack. "You missed out coffee."

"I'm more concerned about what's creeping onto the city's streets."

"Specifically?"

"Drugs and counterfeit goods."

"Then stop selling them."

"I'm not talking about my lawful businesses."

"What about your unlawful ones?"

Gregor smiled. A flick of his eyes towards his ogres was an obvious threat.

"Let's not get too clever with each other," he said softly.

"What's the problem? Is someone muscling in on your patch?"

"I'm saying there's a new player in town. I don't know who it is but I don't like it."

"Is there too much competition for you?"

"Let's just say that the older generation operates by a proper set of rules. These chancers who try their luck don't appear to have any morals. It needs to stop."

"I'm not sure what I can do to help with that."

"All I'm asking is for you to do a bit of digging."

"I'm not your private detective, Gregor. I work in the public interest."

"This is in the public interest. It's called pre-emptive policing. By stopping a minor crime, it prevents a major one from happening."

"You mean when you catch them."

"I never said that. Just find out what's going on for me, will you? Call it a favour between mates."

"I don't do favours," growled Jack.

"And you don't have any mates," laughed Gregor. "Call me when you have an answer."

Before Jack could respond, Gregor left the table. He ordered his ogres out of the cafe.

"Just make sure you pay for your breakfast. I'm not picking up the tab for your lot," growled Jack.

It was too late. Gregor had already gone, leaving Jack with a bill to pay.

***

Jack made it to the station just after eight o'clock. Still irritated at being left to pick up Gregor's bill, he marched upstairs. A quick conversation with Brian Wilkes was enjoyed at the coffee machine. Both men bemoaned what was on offer and then happily took a cup of the tasteless liquid back to their desks.

Lisa arrived twenty minutes later. After speaking to DCI Louth, they headed out to Lisa's car. They were both eager to get over to the auction house to see Simon Hayton. As they left the station, Jack could not help but wonder what Cathy Duggan was thinking. Was she angry with Jack for intruding on her new life or was she having second thoughts about her boyfriend?

"I take it you didn't fancy staying around until I woke up," said Lisa bluntly.

"I needed some fresh clothes," insisted Jack.

"Really?" frowned Lisa. She stared at what Jack was wearing.

"It takes a whole new wardrobe to look this good."

"I would get your money back," scowled Lisa. "I thought you were staying for breakfast."

"Another time," replied Jack.

"And when's that?"

"When you're not serving fruit and yoghurt," muttered Jack under his breath. Outwardly, he just smiled and hoped that Lisa's attention would be taken by the traffic.

They drove through the city to the auction house. Parking directly outside the front door, Jack and Lisa surveyed the car park. Half a dozen cars were dotted around, including the one that had been on Simon Hayton's drive. Jack half-expected Cathy Duggan's car to be there beside it. Hopefully, she would be wearing more than a towel.

At the reception, Jack performed the introductions. He told the girl behind the desk that Simon Hayton was expecting him. It did not take long for Simon to appear. Dressed in dark blue jeans and a white shirt, he beckoned the two detectives into a meeting room.

"We haven't met," said Lisa. "I'm DS Lisa Ramsey."

"Simon Hayton. Please call me Simon."

"Did you manage to get me the details of the seller?" asked Jack. He was keen to move the conversation along.

"His name is Paul Colyer. He sells a lot of furniture through us."

"Is he local?"

"No, he's based over in Hull."

"So why does he sell items in York?"

"The prices are a lot higher. It's an attractive market in York. We have a few dealers who bring their better items over from the coast."

"What about the staff who were here for the auction? Are they all available?"

"They are on standby for when you need them."

"Perfect," nodded Jack. "Can we start with a list of their names?"

Simon Hayton nodded compliantly. "Firstly, there's myself. I'm the auctioneer at all of our auctions. The only time anyone else would do it is if the auction is a large one. For those, Dean and I will take turns."

"Dean?" queried Lisa.

"Dean Lucas is our valuer. His job is to assess each of the lots and put an estimate on their value. He's very good at what he does. As I said, he also steps in to do some of the lots on the larger auctions."

"Who else is there?"

"We have two auction porters, Billy and Finn."

"Second names, please," said Jack.

"Billy is Billy Ellis. He's only been with us for a year or so."

"Hang on; I know a Billy Ellis," said Jack. "I hope it's not the same one. He spent half his upbringing in a young offenders' institute."

"That will be him," nodded Simon. "We took Billy on as our contribution to a program to help rehabilitate offenders. It's designed to give those that perhaps don't deserve it a second chance."

"That one would need a twenty-second chance," said Jack. "He couldn't go more than a week keeping his nose clean."

"We did have some problems with him in the early stages. He's settled down now and does a good job for us."

"What exactly does he do?" asked Lisa.

"He's an auction porter, which, in simple terms, is a lifter and a shifter. Every auction house needs them."

"I'll certainly be keen to meet him," confirmed Jack. "I'm not sure he'll say the same about meeting me."

"And then our other porter is Finn Mann," continued Simon.

"Finn...Mann," repeated Jack.

"I know," laughed Simon. "I have no idea what his parents were thinking."

"You couldn't make it up," sighed Jack, with a shake of his head.

"Finn has been with us for three or four years. He's quiet and gets on with his work. The only other permanent staff are the two girls in the office – Becky and Dawn. Do you want to speak to them as well?"

"We'll take a statement for completeness. We won't need long with them," confirmed Lisa.

"That's fine. Where would you like to start? The room is yours for as long as you need it and the staff are at your disposal."

"I think we should start at the top," confirmed Jack. "We can work our way down from there."

"Do you want me to get one of the girls to send some coffee in?"

"That would be great," nodded Jack. "I think we might be here for a while."

For the next half an hour, Simon Hayton offered surprisingly little. His involvement with the lots was minimal until it came to selling them. He would review the catalogue and then take the podium on auction day. Other than that, it was hard to know what he did. As Jack questioned him, his mind drifted back to

Cathy Duggan. There would be harsh words coming his way when she found out he had been interrogating her boyfriend.

Lisa's softer approach did not reveal anything more. Her glances across towards Jack told him she was running out of questions. They ended the interview and advised Simon that they might need to talk to him again. First, they would speak to the others. Somebody had to know more about the auction house than Simon.

Dean Lucas was a far more interesting man. He came alive when he spoke about some of the lots he had seen. He was the valuer at the auction house and had worked there for six years. During that time, he had worked his way up from being an auction porter. With little formal training, his knowledge had been gained the hard way.

"Tell us about the lot in question," said Jack.

"It was a nice lot. Not my sort of thing but sought after. We don't get much coming across from China, particularly around that period. That probably explains why it went for so much."

"What do you mean?"

"It was listed as five to seven hundred pounds. That was a bit of a guess because we don't see many of them. Most of the trunks we get are Victorian or earlier English examples. It was nice to see something different."

"What did it sell for?"

"I think the final price was eighteen hundred pounds or something like that. It must be the rarity of it. Once the premium is added, you're going to be into it for well over two thousand pounds." Dean puffed out his cheeks to emphasise his point.

"What do you think the buyer will sell it for?"

"I don't see how it could go for over a thousand pounds. He might be lucky to get that."

"So why pay that much?"

"Unless someone knows something I don't, the bidders must have got carried away. There was plenty of interest and it did get a bit feisty. Simon plays on that to our advantage."

"What do you mean?"

"The higher the price, the more commission we make. We aren't going to tell anyone to stop bidding. We represent the seller."

"Did you open the trunk when you looked at it?"

"I couldn't. The trunk was locked when we got it and it was still locked when it went out of here. It was one of the last lots to come in, which is why it was the final item in the catalogue."

"Did anyone open it?"

"I doubt it. The only person who would want to open it would be me. I would be looking for a maker's mark and to see what condition it was in. Because it was late in the day, I just did a quick once over and then went online to find out more about it. As I said, the valuation was a bit of a guess on this one. I hope that doesn't put me in trouble."

"We appreciate your honesty," said Lisa, allowing a sense of relief to flush across Dean's face.

Billy Ellis was the next to enter the room. Jack was primed to interrogate him, something the lad would be expecting. When Jack saw his rat-like features and shaven head, he knew he had his man. Billy had plenty of previous convictions and had been arrested by Jack on multiple occasions.

"Shall we just charge this one now?" grinned Jack when his eyes made contact with Billy.

"I ain't done nuffin'," squeaked Billy.

"That would be a first," laughed Jack. "My colleague has not had the misfortune to come across you before, so shall we give DS Ramsey your list of previous offences?"

"If you like," shrugged Billy. "That was in my past. I've gone straight since then."

"Does 'straight' include sticking bodies in trunks?"

"You can't pin anything like that on me. Burglaries were my game; not violent stuff."

"Maybe you've been promoted since then," laughed Jack.

"I told you; I've gone straight."

"Yeah, and I've started flying," said Jack.

Once the initial sparring was over, Billy did not offer much. His insistence that he had turned his life around mirrored the account that Simon had given them. Both referenced a few problems in the early stages but nothing since. Billy was now a hard-working tax-payer who was making his contribution in life. As Lisa looked at him, Jack offered a sceptical eye. He was not being fooled by Billy's protestations for a second.

Once Billy was finished, Finn took his place. Before he came in, Lisa issued a stern warning to Jack. There were to be no quips about his name or attempts to plant hidden puns. The lad was likely to have heard every one of them. Nobody had a name like his without being the butt of the jokes for most of his life.

When Finn sat down, he looked nervous. The lad was meek and spoke in a quiet voice. He confirmed that he had helped bring the trunk into the auction room though had not been there when it arrived. He had also taken it out when Henry Davenport asked for someone to load his van.

"Was it heavy?"

"No more than any other bit of furniture," shrugged Finn.

"Did you open it?" asked Jack.

"Why would I do that? I just carry things back and forth. Dean does the clever stuff."

"Weren't you curious? After all, you don't get many Chinese items."

"Don't we? They're all bits of furniture to me."

Jack smiled at Lisa. They were wasting their time by continuing the line of questioning.

The same feeling came when Becky and then Dawn came in. Neither offered anything of note to assist the investigation. They both worked in the office and rarely ventured into the auction room. Neither had seen the trunk other than in the catalogue.

At Jack's insistence, Simon was summoned for a second time. Jack wanted to know who the bidders were. Why had they bid so much for something that was not worth that amount? Nothing about the auction lot made sense.

"It got personal," admitted Simon. "I'm sure Daniel Voss was just trying to bid them up. He drove the early action and then stepped away to leave Henry Davenport and Charles Rickton to go at it. Once those two get into a feud, there's no stopping either of them."

"Have they got form for it?" asked Jack.

"They've been adversaries for years. They are probably the two most pre-eminent dealers in York. They fell out a few years ago. Now, they hate each other."

"Do they have a confrontation at every auction?" asked Lisa.

"Not always. We tend to have a flare-up once in a while. This was the worst I have seen recently."

"We'll need details for Charles and Daniel," insisted Jack.

"I'll ask the girls to get them for you. They'll include Paul Colyer's contact details with them."

"Thank you," said Jack. "You've been very helpful this morning."

Simon Hayton smiled. The whole experience had not been as bad as the warnings Cathy Duggan had offered.

***

The afternoon was spent doing background checks on each of the auction house staff. Lisa told Nathan to ask the other two bidders to come into the station the following morning. If either proved difficult, she told him to get tough. It brought a look that suggested he was scared of his own shadow.

Jack took the opportunity to leave others to do the desk work. He grabbed his jacket and headed out onto the streets. He went door to door with some of his older contacts. The body parts screamed of a vendetta, which would have sent ripples through the underworld.

When nobody offered anything, he returned to the station with a coffee for Lisa. By the time he got there, she had already left for the day. Jack frowned and checked his watch. It was approaching six o'clock, which was close to drinking time at The Cellars.

He sat down at his desk and powered up his computer. Jack flicked through the case notes to get an update on the work so far. Sitting alone in the station, he heard some distant footsteps approaching. When he turned, Cathy Duggan was standing behind him. Her distinctive blonde hair and weathered face appeared racked with concern.

"Jack, have you got a minute?"

"Grab a seat. There's a spare coffee if you want it."

"How come?"

"I got it for someone who has gone home."

"Lisa?"

Jack smiled. He pushed the coffee across the desk towards Cathy. She picked it up, checked under the lid, and then sipped from it. It offered a momentary pause ahead of the awkward conversation that was coming.

"About yesterday," she said quietly.

"I didn't know he was your boyfriend," interrupted Jack. "I was a bit surprised when I saw you."

"Not as surprised as I was. I'm just glad I put a towel on." Cathy blushed when she realised the implication of what she had said.

Jack continued to read through the information presented on the screen. When Cathy edged closer, he took the report out of sight. A frown was offered from a woman he could read easily. Their time as a couple had made them understand each other's thoughts.

"You don't trust me, do you?" said Cathy bluntly.

"It's not that," said Jack.

"Let me help you with the case."

"I can't, Cathy. You know that."

"Do you think Simon has got something to do with it?"

"That's not for me to say."

"Come on, Jack. We've known each other long enough to be a bit more open than that."

"Based on what he said, all he did was auction the trunk."

"And you don't believe him," said Cathy, with one of her harsher looks.

"Do you?" replied Jack. He raised his eyebrows to make his point.

The silence Cathy offered was telling. Her look of concern came as a surprise. Jack had expected a staunch defence of Simon and yet nothing was forthcoming. She was staring at Jack, almost pleading with him to tell her that everything would be alright. Not for the first time in their lives, Jack was not going to give Cathy what she wanted.

"I was hoping he might be the one," sighed Cathy.

"He may well be," insisted Jack. "I wouldn't jump to any conclusions."

"Let me help, please."

"Sorry, Cathy. This is one case you cannot get involved in."

Cathy's face tightened up to inform Jack what she thought of his words. She was close to telling him exactly what was going through her mind.

Chapter 4

Lisa arrived at the station dreading the day. Her mind was riddled with doubts about Jack. He had not invited her to The Cellars for that drink they had spoken about. He had not even made the effort to see her.

Maybe the old Jack Husker had returned. If he had, they would return to their distant ways and those awkward moments of silence. She had not slept, with a long soak in the bath having done little to curb her frustration. Finally, the wine bottle had called her. Even that had not helped her to relax.

The only good thing Jack had done was not turn up early. It allowed Lisa to get started on a case that would get her out of the station. The pile of folders on her desk demanded attention. She picked one up and then placed it back down when she remembered her morning was already booked up.

Lisa headed downstairs with an uneasy feeling circling inside her. She saw Jack standing by the coffee machine, which did nothing to improve her mood. He smiled and then turned back to collect his drink. Lisa shook her head when Jack tried to hand her a cup of the unpleasant offering. She went into the meeting room, with Jack following behind.

They barely had a chance to exchange pleasantries before Nathan Lewis arrived. To their surprise, he had achieved the full task Lisa had given him. Both Charles Rickton and Daniel Voss were coming into the station that morning. They would be arriving one hour apart, allowing plenty of time for each to be interviewed.

"Did either give you a problem?" asked Lisa.

"Charles was a bit awkward," admitted Nathan.

"Did you threaten to send a search team to his shop?"

"No, I just mentioned Henry Davenport's name and he suddenly seemed keen to offer his opinion."

"That's good work. What about Daniel?"

"He was very relaxed about everything. Whether he'll turn up is another question."

"Have we got someone to stand in with us?"

"Yes," smiled Nathan. His uncomfortable expression hinted at someone trying to conceal a secret.

"Don't tell me, the DCI is getting involved," groaned Lisa.

"Better than that," he grinned. "I've got a new uniform for you to meet."

Suddenly, Kelly Knox walked through the door. Kitted out in a pristine police uniform, she smiled towards Jack and Lisa. Lisa had tried to keep in contact with her since her suspension. As with most things, her good intentions had soon subsided.

"Morning, Kelly," offered Lisa.

"Good morning," she smiled, with a genuine look of calm across her face.

"It's good to see you," nodded Jack.

"I'm pleased to be back. It's my first day. The inquiry said I could return as a uniformed officer but not as a detective."

"Are you happy with that?" asked Lisa.

"I'm delighted to have a job. Let's be honest; I don't deserve one."

"I wouldn't be too harsh on yourself," said Lisa. "You were put in a position that you should never have been in. The DCI has to take the majority of the blame for that."

"Perhaps Louth should be the one in uniform," grinned Jack.

"That's enough of your fantasies," laughed Lisa. "It's great to see you back, Kelly."

"Thanks. Now, if you don't mind, I have work to do. I think your first visitor is here."

"Then show him in, PC Kelly Knox," instructed Lisa. "Nathan, can you continue with the background checks while we interview the two men?"

"No problem. I'm on it."

Jack and Lisa exchanged smiles as Nathan and Kelly left the room. Kelly was not gone long before she returned with an irritated Charles Rickton. His rounded face was flushed red and sat on an overweight body that appeared to have outgrown his trousers. Just the effort of marching into the room had left a bead of sweat on his forehead.

"This had better not take long," snarled Charles even before he had sat down.

Jack performed the introductions and made a great play of offering his thanks to Charles for coming in. It was deliberately insincere and came with a slightly mocking tone. Lisa allowed herself to enjoy the spectacle of Jack antagonising an obnoxious man. A master was at work. She was not going to interrupt him.

"Get on with it," growled Charles.

"Why don't you tell us about yesterday's auction?" asked Jack.

"What is there to tell? I turned up, bid on some lots and took away those that I won."

"Did you win many?"

"Yes, I did."

"Have you got a list of your winning lots?"

"The auction house will hold those records."

"You must know what you bought."

"Of course, I do, but not in the detail you'll insist upon. You have to remember, I buy and sell many items every day. They pass through my hands quickly. I am a dealer, not a collector."

"Tell me about the Chinese trunk," said Jack.

"Which trunk?"

"I think we both know which one I am referring to. The final lot was a nineteenth-century trunk, which you bid on."

"I bid on it and I lost. That is the way auctions work."

"Why did you lose it?"

"The price was too high. It's as simple as that."

"What do you think it's worth?"

"Not as much as that fool paid."

"Humour us with a figure," insisted Jack.

"I don't know. Chinese trunks are not my area of expertise."

"You know enough to bid on them."

"I was curious to find out more about the item. I don't know; maybe I would have got fifteen hundred pounds for it."

"And yet your highest bid was seventeen hundred," said Jack.

"Was it?"

"It was according to our records."

"Then I must have got carried away. That isn't a crime; is it?"

"According to the auction house, the trunk is worth a lot less than that."

"That is an opinion. With all due respect to them, they are operating in a different market than I am. My clients are high-end investors who are always on the lookout for something special."

"How does that differ from what Henry Davenport does?" asked Lisa, interjecting into the conversation.

"I do it better," snarled Charles.

"Are you aware of the problem Henry has encountered with the trunk?"

"I am," he grinned. "Everyone has heard about it. Word travels fast in our world."

"You don't sound particularly upset by it."

"I will never be upset by something that causes *that* man a problem."

Charles Rickton said little else. He glanced at his expensive watch and declared that he was finished. Rather than have a row, Jack nodded that he could go. For now, Charles had nothing more to offer.

His place in the room was taken by Daniel Voss. Kelly brought the younger lad in ten minutes later. He was so different to both Henry and Charles. Engaging in personality, he stopped in the doorway to chat with Kelly. With his long brown hair and thin body, he looked more like a band member than an antique dealer.

It took some introductions from Lisa to bring Daniel to the table. He smiled and sat down while flicking his hair off his shoulders. On his t-shirt, some faded writing offered something of relevance in his world. To Jack and Lisa, it was akin to clothing they might have worn as a student.

"What do you want to know?" he asked eagerly.

"Let's start with the auction yesterday. How was it for you?" asked Lisa.

"Yeah, great. I picked up a couple of pieces, which I've already sold."

"What were they?"

"They were silverware; both early Victorian."

"Is that your speciality?"

"Yes," he nodded. "I do a bit of artwork as well. I prefer sculptures though I do better with paintings."

"Is that through a shop?"

"No, I'm online only. I have a website and I do a fair bit through Instagram."

"Why did you bid on that Chinese trunk?" asked Jack. "That isn't in your domain."

Daniel smiled. He flexed his mouth and glanced across, first at Lisa and then back to Jack.

"I wanted to teach those two muppets a lesson."

"Which two?"

"Henry Davenport and Charles Rickton. The way they behave is pathetic."

"What did you do?"

"It was obvious they both wanted it, so I ran the bidding up. Once it was beyond what it was worth, I sat back and enjoyed the spectacle. I didn't think it would go as high as it did."

"What do you think the trunk is worth?" asked Jack.

"The retail price for me would be five to six hundred pounds. Henry and Charles would get more than that because they've got a shop. They would get tourist prices."

"Which is how much?"

"I don't know. I guess they might get anything up to nine hundred on a good day."

"Charles Rickton said the trunk was worth fifteen hundred pounds to him."

"Not a chance," laughed Daniel, with a shake of his head. "Remember, the trunk was locked shut. He would have to force it open and either make a key for it or replace the lock. Whatever he does, the cost of preparing it for sale is going to be another couple of hundred pounds. Then there's the risk of damaging it when you open it."

"Are you saying he wouldn't have any chance of making money on it?" asked Lisa.

"Unless you're getting it for the lower end of the catalogue price, that one is a dud."

Jack rubbed his hand across his chin while Lisa brought the interview to an end. Somebody was telling them lies.

***

Louth was waiting for Jack when he returned to his desk. The scowl on his face told everyone he wanted some answers. Jack waited for the inevitable argument that was coming. For once, the DCI's manner was surprisingly calm.

"What's the story with the other bidders?" he asked.

"Charles Rickton is a pompous arse and Daniel Voss is a wind-up merchant."

"Neither of which is a crime," noted Louth. "Otherwise, I would be losing my best detective, wouldn't I?"

"I wouldn't describe Lisa as pompous, sir," grinned Jack.

"I wasn't," replied Louth as he offered his stare to deliver a warning.

"The next step is to have a look online for similar trunks," said Jack.

"Why?"

"Charles Rickton insists the trunk is worth at least fifteen hundred pounds. Daniel Voss is at a fraction of that. Someone must be telling the truth."

"Or maybe neither of them knows much about Chinese trunks."

"That's possible too," nodded Jack.

"You want my advice, Jack. The best place to find Chinese trunks is on Chinese swimmers," grinned Louth. He looked over pleased with his effort.

Jack ignored him and turned to his computer. Satisfied with his joke, Louth moved away. It left Jack wondering whether he preferred an angry DCI or one who thought he was a comedian.

Finding an equivalent trunk proved difficult. Few examples provided a fair comparison. Most were either badly damaged or in an overly-restored condition. In the absence of information, Jack turned to the dealers he had met in the past.

A series of calls suggested the trunk was worth no more than eight hundred pounds. Even if it was a pristine example, it would hold limited appeal. The demand was not there, making it purely a decorative item. Nobody would pay a four-figure sum for it. That did not sit alongside the valuations Henry Davenport and Charles Rickton had put on it. Both men had seen far more potential in something the market did not want.

Jack got up from his desk and headed out of the station. Unable to face another of the pool cars, he walked across the city to Henry Davenport's shop. It took him over forty minutes to get there. A detour to a coffee shop did not help.

When Jack walked in, he smiled at the older lady behind the counter. She peered up from a book she was writing in. A smile was offered, which turned to a look of concern when Jack showed his warrant card.

"Is Henry Davenport in?"

"Henry...you want to see Henry?" she frowned quizzically.

"Yes, please."

"I would have to see if he is in."

"Why don't I just go through and check?"

"I'm not sure Henry would like that."

When the lady glanced towards the door at the back of the shop, Jack made his move. He was confident the lady would not be chasing him. That would require a moment of decisiveness she had not managed in years.

Once out of the shop, Jack followed the corridor to an office. He knocked once on the door and entered. A man who looked similar to Charles Rickton was sitting at a desk. He had a phone to his ear and glanced up with consternation.

"Do you mind? This is a private call," barked the man with his hand placed over the end of the phone.

"I'm DI Jack Husker. Please can you end your call? I would like a word with you."

"No, I cannot. You will wait until I am finished."

"Fine, I'll take a look around while I wait."

"You will not!" growled Henry. It was said in the direction of a door which had closed behind Jack on his way out.

By the time Jack was back in the shop, Henry was alongside him. His angry red face was threatening to explode. His attempt to force out his words only resulted in exasperation. Jack smiled and turned towards him.

"I see your call has ended," grinned Jack.

"You need a warrant to be in here," insisted Henry.

"We're in a shop," shrugged Jack. "You won't get many customers if they all need a warrant to come in."

"But…"

"Shall we find somewhere comfortable to sit down for a chat?"

"I cannot spare the time. Come back when you have made an appointment."

"Fair enough," shrugged Jack. "We'll search the place at the same time."

"What do you mean?"

"It's obvious you have something to hide. Why else would you refuse a five-minute chat?"

"Five minutes, you say?"

"Probably less."

Henry looked across towards Margaret and shook his head. He was not going to get any help from her.

"It will have to be quick."

Jack allowed Henry to lead him back to his office. Once inside, they both took a seat. At Henry's insistence, Jack introduced himself for a second time. He then interlocked his fingers across his oversized stomach.

"I don't know why your colleagues didn't cover everything when they were last here."

"I can't comment on that, Mr Davenport. I guess we're looking at this from multiple angles."

"Just ask your questions and then I will ask one of my own," barked Henry.

"Mine is a simple one," said Jack. "Why did you pay so much for the trunk?"

"Because I wanted to buy it. Are we done?"

"It's worth less than half of what you paid for it."

"Says who?"

"Says every dealer I have spoken to."

"And tell me, DI Husker, are they York's premier fine antiques dealer?"

"They are pretty high up in the business."

"They do not know the York market. What might be valuable to them will not be to me and vice versa."

"What price are you going to sell the trunk for?"

"It will be priced at two-nine-fifty, with the expectation I will achieve a hundred or so less. It will be sold within a week."

"I don't believe you."

"That is your prerogative, DI Husker. May I ask my question now?"

"Of course."

"When can I have my trunk back? I need to get it into the window for Saturday."

"Mr Davenport, that trunk is evidence relating to a serious crime. It will not be returned to you until we have finished with it."

"How long will that be?"

"It will be as long as it needs to be."

"That is ridiculous," complained Henry, who was suddenly sitting bolt upright. "It is mine and I want it back."

"Is that with or without the body parts?"

The look Jack gave Henry Davenport dared him to respond.

***

After a day which offered no clues, Jack headed home. A text from Lisa came with an invitation to the pub. Abandoning all thoughts of any previous plans, Jack walked straight to The

Cellars. He went there armed with enough cash to clear the tab that was causing Alf to complain.

As soon as he walked in, Jack thrust one hundred pounds over the counter. Alf swept it up and replaced the money with a pint. The notes were pushed into Jack's kitty under the bar. For the first time in longer than Alf cared to remember, Jack was in credit.

"No Lisa tonight?" queried Alf.

"She's on her way," smiled Jack.

"Doesn't the girl get one night off for good behaviour?"

"She had that last night. I'm not going to risk another. She might realise she has better things to do on an evening than come here," laughed Jack.

"What could be better than a night in the pub with Jack Husker?" smiled Alf.

"My thoughts entirely. Pop her glass of wine on my tab when she comes in," instructed Jack.

He took his pint over to the corner. He had barely sat down when Lisa came striding through the door. She went straight to the bar and ordered a glass of wine. She beckoned towards Jack who confirmed he was ready for another. That was better than getting up in a few minutes when his pint was close to being finished.

Lisa brought the drinks over and pushed Jack's glass across the table. He took it and held it up to toast her. He lined up his refill behind the one he was drinking.

"Thanks for the wine."

"I try my best," said Jack.

A LOT TO DIE FOR

"How did you get on with Henry Davenport?" asked Lisa.

"Probably about as well as you did. I can't decide whether I find him or Charles Rickton more contemptible. You can understand why Daniel Voss took such delight in bidding them up on that trunk."

"Do you think either Henry or Charles knew what was in it?"

"No," said Jack. "I think they were just battling for an unusual item."

"What about Daniel?" asked Lisa.

"I reckon his story stacks up. He saw an opportunity to wind them up and took it. I would probably do the same," admitted Jack.

"Then who put the body parts in there? Do you reckon it was somebody at the auction house?"

"I can't see why they would. As soon as the trunk is opened, it's going to get linked back to them."

"We need to look at the seller," said Lisa.

"Simon said he's a regular seller through the auction. It would make no sense for him to do something like that either."

"Let's make him a priority for tomorrow," insisted Lisa. "That trunk must have been unlocked recently when the body parts were put in. They weren't that old."

Jack nodded to confirm his agreement. First, he had other things on his mind. His thoughts were already turning to his second pint and whether there would be a third one to follow it.

Chapter 5

Jack woke with a clear head. He rolled over in bed and realised Lisa was not there. He had walked Lisa back to her flat and had then gone home. It was her idea to stick to one glass of wine and get an early night. She had a dentist appointment she needed to get up for. A drinking session that would continue back at her flat would mean alcohol-laden breath. The dentist deserved better than that. Her sense of pride did too.

Having kept his intake to three pints, Jack felt refreshed. He had a shower and put on some relatively clean clothes. They had been on the back of his chair for less than a week. The usual hunt for socks saw him rewarded with a pair which matched. Something in his life was changing if he was wearing two of the same colour and similar length.

Jack made himself a cup of black coffee. He glanced at the box of aspirin beside the jar and ignored it. They were now an occasional treat that followed one of his heavy sessions. In recent weeks, Lisa had needed more of them than he had. Hangovers were not something she did well.

With nothing to eat in the house, Jack vowed to pick something up on his way to work. It would only be a couple of slices of toast to line his stomach. A meeting with the pathologist came with too much unease for anything more. Thankfully, it was not to see the post-mortem. It was just to go through the findings.

The strangest thing about it was that he was not seeing Cathy Duggan. The usual pathologist on major crimes had been assigned elsewhere. Her conflict of interest was obvious and yet it still felt odd. Jack would miss her bluntness. He would have to accept a pathologist brought in from outside the city. Whether Ray Chapple would be as good as Cathy was hard to say.

Jack drank his coffee and headed out of his house. Thankfully, he had persuaded Ray to come to the station with his findings. That was something Cathy Duggan would never have agreed to. She was clear that any favours would require others to make the effort.

Jack collected some toast and another cup of coffee from one of his usual cafes. He clutched the bag and cup in his hands and continued on his way. Eventually, the temptation of them became too much. He settled down on a bench and opened up the warm offering. The white slices covered in butter were soon dealt with. Jack washed it down with a mouthful of the over-hot coffee. Despite the heat, he managed to force it down.

He placed the cup at his feet and glanced at his phone. There was a message from Gregor Banks. He was insisting on an update for an assignment Jack had no intention of carrying out. He would not dance to Gregor's tune unless there was something the investigation needed from him.

A quick exchange of texts with Lisa offered more joy. She would be heading into the station once she was finished at the dentist. They needed a meeting with the seller of the Chinese trunk. Lisa had asked Nathan Lewis to set one up. If he could arrange it, she would drive straight over to Hull.

Jack made a loose promise to meet her later for a drink. If Lisa ended up going to Hull, it was a date she had little hope of keeping. Both of them were comfortable with that. They knew the job came first. Their time together would always have to fit around a major case.

He allowed Lisa to have the last word and then picked up his cup. Gregor did not even get the courtesy of a response. Jack eased himself up and continued on his way, tossing the empty paper bag into a bin on his way past. Gregor was forgotten about by the time he had covered the distance to the station. With his coffee still piping hot, Jack climbed the steps at the front of the building.

Once inside, he went into the meeting room he had booked. He was not about to make the mistake of going up to the main office. DCI Louth would be there with a list of tasks he wanted to delegate. It was the same every morning. Whoever caught his eye would be the unfortunate recipient.

Jack had barely settled down when an old man walked in. He looked like a retiree who should be queuing for his pension outside the Post Office. When the man held out a hand, he was surprisingly spritely. He moved quicker than Jack often did.

"DI Jack Husker; I'm Ray Chapple. We haven't worked together before."

"Pleased to meet you, Ray," smiled Jack in a rare display of welcoming behaviour. "Call me Jack, please."

"Jack, it is," confirmed Ray.

"Do you want to grab a coffee?"

"No, thanks," laughed Ray. "The stuff in here would kill me. The doctor says I have to watch what I eat and drink or I might not make old bones."

"I'd change your doctor, Ray. If you eat healthily, give up drink and women, you'll live forever. It'll certainly feel like it," laughed Jack.

"True enough. Mind you, I don't think there is much pleasure to be gained from breaking the rules for a cup of station coffee."

The two men smiled to confirm their agreement. Despite the friendliness of their encounter, Jack was eager to move the pace along. He wanted to see what Ray had to say. Part of it was driven by the cynical thought that Ray might not last much longer. If his doctor was looking for 'old bones' from Ray, he was expecting him to turn into a museum artefact.

Ray got out a file of papers from a tired-looking brown leather briefcase. The bronze lock was tarnished and took some effort to force open. He wrestled with it until he was able to force a clunk to confirm the mechanism had been released. With a smile, Ray eased out a folder. He placed it on the desk and looked across towards Jack.

"Everything you need is in there," said Ray. He pushed it across the desk.

"Do you want to give me the highlights?" asked Jack. "I'm not a great reader at the best of times."

"I think that is a generational thing with you youngsters," nodded Ray, to which Jack looked in shock at the pathologist.

"It's been a while since I've been called a youngster."

"You're all young to me," laughed Ray. "Some of these recruits I see are the same age as my grandchildren. One day, it will be the same for you."

"I might be pensioned off before then. Go on; what can you tell me about the body parts?"

"They are from a man called Shane Keyson. He is, or was, based on what he has missing, a dock worker from Immingham. Quite what he is doing in the trunk or over in York is anyone's guess. All I can confirm is that we have his four lower limbs, being the bottom half of his arms and legs, plus his head."

"I don't know the name," admitted Jack.

"His only criminal activity is over in the Humberside area. His DNA is on record from some petty crimes a few years ago. The most serious was a fight outside a pub. He received a suspended sentence. By all accounts, he was lucky not to end up in prison."

"What's he got to do with the trunk?"

"I have no idea, Jack. My job ends with the body parts."

"How long ago do you think he was killed?"

"It's hard to say. I don't think he died more than a day before he was put in the trunk. He was probably in there for a few days. Of course, there is another question."

"Which is?"

"Where's the rest of him?"

"If he's from Immingham, my instinct tells me the rest of his body would be dumped in the sea somewhere," offered Jack.

"Whoever did this must have disposed of anything they couldn't fit inside the trunk."

"You're probably right. Finding the rest of him and why this was done will be the hard part," admitted Ray.

"I can't help feeling the answer will lie somewhere over on the coast," said Jack. Already, his thoughts had turned to a trip to the seaside with Lisa.

***

Lisa was in a bad mood when she walked into the station. It was nearly ten o'clock and the aching from the dentist was still there. He had prodded her gums and made disappointed noises each time his pointed implement was poked into her. The finale of the painful experience had been a follow-up session with a brutal hygienist. Despite her obvious discomfort, the middle-aged butcher had inflicted her special brand of suffering on Lisa. For that, she had charged as much as the dentist and left Lisa's entire mouth numb.

The pain had only got worse when she saw the bill. Forced to use a private practice, the cost was akin to the debt of a third-world country. She could imagine Jack's response if she sought any sympathy. He would just shrug and then ask her what a dentist was. Maybe his false teeth needed nothing more than a glass of water to soak in by the side of his bed.

Her mood did not improve when she spoke to Nathan Lewis. He had failed to track down the seller of the trunk. Paul Colyer's phone had gone unanswered while his address looked like nothing more than a yard. At least Nathan had enough about him to perform those basic checks.

"Is there nothing you can find for him?" demanded Lisa.

"At the most, he has somewhere for storage. I can't find anything to suggest he has a shop or sells online," insisted Nathan.

"He can't sell all his items through auctions," said Lisa. "They wouldn't take everything."

"I'll keep looking," said Nathan, aware that Lisa was agitated.

DS Frank Campbell allowed his eyes to drift over the partition between their desks. He sensed there was a moment to have some fun. Put on the planet for a combination of his wit and as a gift to the female race, he never failed to make others envious of what he could offer. Just one bite was all he was asking for when he dangled his bait towards their desks. Both Lisa and Nathan would find it hard to resist his charm.

"What's the problem?" he said with a cheery grin.

"Nothing," insisted Lisa. She looked over the low divide and scowled. The last thing she was going to do was dance to Frank Campbell's tune.

"Hey, Chucky, what's the problem? I might be able to help," said Frank with a wry smile.

"It's this Chinese trunk," sighed Nathan.

"What's up with it?"

A look from Lisa tried to divert Nathan's attention away from Frank. It was too late to save him. He was hooked and Frank and was not about to let him go.

"We're trying to locate the seller," insisted Nathan.

"Do you know what I do when I'm faced with furniture containing a severed arm?"

"What?" asked Nathan enthusiastically.

"I go looking in second-hand shops," mused Frank. "Let me know how you get on."

As Frank got up and walked away with a grin on his face, Nathan began the search on his computer. He would go through every second-hand shop in the Humber area. Or he would have until Lisa stepped in to rescue him.

***

Jack spent the day trying to find out everything he could about Shane Keyson. It was slow methodical work. He found an address and obtained confirmation from his landlady that he had rented a studio apartment for the past two years.

Shane had moved into it as a temporary measure when he split up from a relationship. He was now the longest occupant of the apartment and somebody she never had any problems with. He always paid his rent on time and never complained about anything.

When she tried to ask whether something had happened, Jack offered as little as he could. He brushed off her questions as needing to do some background checks for a case he was working on. To reassure her, Jack confirmed that Shane was not the one under investigation. That appeased her and allowed him to move the conversation on to when she had last seen him.

The answer provided a dead-end. The landlady lived away from the area and had not been back for over two months. She only went there if there was a maintenance issue or to arrange for somebody else to move in.

Just as Jack was about to give up, the landlady offered a moment of inspiration. She could give him the contact details of his boss. He had been the one to provide a reference when Shane moved in. Jack played down the significance as he jotted down the valuable information on his notepad.

After thanking the landlady for her time, Jack tried the number and was met with a voicemail. He did not leave a message but instead circled the number as one he would call later. First, he wanted to find out more about Shane Keyson and who he might have links to. There had to be someone in his life who held a serious grudge against him.

A call on Jack's mobile from an unknown number provided a moment of intrigue. It came within minutes of him phoning Shane Keyson's boss. Hurriedly, he answered it, hoping it might be the man he wanted to speak to.

"DI Jack Husker speaking."

"Hi, Jack. It's Cathy."

"Cathy?"

"Cathy Duggan. You know, the woman you saw walking around in a towel."

Jack blushed and then laughed out loud. His reaction caught the attention of those around him. With Jack's reputation and seniority, none of the youngsters were going to say anything.

"I'm not sure that narrows it down," laughed Jack. "At my age, you see so many."

"In your dreams, you dirty old man."

"Even my dreams aren't that exciting," smiled Jack. "What can I do for you?"

"I want to see you, Jack."

"Excuse me?"

"Not in that way," laughed Cathy. "Can we meet? I need to speak to you about something."

"When are you thinking?"

"Meet me for a drink after work. Somewhere well away from the station."

"Okay. Tell me where and when and I'll be there."

"I'll text you a location. Does five-thirty work for you?"

"That's fine."

"And don't worry; I'll be wearing more than a towel," laughed Cathy. "That might just mean I put on some socks to go with it."

Jack forced a polite response. Cathy's words were making him feel very uncomfortable.

***

After a frustrating day, Jack left the station at five o'clock. Lisa had texted him to say that she would not be able to see him that night. Her parents would be calling and it was likely to take at least an hour. Once her mother started chatting, it normally wrote off most of the evening.

Jack was pleased that she was busy. His history with Cathy meant that meeting her didn't sit comfortably with him. He could also sense Lisa's unease with her. No matter how many times Jack had tried to reassure her, that nagging doubt was still there.

He walked into the pub at five-twenty. A quick look around confirmed that Cathy was yet to arrive. Jack texted her to find out what she was drinking and was told to order a glass of white wine. She was running late, with one of her post-mortems having gone on longer than expected.

Jack went to the bar and gazed at the selection on offer. There was an eclectic mix of modern trendy lagers and a broad selection of wines. An overly fashionable man in his early thirties greeted Jack with a smile. He had an impressive moustache that was twisted up at the ends and a manicured goatee beard to go with it.

"What can I get you, sir?"

Jack puffed out his cheeks and prepared himself for a lifetime of disappointment.

"Dare I ask whether you have any hand-pulled ales?"

"They are over there. Take your pick from the row. I recommend the guest ale on the end."

Jack looked across to see the row of pump handles tucked away in the corner. Maybe he had misjudged the lad based solely on his appearance.

"Why are they hidden over there?"

"They were there when we bought the place. We haven't got around to relocating everything yet. We're hoping to add a couple more options when we do the work. If you want to try any of them before you decide, I'll get you some tasters."

"No need," confirmed Jack. He had warmed to the lad's hospitality. "I'll have a pint of the guest ale, please. Can you also do me a large glass of dry white wine?"

"No problem."

Jack waited for the drinks to be served and then paid for them. After offering genuine gratitude to the barman, he went to sit down. Taking a bench in the corner, he made sure the choice of seating would not offer anything too intimate. The L-shaped seat was accompanied by a single chair. No matter where Cathy decided to sit, she would not be getting too close to him.

Cathy Duggan came into the bar like a whirlwind. She swept in with a folder tucked under her arm and spun around until she saw Jack. As soon as she set eyes on him, she marched over and sat on the adjacent side of the bench. With a smile, she looked at Jack who had not risen more than a few inches from his seat. To go any further would risk them needing to embrace.

Cathy took a large swig of her wine. In so many ways, it resembled Jack's approach to a pint of beer. She savoured the taste and then eased back to enjoy a more relaxed sip. A deep release of breath was followed by the glass being placed down in front of her.

"Bad day?" asked Jack.

"Not one of my best. I'll spare you the gory details. All I'll say is this one wasn't fresh."

"Thanks for that," replied Jack, with a grimace.

"How was your day?"

Jack thought for a minute and then held back the response he would naturally offer. Everything he had done involved a case that Cathy Duggan could be no part of.

"It was fine. Just another day in crime town."

"It's okay. I know you can't tell me anything more."

"You know how it is," shrugged Jack.

"I do," sighed Cathy. "Thanks for agreeing to come for a drink. I know it doesn't put you in an easy position."

"Come on; don't keep me waiting. What was it you wanted to talk to me about?"

Cathy Duggan pursed her lips and thought for a moment. With each second that passed, Jack became more concerned.

"It's about Simon."

"Cathy, you know I can't talk about the case."

"It's not the case. I want your opinion. Am I making a big mistake with him?"

"I don't know," said Jack. "I barely know the guy."

"That's the thing. I don't think I do either."

"What do you mean?"

"Well, I thought I did. Then, when I saw you in the house, it made me realise that I'm not as close to him as I thought I was."

"I'm not sure I understand."

"You probably wouldn't, Jack. That's the best bit about you."

Chapter 6

The evening with Cathy Duggan had extended to two drinks. For Jack, that meant two pints of the trendy barman's guest ale while Cathy followed her glass of wine with sparkling water. The only closeness had been a brief hug when they went their separate ways.

Jack had enjoyed one more pint in The Cellars on his way home. It had given him time to reflect on what Cathy had said. Why did the case have to involve her boyfriend? Life had been so much simpler when she was loved up and looking forward to a future with Simon.

After exchanging some messages with Lisa, Jack had gone to bed. He was awake early, allowing him to head into the station long before he needed to. On the way, he picked up a bacon butty and a coffee. By the time anybody else arrived, the only evidence would be the aroma wafting through the building.

Jack settled down at a desk by the window. He spent some time looking up Simon Hayton while he ate his butty. Until the case, Simon had not appeared on any police records. And yet his presence on the internet was notable. There was a news article about him at the auction house and a series of features that were akin to free advertising.

The search also offered up some upcoming auction dates. A clearance auction caught Jack's attention. It started at ten o'clock and would provide Jack with an opportunity to see Simon in action. It would also corroborate the stories of the other workers' descriptions of their roles.

Jack was finishing his coffee just as Lisa arrived. They smiled at one another and then sat a respectable distance away. The last thing anybody wanted was a couple displaying closeness at work. They had a job to do and that meant putting relationships to one side.

"Bacon?" asked Lisa.

"Don't mind if I do," grinned Jack.

"I meant the butty you've just had."

"What gave it away?"

"You mean other than the smell when you come out of the lift, the grin on your face and the screwed-up wrapper beside you? Nothing at all."

"That's the problem with dating a detective," he smiled.

"Or being so predictable," she grinned back.

Their exchange was ended by the sight of Frank Campbell waddling towards them. It changed the mood and put them on notice that wisecracks would soon be coming their way. Frank never missed a chance to test out unwary colleagues. His remarks had seen him get into trouble on several occasions. It never seemed to change him.

"Morning, Mr and Mrs Husker," he grinned inanely.

"Morning, Frank," offered Jack and Lisa, a little too harmoniously for their liking.

"You found the rest of your body yet?"

"Not yet," confirmed Lisa.

"Don't bother checking in Jack's bedroom. Nobody goes in there."

Jack shook his head at Lisa to advise her not to respond.

"If you've been working on that one all night, you've wasted a lot of time," growled Jack. "Anyway, we think it was suicide."

"Suicide?" frowned Frank. "The bloke's been cut into multiple pieces."

"That shows his desperation to die after hearing one of your jokes."

Frank muttered a few expletives under his breath. He settled his large frame down at a neighbouring desk and released a sigh from the effort. The smell of bacon had caught his attention. His eyes scanned around to see if there was any going spare.

Nathan Lewis was the next to arrive. He saw Frank and immediately diverted to a desk as far away from him as possible. Lisa watched him sit down and made her way over to speak to him. It would be done in a whisper to ensure Frank did not get involved in their conversation.

While she was gone, DCI Louth called Jack into his office. He walked over and accompanied him to his door. Too wise to allow Jack out of his sight, he closed the door behind him. As Louth sat down behind his desk, Jack felt like he was being watched by a teacher.

"Where are we up to with this Chinese trunk?"

"We know the body is Shane Keyson, a dock worker from Immingham. I'm waiting for a call back from Keith Elton, who was his boss. I have also spoken to his landlady."

"Is that another excuse to go into a pub?" grinned Louth.

"I'm talking about the landlady of the apartment he rents. There are two types of landlady."

"I know that, Jack. I'm just surprised that you do. What about the auction house?"

"So far, we have nothing from them or the bidders for the trunk. We're still doing the background checks on them all."

"Have any of them got previous?"

"Billy Ellis, one of the auction porters, has. That scrote has been arrested more times than I've been in a pub."

"That's impressive," laughed Louth. "What's he got form for?"

"Petty stuff. Burglary, driving offences, assault and the odd spot of GBH thrown in for good measure."

"What about butchery?"

"As much as I would like to pin it on him, I can't see it."

"What about the auctioneer? Did I hear that Cathy Duggan is dating him?"

"Yes," blushed Jack.

"That's a bit unfortunate. How is she?"

"She's okay. She knows she can't get involved."

"Do we think he's got anything to do with it?"

"I can't see how. I'm going to have a look at the auction he's running this morning and see if anything strikes me as odd. I wouldn't hold your breath on that one."

"What about the Immingham connection?"

"As soon as I can speak to Shane Keyson's boss, we'll head over to see him. We also need to track down the seller of the trunk. He doesn't seem to have anything other than a mobile number and some premises on the outskirts of Hull. We'll try to cover that off when we're over there."

"Keep me informed, Jack."

"Will do, sir."

"And next time, if you're going to stink the station out with one of your bacon butties, make sure you bring me one. That bloody wife of mine has got me on rabbit food again. I'm expecting to grow long ears at this rate."

"No problem," smiled Jack. He could already picture DCI Louth and his long ears bouncing around his office.

***

After a quick stop-off at a coffee shop, Jack and Lisa headed to the auction house. Lisa drove while Jack checked his messages. There was still nothing from Keith Elton who would soon be getting another call. Jack was irritated at being ignored.

"What auction are we going to see?" asked Lisa as she navigated carefully through the roadworks.

"I'm guessing it will be house clearance stuff from the description."

"You could buy some of it," grinned Lisa. "It'll be an upgrade on your current furniture."

"Or I could rent my house out as a museum and move in with you."

"You wouldn't like my flat. It's modern and tasteless."

"You mean, warm, modern and tasteless. At this time of year, there's a lot to be said for that."

"True enough," smiled Lisa. "And remember, I already have an old item in the corner to add character."

"Don't even think about saying the punchline," growled Jack.

Lisa turned into the car park and was shocked by the number of vehicles. It was packed full, forcing her to park in the far corner. She reversed expertly into a space while Jack said nothing to distract her. Even he had to admit it was done with far greater skill than he could have managed. His slow nod was seen by Lisa who could not help but feel pleased with her efforts.

Navigating past a crowd of people, they went inside the building. They greeted Dawn who was looking stressed behind the desk. They declined her offer to call Simon. They were only there for background information, not for anything formal.

Despite their refusal, Simon Hayton appeared just after they had sat down. He took a seat beside them and offered his hand to shake. With others around them, he spoke in a whisper. The last thing he wanted was to scare away his audience. The demographic would see them scurrying back to the bus stop with their free passes if there was a hint of anything gruesome.

"What brings you here?" he asked.

"Just to find out a bit more about how auctions work. It's not our field of expertise," said Lisa.

"You should have said. I could have given you a tour."

"That's very kind but we don't want to waste your time," she replied. "We thought we would pop in for a few lots and then head on our way."

"If you see anything you like, make sure you've registered. You need a number to bid."

"We won't be bidding on anything," confirmed Jack. "Where are the three amigos?"

"You won't see the likes of Henry or Charles at these auctions. This is clearance stuff, which is way beneath them. Daniel Voss occasionally pops in if there is some silver in the catalogue. You won't see him today. The only thing of any value on this one is a toy collection. The deceased had several Tri-ang vehicles."

"What are they?" asked Lisa.

"They're tinplate toys from the nineteen fifties and sixties. They can be highly collectable if you're into that sort of thing, which a lot of people are. It reminds them of their childhood, often things their parents couldn't afford. Other than that, it's old furniture and kitchen items. Most of it will go for a few pounds at best."

"Who buys that sort of stuff?"

"Look around you. It's a day out for most people. They go away with a couple of items for not a lot of money. They normally come with little intention of buying and get tempted by something. It's very fast-paced compared to the antiques auctions because we have a lot to get through."

Simon left Jack and Lisa to contemplate his words. A check of his watch told him that the auction time was approaching. The room was nearly full and a hum was starting to go through the space. To Jack and Lisa, it felt like a foreign world. The closest Lisa had seen to such a tense environment was ahead of the Boxing Day sales.

On stage, the first lot was being carried out by Billy Ellis and Finn Mann. It was a modern table, which was soon joined by four accompanying chairs. Even from the back of the room, the tatty set looked unimpressive.

Simon Hayton walked to the podium at exactly ten o'clock. He did a quick introduction and confirmed the rules of the auction. Without delay, the first lot was offered to the room. It brought a couple of reluctant bids that suggested nobody truly wanted it. Despite Simon's best efforts, the table and chairs only made twelve pounds. That was ten pounds more than the single chair was sold for on the following lot.

Jack and Lisa watched as a series of items were brought in. The 'lifter and shifter' definition for Billy and Finn could not have been more accurate. All they did was bring in the items and take them away just as quickly. The only person missing from the action was Dean Lucas.

They remained in their seats while a series of depressing items came and went. None of them offered much appeal or any recognition of the part they had played in someone's life. They were probably much-loved by whoever had passed. Now, they were being flaunted on stage to an audience greeting them with utter indifference.

A flurry of bids on a side table provided a moment of optimism. Twenty-six pounds was the highest price paid to date and saw fierce competition between two older ladies. Bidding in two-pound increments, each decision was made in a manner to suggest they were contemplating the purchase of the Crown Jewels. When the table reached its sale price, the losing woman looked aghast at the cost of the item. She could not possibly find another two pounds in her purse to secure her treasure.

"Come on; let's go," groaned Jack. "I've seen enough."

"Don't you want to wait for the toys?" grinned Lisa. "They'll be from your childhood."

"All I had was an empty box," growled Jack. "And I was grateful for that."

Lisa tried to respond and was left shaking her head. It was too late. Jack was already leaving. Ignoring tuts from those he had to squeeze past, he forced his way to the aisle. Lisa mouthed her quiet apologies and followed him out of the room.

She caught up with him on the way to the car. Jack was still muttering under his breath when she got there. Something had riled him. Lisa unlocked the car and waited for him to get in.

"If I ever get forced to put up with that as a day out, you will shoot me, won't you?" he growled.

"I could shoot you now as a preventative measure," laughed Lisa.

"Please do. That was painful. I think Shane Keyson had the right idea by getting in the trunk."

"That's a bit harsh even for you."

"No, it isn't. Speaking of Shane Keyson, let me try to get hold of his boss. He hasn't returned my message."

"Maybe he thought too much excitement in one day was not good for you," laughed Lisa.

***

They were back in the station when Jack received a call from Keith Elton. He was apologetic for not returning Jack's call earlier. He had been out on a sea-fishing boat the previous day and was only just catching up on his messages. On his second day off, he was trying to make up for lost time.

"Is it possible to come over and see you, Mr Elton?" asked Jack.

"Yeah, sure. Does tomorrow work for you?"

"Tomorrow would be fine. Are you working?"

"Yes, I'll be at the docks from six onwards. I'll be there until mid-afternoon. What is it about? I don't normally get calls from the police, let alone you guys over in York."

"We're just after some information about a case we're working on. We'll get over as soon as we can."

"Just mind the traffic. It's murder on a morning. I'll send you an address."

"Thanks, Mr Elton. My colleague and I will see you tomorrow."

Jack ended the call and looked across towards Lisa. She was busy with Nathan who appeared to be eagerly accepting his superior's instructions. Jack wandered across and told her about the trip to Immingham docks. There was a look of panic from Nathan followed by a sense of relief when he realised that he would not be going.

"I take it I'm driving," she sighed.

"Either that or I'm driving your car," grinned Jack.

"I'll drive," she said hurriedly.

Jack agreed to meet her at her apartment early the following morning. He waited for an invite to stay over, which never came. He put it down to the presence of Nathan rather than anything he had done. Jack left the two detectives to continue working and wandered back to his desk. Within minutes of sitting down, he felt the urge to go for a walk.

He was barely out of the station when a sudden wave of cold air hit him. It left Jack wishing he had worn a coat. He pulled his jacket tight around him and hurried quickly through the streets. He headed towards the city centre, keen to seek out a quiet coffee shop. The first that could promise him warmth and a decent cup of coffee would get his business.

His plan was thwarted by the vibration of his phone in his pocket. Fighting against the shiver that went through him, he took it out. A puff of his cheeks was his response. The name displayed on the screen was an irritation.

"Gregor, what do I owe the honour to?"

"I was just wondering whether you fancied meeting up for a coffee."

"When?"

"Now would be good, seeing as you're heading into town," replied an assured-sounding Gregor Banks.

"Are you spying on me?" asked Jack. A shudder went through his body.

"Don't flatter yourself. I've got better things to do than spend my time watching a decrepit detective. Naturally, there are others who I can't say the same about."

"Where do you want to meet?"

"You choose. Pick somewhere nice."

"Only if you're paying."

"Go on, I'll treat you," agreed Gregor.

"I'll see you in The Hawthorn Cafe in about ten minutes. Do me a favour and leave your thugs outside. They have a place to tie up pets."

"How about I send them to the toy shop across the road? I wouldn't want them too far away in case you get a bit boisterous."

"Just keep them away from the cafe. The girl who serves in there is of a nervous disposition."

"Aren't we all, Jack? See you in ten minutes."

Gregor ended the conversation without allowing Jack to respond. The race was on for who could get there first. Whoever did would get their preferred position. Gregor would want his thugs located close enough to be called upon easily. Jack would want a corner seat where nobody could approach him from behind.

Without breaking into a run, both men moved swiftly. They arrived at the cafe at the same time and met at the doorway. Jack refused to go in until Gregor's associates had been sent away. He knew how eager both were to inflict bodily harm on middle-aged detectives.

"They're harmless, Jack."

"Send them on their way. We won't be long."

The thugs were told to wait outside the cafe. While Gregor was speaking to them, Jack took the opportunity to go inside. He took a seat in the corner. It served both their purposes by giving each man what they wanted. Jack had his back to a wall while Gregor was in sight of his bodyguards.

When the waitress came over, she was exactly as Jack had described her. Nervous in manner, the twenty-something girl appeared scared of her own shadow. She was so timid that even Gregor did his best not to frighten her. He spoke softly and offered none of the implied aggression that was synonymous with his usual manner in front of Jack.

They ordered two coffees and a plate of biscuits, which were added at Gregor's insistence. He described them as a treat for Jack. The two men were in the early rounds of jousting. Both were trying to put the other at ease.

"This is nice," smiled Gregor. "I haven't been in here before."

"It's underrated. You just have to get past Nervous Nicky," grinned Jack. "Your thugs would probably give her a heart attack."

"Just to be clear, they are business colleagues, not thugs."

"Sorry, my mistake. It's so easy to get confused when one of them has their hands around your throat."

They paused when Nicky brought over the drinks. The plate of biscuits went between them. It was a good selection of homemade options. Jack smiled when he saw the chocolate shortbread, which would be the perfect accompaniment to his mug of coffee.

"I knew you wouldn't be able to resist them," said Gregor when Jack picked the first one off the plate.

"It would be a shame to let them go to waste."

"But not to your waist," laughed Gregor.

"It also means you can do the talking while I tuck in," confirmed Jack.

"I thought I was here to ask you questions," frowned Gregor.

"I'm occupied with these delicious biscuits, so you might as well fill the void with some information."

"Go on, what do you want to know? As long as I get my turn afterwards, I'll talk first," nodded Gregor.

"Shane Keyson," said Jack.

"Who's he?"

"A dock worker from Immingham."

"Sorry, that's out of my jurisdiction," shrugged Gregor. "I don't know him."

"What about Billy Ellis? Do you know him?"

"As in the kid at the auction house?"

"That's him."

"I know him. He's a right little scrote. I haven't heard much from him recently. In his day, he was a horrible little oik. All petty stuff but a pain in the arse to go with it."

"Did you have any dealings with him?"

"Am I going to have to give you the spiel about being a law-abiding businessman or do you just want an off-the-record answer?"

"The off-the-record bit will be fine," admitted Jack.

"See, we're getting more of an understanding in our old age. I do prefer it that way."

"Don't get too used to it," growled Jack. "What do you know about Billy?"

"I didn't come across him much. On one occasion, we slapped him around a bit when he strayed onto our territory. Other than that, he was mainly a thieving little toad, which isn't my game."

"What's he into these days?"

"The last I heard, he was going straight."

"Billy Ellis going straight? That's a joke and a half."

"That's exactly what I thought," laughed Gregor. "I've not heard about anything he's into recently, so it's possible. People do change."

"He must be up to something," insisted Jack. "Gutter-feeders like Billy Ellis do not change their spots."

"If he is into something dodgy, it isn't on my radar. Maybe I need to diversify more," grinned Gregor.

"Or maybe your standards are slipping and others are muscling in."

"Which brings me nicely to my question. Where are you on finding out who the new player is?"

"I've come up blank so far," shrugged Jack.

"Don't give me that," growled Gregor. "I've played along with your games. I want to know who's running the sideshow. Don't make me ask nicely again. I only buy biscuits once."

Gregor stared into Jack's eyes for longer than was comfortable. He placed a twenty-pound note on the table. He then got up and marched out of the cafe.

Chapter 7

The trip to Immingham began early. At Lisa's insistence, they set off before seven. She would heed Keith Elton's words and beat the early morning traffic. She had set an alarm for six o'clock, hoping the drive would not be as bad as she feared.

Late in the evening, Lisa had messaged Jack to ask him if he wanted to stay over. He had just got settled into his favourite armchair and declined her belated offer. He promised to be at her flat well before they needed to set off. He kept to his word and arrived just after six-forty-five.

"How come you didn't want to stay over last night?" asked Lisa.

"I thought one of us might lead the other astray if I did," admitted Jack.

"That's unusually restrained of you."

"It's old age," said Jack. "I might as well say it before you do."

Lisa smiled. Jack had read her mind and prevented her from scoring an early point.

"What about staying over tonight? Are you planning on being as restrained when we get back?"

"We don't have to get up for work tomorrow, so if you fancy making a night of it, I won't say no."

"Let's see what time we get back. Hopefully, we won't be too long in Immingham. Not that I know much about the place. I've never been there."

"Nor have I," admitted Jack. "Remember, I want to come back through Hull. Let's see if we can find where Paul Colyer hangs out."

"That's fine. Nathan gave me the details."

The conversation ended when Lisa put on the radio. It launched a musical assault on Jack's ears. He didn't mind. It gave him time to think about the case. With little coming from their work in York, he needed Keith Elton to offer something.

While Jack remained deep in thought, Lisa pressed her foot down. The warning about the traffic felt misguided. There was barely a car on the road. They got to the docks and followed the instructions Keith had given them. After showing their warrant cards, they were told to park up and go on foot to a portacabin.

They knocked on the door and entered when a loud voice instructed them to do so. Inside, a man was sitting at one of three desks in an overly heated office. The contrast to the cold whistling wind outside could not be understated. Nobody was going to freeze when they stepped inside. They had a reasonable chance of being roasted.

"Keith Elton?" enquired Lisa.

"That's me," confirmed a short stocky man who looked no taller when he stood up.

"Mr Elton, I'm DS Lisa Ramsey and this is DI Jack Husker, who you spoke to on the phone."

"Call me Keith, please. You're here early."

"The traffic was nowhere near as bad as I was expecting."

"Sorry, that's my fault. I forgot it was Saturday. In this job, you grab your days off when you can. You lose track of the week. If you had come yesterday, you would have been stuck for hours. There was a pile-up on the M180."

"Did you do much while you were off?" asked Lisa.

"I had a fishing trip off the coast on Thursday."

"Did you catch anything?" It was asked in preference to a question about whether Keith had disposed of anything over the side.

"We did alright. We had some nice cod and a large ling over one of the wrecks. Can I get you some tea or coffee?"

"Coffee would be great," said Lisa.

"It's only instant and it'll have to be black. The muppets didn't leave me any milk. I'll have to grab some later."

"Black is fine," confirmed Lisa.

The act of making it was swift. A kettle was reboiled and poured over a heaped spoonful of cheap own-brand powder. Jack feared what he would be given. His golden rule about any coffee being better than none was about to be tested.

"I'll let the lady have the unchipped cup," said Keith.

"Thank you," smiled Lisa.

Jack was handed a dirty cup with a crack down one side. He thanked Keith and placed it on the desk the squat man had been working at. Once all the drinks had been made, Keith sat down.

He made no attempt to find out what the conversation would be about.

"Thank you for agreeing to see us," began Lisa. "It's one of your employees that we want to talk to you about."

"Which one of them is in trouble?" sighed Keith.

"It's Shane Keyson."

"Go on, what's he done?"

"We believe he might have been murdered."

"Murdered!" barked Keith. His eyes opened wide in horror. "He can't be murdered. He's due back on Monday. He's supposed to be on holiday."

"Unfortunately, we believe something may have happened to him while he was off."

Keith Elton took a series of deep breaths as he struggled to come to terms with the news. He held up his hand to request a moment to compose himself.

"How sure are you?"

"We have a DNA match to a body we found."

"Oh, fuck," sighed Keith. "Sorry," he added when he looked across at Lisa.

"It's fine; take your time," she assured him.

"Those tests are pretty accurate, aren't they?"

"I'm afraid so," she nodded.

Keith took another few seconds and then rubbed his face in his hands. A swig of his coffee did nothing to improve how he was feeling. He placed his cup down and sat back. He shook his head and muttered under his breath.

"How?" he asked meekly.

"Sorry, we can't go into the details. We're in the early stages of the investigation, which means we have to be careful about what information we offer. All I can say is it appears to be a violent act."

"Oh no," sighed Keith. "The poor sod."

"It would help us enormously if you could tell us a bit about Shane and anyone else who works here."

"You don't think any of our lot were involved, do you?" Keith looked aghast at the possibility.

"We have nothing to suggest that. At this stage, we're just trying to find out more information. We don't even have his next of kin or anything like that."

"You might struggle with that. His parents died in a car accident ten years ago. I don't think there was anyone else."

"What about a partner?"

"He has a girlfriend. I wouldn't waste your time on her. She's a complete airhead. He's only with her because she looks the part."

"Have you got any details for her?"

"I can find them. If I haven't got them, someone will."

"That would be useful, thanks."

"I'll send those on to you as soon as I get a moment to hunt them down."

"That's fine. Can you tell me who else works here?"

"There's four of us. I manage the place and have three lads working shifts. As well as Shane, I have Olly Hakings and Liam Nicholls. All of them are good lads and work hard. I wouldn't be able to say a bad word about any of them."

"Do any of them ever get into trouble?"

"No more than any other lad in his twenties. I'm sure you know about the fight Shane ended up in. I think he also had some other bits and bobs in his past."

"Do you think there might have been any grudges held over from that fight?" asked Jack.

"I doubt it. The lad he put in the local hospital had it coming. He was a low life. I know that doesn't justify it but nobody would shed a tear for him."

"Do you think he might have come back for revenge?"

"No. He drowned in an accident a couple of years ago. The stupid sod went out in a rowing boat in the middle of the night. He was high on drugs."

"What about the other lads?"

"Olly would be the only other one with any previous. He got charged for dangerous driving last year. Other than that, I think he would be clean. Liam is a Mummy's boy. He has never even gone out with his shoes unpolished."

"Would any of them have any problems with Shane?"

"Definitely not. They're on shifts, so they hardly see each other."

"When was the last time you saw Shane?"

"I can get you an exact time and date. It will be just over a week ago before he went on leave."

"Where was he going?"

"He wasn't going anywhere. Like me, he spends a lot of his spare time fishing. He would have been on a pier somewhere with a rod in his hand."

"And can you think of anyone who might want to cause him harm?"

"Absolutely not. I can't think of anybody who would want to hurt Shane. He's such a good lad."

Jack and Lisa thanked Keith for his time and headed back to the car.

***

They said nothing on the way to Lisa's car. Keith's endorsement of Shane's virtues was still ringing in their ears. It was hard not to be cynical when the job had taught them to have a sceptical eye. It had also taught them not to discuss people they had met until they were well clear of the site.

Lisa waited until she was on the main road. She pulled into the flow of traffic and then turned towards Jack. He was deep in thought and processing the conversation with Keith Elton. So little had been said to help them.

"What do you think?" she asked.

"I think Shane was the nicest man in the world. The only way he would have ended up in that trunk was through a terrible accident. Maybe he slipped and fell through a cheese grater."

"That's one option," nodded Lisa sarcastically. "What did you make of Keith Elton?"

"He serves the worst cup of coffee I've ever had and it was in a cracked mug."

"That must make him guilty," laughed Lisa.

"It's definitely worth ten years inside," added Jack.

"Did anything else catch your eye when you weren't arresting him for crimes against beverages?"

"He's being protective of his lads, which is understandable. Despite what he served me, I can't see him doing that to Shane."

"Which brings us back to square one," sighed Lisa.

"Not yet, it doesn't. We haven't found Paul Colyer. Let's head over to the address Nathan gave us."

"I'm on my way."

"Step on it, driver," grinned Jack.

Lisa floored the accelerator to send Jack jolting back in his seat. She eased off immediately and turned in the direction of Hull. A trip over the Humber Bridge would be a rare experience. Lisa had only been over it once before and remembered being shocked by its scale. Spanning a wide estuary, it stood impressively across the two shorelines.

Some had marked it out as one of the most impressive in the world. And yet the murky brown colour below did not offer the same allure as its equivalents in San Francisco and Sydney. It was hard to imagine tourists flocking to see it when a cold sweeping wind was added in. This was the Humber estuary, not a tropical sea with a matching climate.

It took less than an hour to get across the bridge and into Hull. Jack punched the address into the satnav and sat quietly while Lisa worked her way through the streets. They drove to an industrial area, with warehouses and yards surrounded by security. Every entrance seemed to be protected by barbed wire and cameras.

Lisa stopped the car when she reached the destination. All she saw was a small empty yard and a tatty caravan tucked into the corner of the site. Some broken pallets were strewn across the space. There was nothing that would hint at an antiques business. The metal gate was locked with a large padlock. The site appeared abandoned.

"What do you think?" asked Lisa as she maintained a watchful eye on her mirrors.

Jack gazed at the caravan and smiled. "I've stayed in worse holiday accommodation. I doubt the evening entertainment will be up to much."

"We must have the wrong address," insisted Lisa.

"I don't think so," said Jack. "This is a front for something dodgy. Let me ask the guy over there. There's someone in the hut over the road." Jack pointed to a site diagonally opposite where a raised portacabin was overlooking a haulage yard.

"If you don't mind, I'll stay here and keep the engine running," said Lisa.

"That's fine. If there's any trouble, you go and call for backup. I'll hide up there."

Jack got out of the car and walked across the road. A broken-down car had been abandoned at the side of the compound and had been targeted by youths. All the windows were smashed while anything of worth had been stripped from it. The state of it resembled the first car Jack owned. Just fifty pounds had bought it. He had doubled its value by filling it with fuel.

He entered the compound and walked straight up the metal stairs. At the top, he knocked on the door and went in. Immediately, a man spun around in his chair and stared venomously towards Jack. There was no warmth coming from anywhere other than a cheap plug-in heater.

"What the fuck do you want?" growled the man.

"I would like to ask you a question."

"Is this a wind-up?" snarled the man whose presence appeared to be growing behind his desk. "Get out. This is private property."

"Only when you've answered my question."

The eyes of the man narrowed down. He stared at Jack with so much ill intent it felt contagious.

"I don't know who you are but I suggest you take a walk. I won't ask you again."

"Cut the hard man routine and tell me who has the site across the road."

"Fuck off."

"Fair enough," shrugged Jack. "We'll do this the hard way."

Jack took a step closer to the man. It forced him up from his chair. As he stretched, his size appeared to inflate by the second. By the time he was fully upright, he looked well over six feet tall and his shoulders appeared wider than his height. He cracked his knuckles and stepped out from behind the desk, ready to go to war.

"Please to meet you," said Jack while offering out his hand. "I'm DI Jack Husker."

His hand was left hanging in mid-air. The anger of the man seemed to linger between them. Jack glanced down and saw that his fist was still curled tightly shut. Either the man was going to hit him or he would need to back down quickly.

"You're a pig?"

"I'm a detective inspector if that helps you," said Jack.

The thug flexed his jaw and looked coldly at Jack. He seemed to spend an inordinate amount of time processing the information.

"What do you want?"

"I want to know who owns the yard across from you."

"Which one?"

"The one over there," pointed Jack. "The empty yard with the caravan and broken pallets."

"No idea."

"What's it used for?"

"I don't know."

"Does anyone visit it?"

"How would I know?"

"Fine, I'll get some uniforms down here to investigate. That feels like a lot of wasted time to me. Thanks for your help." Jack turned and headed towards the door.

"Wait," growled the man.

Jack made sure he was at a safe distance before he turned. The last thing he wanted was a solid fist to connect with his jaw. On enemy territory, he would stand little chance against a man built for violence. He stared back towards him and raised an eyebrow to offer a half-interested look.

"Well?"

"It's used as a transit drop-off."

"What does that mean?"

"Stuff is dropped off and onward shipped as soon as it can be loaded."

"Is that for stolen goods?"

"Probably," shrugged the man.

"Who owns it?"

"I've no idea and I don't want to know. The first rule of business is don't get involved in stuff that doesn't concern you."

"Do you know a Paul Colyer?"

The man thought for a moment and shook his head.

"Never heard of him."

"What sort of goods get dropped off there?"

"I don't know. Whatever it is comes in solid wooden crates. That means it's probably been shipped in from abroad."

"Through Immingham?"

"Possibly, or Hull, or Grimsby. It could be anywhere. There are plenty of ports."

When did the last shipment come in?"

"I don't know. I don't watch over them. I've got far too much to do in here."

"What is it you do?"

"I run a small fleet of trucks. It's all legit before you ask."

"I'm sure it is," grinned Jack.

His smile seemed to antagonise the man who had walked back to his desk and declared the meeting over. Jack looked at him and thought better of pushing his luck. He offered a token word of gratitude and headed out to find Lisa. The industrial estate was not a place to hang around, especially in a car that you cared about.

***

Lisa was still waiting in the same place when Jack descended the stairs. He could feel the tingle in his spine that told him he had come close to a confrontation. The man would be capable of doing some serious damage and would have an alternative plan if things went wrong. You could not work in a place like that without having others close by or a weapon to pick up.

He approached the car, with his head swivelling like an owl. On high alert, he was waiting for something to hit him from behind. When nothing came, he got in and insisted that Lisa drive off. She seemed calm and unconcerned by her surroundings.

"Any problems?" asked Jack.

"Nothing," she shrugged. "One kid came down the road doing wheelies on a BMX. Other than that, I saw nobody. What about inside?"

Jack recounted the information he had been told. He offered some details of his encounter with the man in the portacabin. Lisa looked concerned and then appeared to relax when Jack confirmed that only words had been exchanged.

"Do you think the man you spoke to has any involvement in it?"

"Quite possibly. He insists his business is legit but don't they all?" smiled Jack. "A haulage business would be the perfect way to shift stolen goods around."

"Did he say where the goods were coming from?"

"He said it was from abroad. The giveaway is the wooden crates."

"What about our man, Paul Colyer?"

"He said he hadn't heard of him. For all I know, it could be him. We need to get Nathan to look at the registrations of all the businesses around here. I want to know who owns them, who runs them and what they do."

"I don't think any of them are going to say 'import of stolen goods' on the registration," smiled Lisa.

"There goes my main investigative technique down the drain," sighed Jack.

"I'll speak to Nathan. He can get started on it right away."

"We also need to have another look at that trunk. If everything I've been told is correct, there's a fair chance it's stolen."

"From where? If the man is to be believed, that trunk has come in from the continent."

"Or direct from China," noted Jack.

"Do you think it came through that yard?" asked Lisa.

"That's a good question," nodded Jack. "All the evidence says to follow our nose."

"And where is your nose pointing?"

"To The Cellars, of course. It is Saturday. That means serious drinking time." He grinned with a mischievous glint in his eye.

Chapter 8

A noise from the road outside woke Lisa. It rippled through her fragile head and offered an excruciating feeling. She rolled over in bed and forced her face deeper into the pillow. The movement only made things worse. She released a groan and tried to open her eyes, an act which felt like knitting needles were being pushed through her forehead. A second attempt brought nothing but pain.

"Why?" she moaned. "Why do you do this to yourself?"

The noise was getting louder. Whatever was reversing sounded like it was coming into the bedroom. She expected it to crash through the wall at any moment. If it did, she was not going to get up. It was too early.

Another attempt to block it out made no difference. The pillow was dragged over her head and held onto the side of her face. Any touch was increasing the anguish. She had to fight her way through it. She had to force herself to move and accept the torment that came with it.

Lisa reached down and pushed herself up in the overly soft bed. It felt unfamiliar, with the musty smell only increasing that feeling. With a Herculean effort, she propped herself up against the lumpy pillow. It allowed her to force an eye open. She frowned when she did not recognise her surroundings. It was not her flat. She was in a bedroom she had never been in before.

A wave of panic went through her. The sudden moment of reality was enough to jolt her awake. Staring wide-eyed, she fought with the pain that was trying to invade her head. Lisa tried to blink it away and only succeeded in intensifying her discomfort. Around her, she saw the dated decor of a room that appeared like it had never been lived in.

"Where am I?" she croaked through a pair of lips that were like an arid desert.

Forcing her legs out from under the covers, Lisa swung them over the side of the bed. Her eyes tried to focus on her bare legs and the one sock that was covering her left foot. She pushed herself upwards and fought the urge to collapse back onto the bed. Dressed in her shirt from the day before, her underwear and one sock, she gazed around in search of her remaining clothing.

A single step felt like a journey. The side of her leg throbbed above her knee. A glance down offered up an impressive series of bruises and a patched-up cut. Sticking out from beneath her shirt, her leg looked like it had been in a fight.

Tentatively, Lisa made her way to the door. There was no sign of her jeans or her stray sock. Her jacket and shoes were also missing. More worryingly, her location remained a mystery. With a nervous feeling, she reached for the door. She closed her fingers around the handle and eased it open a few inches. Fearing the worst, she braced herself for what she was about to discover.

All that greeted her was an empty corridor and silence. She stepped out and looked in both directions. A smile went through her when a sense of familiarity returned. She had slept in the spare bedroom in Jack's house. A sigh of relief was tempered by the soreness inside her.

She walked slowly over to the door of Jack's bedroom. She pushed it open and saw an unmade bed. With the duvet hanging off, the space had been vacated. Just the act of looking at it was painful. It forced her to seek out the kitchen. She would inflict untold suffering on Jack if he was wide awake and without a hangover.

Lisa walked slowly down the stairs. She picked up her missing sock from the top step. It was slipped on as she descended towards the kitchen. When she got there, Jack was nowhere to be seen. He was not in the lounge and nor were her jacket or jeans.

"Jack, where are you?" she groaned.

The hand she placed on the side of the kettle provided no clues. It was stone cold to the touch. Lisa filled it up and switched it on. She then went to a place she knew too well. She took two tablets out of Jack's stash of aspirin and downed them with a glass of water. The invasion in her raw throat almost saw them come straight back up. It was a battle she had to win.

Lisa made herself a coffee and took it through to the lounge. Her jacket was hung on the back of the door. Lisa picked it up and noted the dirt on its arm. She brushed it down and took her phone from her pocket. Everything she did felt like hard work.

"I'm going to kill you, Jack," she groaned as she typed out a text.

Jack, where are you?

Once sent, she slumped down on the sofa and wished the day would end right now.

***

Jack was woken by the sound of his phone. He blinked himself fully awake and felt the heaviness in his head. It had been a long night, with the lock-in at The Cellars doing him no favours. At least his sleep had been undisturbed. The bed had been comfortable and the warmth around him had allowed him to rest.

Jack forced himself out of bed. He dressed quickly and wandered through into the lounge. The light was still on as was the one in the kitchen. Jack shook his head and focused his attention on the coffee machine. He stared at it and then decided his fuzzy state could not cope with its complexities.

He made himself a cup of instant and took it back to the bedroom. The repeated buzzing of his phone was not something he needed to hear. He grabbed the handset out of his jacket and stared down towards the screen. After a few seconds, his eyes focused on Lisa's name. With a puff of his cheeks, he pressed the phone to his ear.

"Morning," he said softly.

"Is it?" groaned Lisa, with her hung-over feeling permeating through her words.

"It is here," said Jack as he walked back through to the lounge. "Where are you?"

"I'm in your flat. Where are you?"

"In your lounge."

"What are you doing there?"

"I don't know. What time did we leave The Cellars?"

"I don't know that either. It was late."

"Why aren't you here?"

"Lisa, please, stop with all the questions. You're making my head hurt," complained Jack.

"Only if you answer one more for me."

"Which is?"

"Have you seen my trousers?"

Jack shook his head and then stared over towards the sofa. Hung over the back were the jeans that Lisa had worn the night before.

***

The day made more sense the longer it went on. Jack walked over to his house with some fresh clothes from Lisa's wardrobe. He collected some coffee and pastries on the way, not that he was confident Lisa would eat them. She sounded in a far worse state than he was.

Lisa's initial idea to get a taxi to her flat had been ended by the absence of her jeans. She was halfway to the door when the reality of her predicament struck her. She was going nowhere until Jack appeared. The prospect of raiding Jack's wardrobe was not enticing. With her wine-infused state, a tatty pair of his trousers would complete her transformation into a tramp.

When Jack arrived, Lisa let him in. She stared at the plastic bag he had stuffed her clothes into and the tray of coffee and pastries in his other hand. It was hard to know which was more appealing. Opposite her, Jack was staring at her leg. He grimaced at the sight that was presented. Even Lisa would admit it was not an alluring proposition.

The memory of what had happened began to be pieced together. Jack remembered Lisa's fall on the way home. She had crashed down onto some steps and had ripped her jeans. It meant diverting to Jack's house as the closest sanctuary.

It took them longer to remember why Jack had taken her jeans back to her flat. Lisa groaned when she recalled complaining about the lack of a needle and thread in his house. As her saviour, Jack had taken it upon himself to fetch them. For some reason, he had taken her jeans with him. He was either a talented tailor or he was just steaming drunk.

"Why didn't you come back?" groaned Lisa.

"I barely remember going," said Jack. "I must have gone to bed when I got there."

"Where was I when you left?"

"After I helped you take your jeans off, I sat you down on the sofa."

"Oh," frowned Lisa.

"Why? Where did you wake up?"

"In your spare bedroom. It was like going back in time."

"I'm not surprised. Nobody has slept in there in years."

"I don't think the bedding has been changed since," she groaned.

"Why didn't you go into my bedroom?"

"I don't know," she sighed. "Maybe I was waiting for you to come back."

"Sorry," smiled Jack.

"I'd better get changed. My leg might scare your neighbours if I'm not careful."

"Why don't you have some coffee and a pastry first? I can live with seeing your booze bruises for a little longer."

"Are you sure it won't put you off your breakfast?"

"Not if I look the other way," grinned Jack.

Lisa forced a smile. She had neither the will nor the energy to argue.

***

After writing the day off, Jack headed to The Cellars for a pint in the early evening. He was only going for one and he was going alone. Lisa had returned to her apartment by mid-afternoon. She was adamant that she was going to bed. Not with Jack and not in bedding that smelled like dinosaurs had slept in it.

Alf shook his head when Jack walked through the door. His most regular customer was the last person he was expecting to see. Alf waited until Jack was within earshot. He then shook his head again.

"Didn't you have enough last night?"

"I'm only having one tonight," insisted Jack.

"Is that one barrel?"

"It's one pint. Just give me something light. It's for medicinal purposes."

"How about orange juice?"

"A pint of best will be fine."

Alf knew better than to argue. He poured the pint and pushed it in front of Jack. His kitty was spent though it was no time to cause difficulties. Jack looked like a man in need of rejuvenation.

"I take it Lisa is being more sensible than you."

"It's just me tonight."

"Just for one," confirmed Alf.

"Just for one," nodded Jack.

The arrival of a group of customers gave Jack the excuse he needed to walk away from the bar. He moved over to the corner seat and slumped down in it. No matter how much he pretended otherwise, he was not at his best. Those late lock-ins were starting to take their toll. He would never admit it to Lisa. The truth was he would never fully admit it to himself.

Jack began to reflect on the night before. Lisa had been so unsteady on her feet when they left the pub. He had helped her walk until she insisted she could manage on her own. He had barely stepped away from her when she crashed to the floor. It was hard not to feel some guilt.

She had laughed it off as she hobbled back to his house. Only the removal of her jeans had offered a clue as to how hard she had hit the ground. Jack had tried to persuade her to go to bed. That was when she insisted on repairing them. From there, it was a blur. It was probably best that neither of them remembered much more.

For once, Jack sipped his pint slowly. There was no urge to down it as if his throat was on fire. There was still some dryness in his mouth from the night before. It masked the taste and limited his appreciation of his pint. He would still drink it. It just took away the temptation of wanting another.

The taste got worse when three men entered through the door. Jack spotted them in an instant along with the peril they brought with them. Gregor Banks led the way, his menacing thugs not far behind. When he saw Jack, he wandered over. The last thing Jack needed was an argument. The second last thing was a conversation with Gregor Banks.

"Fancy seeing you here," smiled Gregor.

"What are the chances?" shrugged Jack.

"Odds-on, based on your recent attendance record."

"I never had you down as the school registration monitor. That must have been a promotion from looking after the milk."

"Sorry, I'm too young for all that. You're back in your era with that one."

"What do you want, Gregor? I'm not in the mood."

"You know what I want. Any update?"

"None whatsoever. It's the weekend."

"I'll remember that. I must commit all these alleged crimes when you guys are taking the weekend off. That way, I'll stay out of prison until office hours on a Monday."

"Rest assured, we'll make an exception for you."

"Only because it will give you some overtime," grinned Gregor.

"Seriously, Gregor, what do you want? I was hoping for a quiet night."

"Then tell me what I want to know. Who's the new player in town?"

"I don't know," insisted Jack.

"Then you need to find out. Don't make me do your job. You know how that will end."

Jack looked at Gregor and shuddered. He could see the menace being projected from his eyes.

Chapter 9

An early Monday morning briefing brought plenty of muttered complaints. DCI Louth had called together his resources for an update on the case. His superiors were starting to give Louth a tough time about the lack of progress. That meant the team beneath him were going to feel the heat.

Jack and Lisa walked into the briefing room ten minutes apart. Lisa was early while Jack took the opportunity to catch up with PC Brian Wilkes on his way in. There was talk of a new real ale pub opening near the station. Brian always had his finger on the pulse of the city.

Buoyed by the news, Jack grabbed a coffee and wandered in after Louth had started speaking. Heads turned when Jack took his usual place at the side. Everybody waited for an apology to acknowledge his lateness. Even Lisa shook her head at his failure to provide one.

"Are you sure you're ready for us?" growled Louth.

"I think so, sir."

"Would you care to offer a reason for your lateness?"

"I didn't get here until a few minutes after nine o'clock."

"That is not a reason. That is a statement of fact."

"Oh, sorry. I must have got delayed on a previous matter."

"Which was?"

"Something which ran over."

Louth let out a deep sigh. Sparring with Jack was like fighting a battle with a marshmallow. Everything you hit him with, he absorbed without damage. The only way to deal with him was to ignore him. When the man was so irritating, it was hard to retain such discipline.

"Right, where are we on these body parts?"

A moment of silence descended on the room. The DCI was not going to allow it to linger.

"Lisa, have you got an update?" growled Louth. He wanted to ask Jack but could not bring himself to do so.

"We know the deceased is Shane Keyson, a twenty-six-year-old dock worker from Immingham. He has no immediate family though he does have a girlfriend who we are yet to speak to. According to his boss, he was on holiday and was due back today. Clearly, that's not going to happen."

"Who's his boss?"

"His name is Keith Elton. Jack and I went to see him on Saturday."

"That sounds like one of Jack's romantic dates," grinned Frank Campbell, with a wink towards Lisa. "Did you take a picnic?"

"What did he say?" barked Louth, offering a cold stare in Frank's direction.

"The usual about him being a fantastic lad who could do no wrong, other than the charges we have on file for him."

"Are there many?"

"The one of interest is an assault charge. Keith reckons that avenue is a dead end. The victim died a couple of years ago."

"In suspicious circumstances?" questioned Louth.

"He fell off a rowing boat and drowned when high on drugs."

"And low in water," grinned Frank to an audience of none.

"Is that all we have?" snarled Louth. "We've been at this for a week."

"We've also made some progress tracing where the trunk came from."

"Go on."

"Paul Colyer, the seller of the trunk, has an address on the outskirts of Hull. It's used to transit goods into the country and immediately off elsewhere. We believe stolen goods are going through it. So far, we've been unable to track him down, which suggests he doesn't want to be contacted."

"Are you saying the trunk is stolen?"

"That's our suspicion. We believe it might have been imported with other stolen items."

"I want that trunk going over with a fine-tooth comb," demanded Louth. "Get a couple of specialists on it and let's see if we can find out where it has come from. For now, let's work on the basis it's stolen. What else have we got?"

"Jack and I are going over to the auction house this morning to see what else we can find out."

"Is that necessary?" asked Louth. "You've already been there."

"This one is the weekly fine antiques auction. All the big players will be there, which means swords will be drawn once again."

***

The difference to the clearance auction was obvious when Jack and Lisa turned into the car park of the auction house. It was not a cheap day out for pensioners but, instead, a place for the high-rollers of York. The car park was crammed full of expensive vehicles, with a few vans hidden away in the corner. They were there for the lackeys to take away their masters' purchases.

Lisa drove past a row of almost identical Range Rovers. Other than the subtle changes of colour, they appeared like a uniform for the high-end dealers to present themselves in. They dwarfed Lisa's VW Golf though offered her an advantage. She could squeeze into a space that had been deemed too small by the elite. It put her close to the entrance but left Jack to squeeze out of the passenger side.

"How thin do you think I am?" he grumbled. "I wouldn't get an anorexic piece of spaghetti out of there."

"Do you want me to back out for you?"

"You'll have to," he groaned.

Lisa eased the car backwards. It was like taking her mother out shopping. She waited while Jack took an age to get out of the seat and then just as long to close the door behind him. By the time he was finished, there was a queue of vehicles behind her. Every one of them was a Range Rover.

"About time," Lisa muttered as she pulled the car back into the space under the irritated stare of the waiting drivers.

Her complaints were forgotten when she tried to get out of the car. It was tight even for her younger frame. Bemoaning her lack of recent appearances in the gym, she contorted her body through the gap. With Jack finding amusement in her plight, she refused to give in. A brush of her leg against the car door forced a moment of pain to go through her. It was another generous helping of payback for her ill-discipline over the weekend.

A final effort saw her push through the difficulty. She closed the door and made her way over to Jack. He was doing well to remain quiet. They both knew that a single word would see her fist crash into his arm. It was better to savour the moment silently than feel the strength of Lisa's right-handed jab.

On the way in, Jack collected a catalogue for the auction. In the busy environment, their presence went unnoticed. It allowed them to take a seat towards one side of the auction room. It was the perfect place to watch the action unfold.

Already in situ was Henry Davenport, with his assistant beside him. He was four rows in front of them. Charles Rickton came in a minute after Jack and Lisa. He took a seat on the opposite side of the room and stared fiercely towards Henry. Only Daniel Voss was yet to appear.

Lisa flicked through the catalogue while Jack watched the room. The auction was relatively small though included lots that would attract the high end of the antiques business. Just forty-two items were up for sale, with the auction expected to take no more than an hour. And yet the room was packed out with dealers.

The atmosphere seemed calmer than the previous auction Jack and Lisa had been to. This was dealers making their living rather than excited pensioners bidding for bargains. Any items bought would be expected to make a profit. Jack wondered whether a series of pre-arranged deals had taken place. It would make sense to ensure that nobody missed out. Such thoughts were dispelled when he saw the ill intent being displayed by Henry and Charles.

When Simon Hayton walked to the podium, the room fell silent. After a quick opening speech, he was eager to get the auction started. Jack watched his eyes flick around the room to identify where Henry and Charles were sitting. He paused briefly when he failed to find Daniel Voss and then smiled as the young dealer strode confidently through the door. Looking slightly unkempt, Daniel remained standing and allowed his frame to rest against a wall.

The first three lots only brought a handful of bids. They were sold without any of the three protagonists getting involved. On the fourth lot, Daniel Voss made his move and secured the first silver item. He pounced again three lots later and leaned back with a contented smile.

Henry Davenport showed his first signs of interest when an early Victorian card table was brought on stage. It was the ninth lot and marked the beginning of the furniture in the catalogue.

A tentative bid brought Charles Rickton to life. Once he had stirred, the first duel of the day ensued.

To watch the two men go at it like schoolchildren was amusing for everyone. Lisa never took her eyes off them while Jack allowed his attention to drift onto Daniel. The younger man saw Jack and winked in his direction. He had mischief in mind but was not quite ready to unleash it.

The early skirmishes did not draw much blood. It was more about marking out territory than a genuine attempt to snatch an item from a rival. Henry was left to fight a battle with a younger dealer. With Henry able to command premium prices, there could only be one winner. His final bid was enough for the hammer to fall in his favour.

"Marvellous," he muttered to Robbie beside him. "That one is a steal."

It almost felt like Charles was owed something back. When he bid on the next lot, Henry offered token resistance. A fierce stare between them signalled what was coming. Unmoved, Daniel Voss waited patiently. He already had the items he had come for. The rest of his day was about having fun.

They were halfway through the catalogue when a pair of Victorian elbow chairs was brought out. Both men sat up straight under the watchful gaze of Daniel. Henry made an early move, causing Charles to follow. Neither man was going to get the opportunity to secure a bargain when Daniel was determined to stoke the fire.

In a tidal wave of animosity, anger erupted around the room. Simon stopped the auction to allow a moment for temperatures to calm. Only two men needed it. Daniel was doing nothing more than raising his hand to bid. Whether he got the chairs or bid up his rivals, he was determined to make his mark.

Henry was the first to declare he was finished. Charles continued though was forced to bow out when the price hit eight hundred pounds. With the premium to add, Daniel would be paying over a thousand pounds for the chairs. It was a breakeven item and yet it was worth every penny to enjoy some sport.

"You are a cretinous individual," barked Charles.

"For once, we agree," snarled Henry.

The purpose of the deed soon became clear. Daniel's interjection had removed all self-restraint from the men. They bid wildly on the remaining lots while Daniel snuck out of the room. Jack went after him. He stopped the dealer on his way towards the front desk.

"What was that about?" he asked.

"I was just bidding for what I fancied," shrugged Daniel.

"You overpaid for those chairs and are now stuck with them," frowned Jack.

"No, I'm not. I'll ship them on to a dealer friend of mine. They'll wash their face."

"What do you mean?"

"We do favours for each other. He'll give me the cost of them and then take a smaller profit on his end. I'll do the same on any silver he gets landed with."

"Why waste your time?"

"It's not a waste," he grinned. "It's all part of the game. Nobody went near me on those silver items. They daren't."

"I take it you'll make a lot on them."

"Plenty. I've probably got several hundred upside on each of them," he grinned. "If I were you, I'd get back in there. It'll really kick off now they're both fired up."

Jack shook his head. As much as he disliked what Daniel was doing, it was exactly what he would do in similar circumstances. Both Henry and Charles were asking for it. All Daniel was doing was having fun at their expense.

He left Daniel to pay for his items and went back inside. It was just in time to see Henry and Charles go at each other with insults. Both men were standing up and hurling abuse across the room. At the front, Simon Hayton looked a long way out of his depth. It was hard not to feel some sympathy for him.

Simon waited for the room to calm down and then continued with the auction. The lot eventually went to another dealer who was prepared to pay a high price. It did not stop Henry and Charles from re-engaging on the next lot. That pattern was repeated until every item had been sold. For Jack and Lisa, the auction felt like an ordeal rather than somewhere pleasant to conduct business.

As soon as the auction finished, there was a scramble for the door. Everyone rushed to the payment desk to get away as quickly as they could. Jack and Lisa remained seated and watched a relieved-looking Simon Hayton tidy away his things. He puffed out his cheeks and looked up to see the detectives smiling at him.

His sense of politeness forced him to approach them. Simon climbed down from the stage and walked over slowly. Jack and

Lisa waited for him to ease into the row in front. He sat down and attempted to smile.

"That was hard work," he sighed.

"Is every auction like that?"

"It's becoming that way. It only takes Daniel Voss to ignite the fuse and those two go off like fireworks."

"I get the sense that he's a bit of a wind-up merchant," admitted Jack.

"The stupid thing is they know he's doing it and they still take the bait."

"Why don't they ignore him?" asked Lisa.

"I guess they can't help themselves," shrugged Simon who looked like the weight of the world was on his shoulders. "Dare I ask why you're here?"

"We wanted to see what a high-end auction looks like."

"And now you know," said Simon.

"We would also like you to check your records again for Paul Colyer. We don't seem to be able to track him down."

"No problem. If you come through to the office with me, I'll give you everything we have."

"Did he have anything for sale this week?"

"No, he only sends stuff over every couple of weeks. There might be something in the next auction."

"Is that another Monday auction?"

"No, it's on Tuesday. We have the contents of a large estate to value on Monday, so we had to bump it back a day."

"Is it a local estate?" asked Lisa.

"It's over near Crayke."

"Where's that?" she frowned. "I'm not local like you guys."

"Do you know Easingwold?"

"Yes," she nodded.

"It's a couple of miles east of there. I think we're being optimistic trying to do it in a day but that's the only time we've been given. Come on; let's get you those details on Paul Colyer.

Jack and Lisa followed Simon Hayton out of the room. They had to push their way through the crowd to get into the back office. For once, some calm appeared to have broken out even though Henry Davenport and Charles Rickton were both in the confined space. Separated by a mass of people, their attention had turned to the front desk.

Simon took Jack and Lisa through to the office where he tapped away at his computer. All he came back with was the same information as before. It was a name, a phone number, an email and a postal address.

"Have you got anything else?" asked Lisa.

"That's it," confirmed Simon. "I take it you're struggling to get hold of him."

"We haven't managed to track him down yet."

"That's often the case with Paul. The girls complain constantly that he'll go weeks without being contactable. When he does respond, it's always by email. He's very apologetic and couldn't be more helpful. He then goes missing again for the next few weeks."

"Where is he in those periods?"

"He's normally abroad. He sources a lot of his items on the continent. That's not unusual for coastal dealers. They have that advantage."

"Does he ever come into the auction room?" asked Lisa.

"Never," confirmed Simon. "He arranges for a full van load to be shipped across. We unload it and value it."

"Doesn't that trouble you?"

"Not really," shrugged Simon. "You have to remember this is an established relationship. We will have met him when he first brought items to our auction, which was well before my time. Since then, we've operated as we do with any other regular account. If the dealer doesn't feel the need to meet, then nor do we unless there is a problem."

"And you don't see the Chinese trunk as a problem?" frowned Jack.

"I see it as a police matter. It has nothing to do with the auction."

Jack looked at Simon and felt an uncomfortable feeling go through him. Something was not right and it didn't need a detective to notice it.

***

They left Simon Hayton in his office. Once outside of the calm environment, they forced their way through the throng. Frustrations were growing, particularly amongst those who had been late out of the auction room. Henry Davenport was one of them. His position at the back of the masses was infuriating him. Normally, he sent Robbie to settle up on his behalf before the final lot. The confrontation in the auction room had knocked him off his stride. He had been caught out. Now, he was being made to pay the price for his mistake.

"Hey, I want a word with you," his voice boomed out as Jack and Lisa slalomed through the crowd.

Only Lisa noticed that Henry was speaking to them. Jack had ignored the noise and was marching towards the door. He had seen enough and would head back to the station with plenty of thoughts in his mind. When Lisa stopped, she pulled on Jack's arm and spun him around to face Henry. Jack was riled when he saw who was sneering at him.

"Can we help you?" asked Lisa before Jack had the opportunity to be rude.

"You certainly can. You can tell me when I am getting my trunk back. You were supposed to release it to allow me to put it in the window this weekend."

"We'll release it when we're finished with it," interrupted Jack.

"That is not acceptable," snapped Henry. "It is my item and I want it back."

Jack shook his head and walked out of the building. He was not going to waste another breath on a conversation with Henry Davenport. As Lisa watched him, she shrugged at Henry whose anger was growing by the second.

"I think you just got your answer," she stated bluntly before following Jack out of the door.

She caught up with him by the car. When she got there, Jack was waiting behind it. A moment of regret went through her when she realised what that meant. The two cars on either side had not got any further away. Once again, she would need all the flexibility her body possessed.

"Why did I park here?" she sighed.

"Because it was closest."

"At least look away while I get in. It's not the most elegant position."

"No chance," he grinned. "I saw you take part in the diving through concrete event on the walk home from The Cellars. Now I get to see your attempt at car entry gymnastics. Remember, artistic merit is just as important as technical content."

"Does that apply to boxing as well?" warned Lisa.

Jack grinned. He didn't have to say anything. One way or the other, Lisa had to get into the car. If he had been driving, he would have parked at the opposite end of the car park and walked.

Lisa eased herself in slowly. Another scrape on her leg offered an untimely reminder of her soreness. Once in, she reversed the car out of the tight space and waited for Jack to get in. She resented the way he seemed untroubled by her difficulty.

"That was impressive," said Jack, without a hint of sarcasm.

"Go on...I'm waiting for the punchline."

"There isn't one. It was impressive. I would have needed to go through the sunroof."

"I haven't got a sunroof."

"Exactly. Just imagine how difficult that would have been."

Lisa smiled. At times, it was not hard to imagine why so many women had left him.

***

They were back at the station within ten minutes. Lisa made a point of parking in the largest space she could find. There was no shortage of them and it allowed them both to get out easily.

"Why do you think Henry is so keen to get that trunk back?" asked Lisa.

"It's hard to say. He might want to ship it on quickly to get some of his money back or he could be trying to hide the evidence. Either way; it's not going anywhere. I want that case looked at in the minutest detail, just as Louth said."

"You think it's stolen, don't you?"

"I do," admitted Jack. "I think it's been pushed through the auction to get rid of it."

"Why would you do that? Any decent auction is available online and would attract attention. Wouldn't you be better selling it privately to keep it low-key?"

"That's a fair point. Maybe Henry doesn't know it's stolen. Something doesn't make sense and I want to know what it is. And why would you put body parts in a stolen trunk?"

"I don't know," offered Lisa. "That doesn't make sense either."

They walked into the station and up the stairs. It was Lisa who was left cursing their decision not to use the lift when she felt the ache in her leg. The bruising was not getting any better. It was her fault and she knew it.

They were grateful that Frank Campbell was on the phone. With Frank busy and no sign of Louth, it allowed them to sit down without any fear of snide comments. They took two spare seats alongside each other and powered up a computer. Somehow, they needed to track down Paul Colyer.

"Have you got a minute?" came a soft voice behind them.

Jack and Lisa looked up to see Nathan Lewis standing nervously behind them. Shifting from foot to foot, he had the appearance of somebody trying to lay an egg. He waited for one of the senior detectives to say something. Lisa was the first to speak up. She feared the lad might burst.

"Have you got something?"

"I think so," he said quietly.

"Go on; hit us with it."

"It's about Shane Keyson. I've done a bit of digging on him and have found something of interest."

"Spit it out, Nathan," insisted Jack. "You're killing us with anticipation."

"Right, okay," he stammered. "Shane Keyson filed a whistleblower report two weeks ago."

"That's interesting," said Jack. "Where did you find that out?"

"I spoke to the HR team at the company he works for?"

"Who told you to do that?"

"Nobody. I just thought some details about his employment record might prove useful. Did I do the right thing?"

"You did more than the right thing, Nathan," grinned Jack. "You might have cracked this case, or trunk, wide open. We need to find out what that whistleblower case was about. Lisa, do you want to work with Nathan on that?"

"Yes, sure," she nodded.

"It was about the import of counterfeit goods," said Nathan calmly.

"What?" asked Jack.

"He reported that counterfeit goods were arriving through the port. I requested a copy of the report. I'll send it on to you."

"Nathan, that's brilliant," smiled Jack. "I think we might have the start of a trail coming together. What were they importing?"

"It doesn't say," said Nathan. "That was as much information as they could give me. Sorry."

"That's fine," said Jack. "That's a good day's detecting by anyone's standards. You know, there's one thing which bothers me about this."

"Which is?" shrugged Lisa.

"Keith Elton."

"What about him?"

"He never said anything."

"Maybe he doesn't know about the report."

"He must know about either the counterfeit goods or the whistleblower report. It has to be one or the other."

"I think we should ask him," said Lisa. "Do you fancy another ride out to Immingham tomorrow?"

"Only if you're going to perform some more of your car gymnastics," grinned Jack.

A look of horror filled Nathan's face as his cheeks blushed the deepest shade of red.

Chapter 10

After a night of self-restraint, Jack and Lisa set off for Immingham at seven-thirty. It had been Lisa's insistence that Jack stayed over and they shared a meal in her flat. The offer of a trip out to The Cellars was declined by Lisa, knowing it would only lead to trouble. Nobody needed to tell her that she had as little self-discipline as her partner.

A bowl of home-cooked spaghetti had been a welcome opportunity to eat something healthy. Lisa was feeling good about not going out. She had slept well, as had Jack, despite him moaning about the lack of beer in her flat. She had chosen not to tell him about the wine in the back of her cupboard. It had been taken out of the fridge to remove any thoughts of temptation.

Jack had informed Keith Elton they were coming. He sounded surprised when they spoke on the phone. Jack had insisted that it was just to follow up on something that had come out of their investigation. A concocted story was offered about being in the area on a separate case they were investigating in Grimsby. Keith had displayed his indifference and told them he would be at the dock for most of the day.

The previous warnings about the traffic soon made sense. Lisa cursed the constant interruptions to their journey. Every junction turned into a car park. Suddenly, her VW Golf felt tiny. With lorries and large vans around her, she had never felt more vulnerable when driving.

Jack's offer to find a better route was refused. The last thing she wanted was for Jack to attempt to read a map. The satnav was set and would come up with a sensible solution. That could not be said about the man who was sitting beside her. Unpredictable at best, he was likely to take her through somebody's back garden if he thought it was quicker.

After an hour of frustration, the traffic began to ease along. At barely more than fifteen miles per hour, it flowed. At least it was moving and, as the time ticked past the commuter rush, their speed increased. They arrived at the docks just before ten o'clock, an hour later than planned.

They got out and headed towards Keith Elton's portacabin. Braced for the heat to hit them when they got inside, Lisa began to unbutton her coat. On the cold dockside, they wasted little time before entering. A quick knock was offered on their way in.

Once again, the wave of warmth struck them. Jack recoiled at the sudden shock of it. Behind a desk, Keith Elton was on the phone. He half-swivelled in his chair and saw them. Enthusiastically, he waved them over to sit down.

The phone conversation continued uninterrupted. Some form of schedule was being discussed. At times, the exchange was heated. Keith's bellowing voice was filling the space with noise. He was determined to get his way and was stubbornly refusing to be flexible. It offered an insight into the busy world he operated in.

A momentary interruption came when a head popped around the door. Jack and Lisa turned to see a large middle-aged man in a fluorescent yellow jacket and a white protective hat. He looked first at Keith and then at the two detectives. He did not need to be told that Keith Elton was busy.

"I'll come back," he growled.

Before anything else could be said, he was gone. Jack was tempted to go after him to find out who he was. A blunt conclusion to Keith's call did not allow the opportunity. Whoever was on the other end of the line had been put in their place.

"Tough day?" asked Lisa.

"It was just the wife," he smiled. "I'm kidding. I never talk to her like that...not since I buried her under the patio. That's also a joke before you get any ideas," he confirmed.

"Thanks for agreeing to see us," offered Lisa, not wishing to engage in futile banter.

"I'm not sure what else I can tell you but you fire away with your questions. Coffee?"

"No, I'm fine," interrupted Jack, in a rare moment of abstinence. It was a direct response to the unpleasant drink Keith had made him on their previous visit.

"Not for me either," said Lisa.

"I'm going to make myself one, so it wouldn't be any bother. I can treat you today. I've got milk."

Jack and Lisa smiled at Keith Elton. Milk was not going to rescue one of his coffees.

Keith got up from his chair. His lack of height was more obvious when he squeezed past. With Jack and Lisa seated, he barely rose above them. The man appeared to have grown sideways rather than upwards.

They waited for him to boil the kettle and make his drink. Another offer was refused when he held up the same cracked mug Jack had been served coffee in before. They smiled and allowed him the time he needed. Only when he returned to his desk would they begin to ask him questions.

"I like it when you guys come," smiled Keith. "It's about the only time I get to have a decent coffee."

"I take it the job is busy," said Lisa.

"Manic would be the word," noted Keith. "It gets tense at times. You're dealing with some fairly down-to-earth blokes in this game."

"I can imagine," said Lisa. She could say the same about some of the officers in the station.

Jack decided the niceties had gone on for long enough. It all felt too cosy for his liking. He wanted information from a man he did not trust. For all they knew, Keith was the one who had put Shane Keyson in the trunk.

"I wanted to follow up on a few things from our previous conversation about Shane," said Jack.

"That's fine," shrugged Keith.

"You said that you couldn't think of anybody who would want to hurt Shane."

"That's right. He was a good lad."

"But you didn't mention the one thing that might have made him a target."

"What's that?"

"Shane Keyson was a whistleblower."

"So?" shrugged Keith, in a manner that told Jack everything.

"I take it you knew from that reaction."

"Shane told me he was going to do it."

"Why didn't you mention it?"

"Why would I? A whistleblower process is confidential. I'm not supposed to know. It was only because Shane confided in me that I did. He trusted me."

"Who else knew about it?"

"I don't think he told anyone else other than whoever he needed to."

"And who's that?"

"The number is on the board up there. You just ring it."

"What was he going to report?"

Keith narrowed his eyes and stared at Jack. It was a stand-off which continued for an age.

"Shane reckoned counterfeit goods were coming in through the port."

"Were they?"

"No," insisted Keith. "He was talking rubbish."

"Why did he think they were?"

"I don't know. It was probably gossip in his local pub or something he had seen on social media. There was certainly no evidence of it from where I was sitting."

"What about the other lads? Did Olly Hakings and Liam Nicholls have any concerns?"

"Not that they told me."

"We'll need to speak to them."

"They're not on shift."

"You can give us their contact details."

"I'll send them on," shrugged Keith.

"No, you'll give them to us now. While you're at it, you can also give us those details for Shane Keyson's girlfriend that you were going to send on."

"Didn't I send those to you?"

"No, Mr Elton, you didn't."

"It must have slipped my memory. I do apologise. Good luck with that one. She's as vacant as they come."

"It will still be nice to speak to her. You know, just to close the loop."

Keith Elton stared at Jack. No longer was he offering a welcoming expression. There was now genuine hatred coming from his squat appearance.

***

Keith took an age to find all the details they wanted. Jack and Lisa sat patiently while the dock manager went through his records. He played for time, offering the illusion that the information was not easy to find. There was not a moment when either detective considered leaving. Despite Keith's protestations that he was busy, they intended to sit in his office for as long as was needed.

Even the offer of another coffee did not break the flow. Jack stared the man down and noted the way his demeanour changed. It left him wondering whether his wife was truly under the patio. It would be a line of enquiry for Nathan to follow up on. It was unlikely and yet offered the opportunity for embarrassment if such a crime was missed.

The final act before they left was for the details of Shane's partner to be scribbled onto a piece of paper and thrust into Jack's hand. It was done with force to send a message that they were close to treading a dangerous line. Jack never blinked. He stared at Keith Elton and promised him they would talk again soon. Jack sensed that might be with Keith under arrest.

They left the office without much of an exchange. A moment of fear went through Lisa. She wondered whether she might be returning to a vandalised car. Any worrying proved unnecessary. The car sat untouched exactly where she had parked it.

They got inside and left the docks quickly. Only when they were clear of the site did Jack punch the details for Shane Keyson's partner into the satnav. The airhead they spoke about was called Chloe Adams and lived in Barton-upon-Humber.

"That got a bit tense, didn't it?" smiled Lisa.

"It was as if he was hiding something," nodded Jack. "Do you think it's the importing of counterfeit goods or the murder of Shane Keyson or both?"

"I had it down as the murder of his wife," grinned Lisa.

"I'm hoping that was a joke," noted Jack. "We should get Nathan to check that she is still alive and kicking, just to be on the safe side."

"Let's head over to see Chloe Adams. We can call Nathan on the way back."

"Is that before or after we've stopped for coffee?"

"You had your chance for one at the docks."

"I had the chance for some brown sludge in a cracked mug," protested Jack. "I would like a coffee."

"You can have one after we've seen Chloe...but only if you behave yourself."

"Yes, Mum," groaned Jack. His protests were not going to change anything.

Lisa was pleased the traffic had subsided. She drove to Barton-upon-Humber in under half an hour. With Jack staring out through the passenger window, the car was quiet. It was preferable to hearing him complaining. She went into the town and pulled up in front of a terraced house, which was situated just off the High Street.

"We better put a note out," she insisted. "This may be residents' parking."

"I wouldn't," said Jack. "That group of kids over there look like trouble. They might not take kindly to the police."

Lisa stared up the street and saw the shaven-headed youths circling on their bikes. The car had not yet caught their attention. It was probably best if it stayed that way. The last thing she wanted was a brick through her window.

Jack and Lisa got out and walked over to the address they had been given. The property was in a line of small terraced houses. It had the appearance of something that had been looked after, with fairy lights adorning the front window. Lisa pressed the bell and waited for an answer. There was a pause, followed by the sound of movement inside.

A bolt was slid across and then the door opened. A young lady peered out over a chain that secured the gap. It was a lightweight effort that would have little chance of holding back a child.

"Chloe Adams?" asked Lisa.

"That's me."

"I'm DS Lisa Ramsey. This is DI Jack Husker. May we come in and speak to you?" They both held up their warrant cards for inspection.

"Is this about Shane? I know about his death," she offered solemnly.

Lisa nodded. When she did, the chain was slipped off and the door was allowed to open.

Chloe took them into a lounge. It was a small front room with a two-seater sofa and a chair. Both looked old as were most of the furnishings. And yet the house was immaculate. Nothing was out of place in a room that appeared barely lived in.

"Can I get you a drink?" she asked.

"I would love a coffee," said Jack as he offered a frown towards Lisa.

"That would be great, thanks," said Lisa.

Chloe disappeared into the kitchen. Lisa went with her under the pretence of offering some help. They went into a small room at the back of the building. Barely six-foot square, there was hardly enough space for the two of them.

"Sorry, the kitchen isn't up to much," sighed Chloe.

"Mine isn't any bigger," said Lisa, omitting that hers was in a modern flat.

Chloe made two coffees and put some milk in under the instruction of Lisa. A moment of mischief made Lisa wonder whether she should put three spoons of sugar into Jack's. She decided not to, knowing he would only complain all the way back to York. She waited patiently for Chloe to finish. The girl took her time as if distracted by everything around her.

"When did you find out about Shane's death?"

"Keith rang me," she said. "It was such a shock."

"Did the local police come to see you?"

"Why would they? We're not that much of a couple. We're more friends with benefits if you know what I mean." When Chloe blushed, Lisa felt her cheeks burning too.

"Do you live here alone?"

"Yes, it's just me. I'm known as the crazy cat lady at work but without the cat," she smiled.

"Where do you work?" asked Lisa.

"In the supermarket on the edge of town. I work shifts there."

"Why do they call you crazy?"

"I've got a reputation for doing dumb things. I tend to do stuff without thinking it through properly."

"Like what?"

"Do you remember the recent flooding that was on the news?"

"No, why?"

"One of the roads around here got badly flooded. There was a car on the local news seen floating away. It was all over social media."

"Sorry, I didn't see it."

"That was my car. I thought I could drive through the water. It wasn't that deep."

"I take it you got stuck."

"Stuck would be an understatement. The car stopped and I had to climb out through the sunroof. It was lucky I had one. The water was up to the windows."

"And you thought you could drive through it?"

"It didn't seem that deep. As my friend said, it only came halfway up the ducks."

Lisa smiled. She picked up two of the coffees and followed Chloe back into the lounge. She hoped the girl was joking. Something told her, she wasn't.

Jack took his cup of coffee and shuffled up to allow Lisa to settle down on the sofa beside him. Chloe sat on the remaining chair and tucked her legs in under her body. She smiled and clutched the warmth with both hands. For someone who had lost her partner, she seemed remarkably calm.

"Tell us about yourself and Shane," smiled Lisa.

"As I said, we were friends and sometimes lovers. We have known each other for a long time. We first slept together five or six years ago. We both had partners for a while and then were single again. Before you ask, yes, we still saw each other occasionally when we were with our partners."

"I wasn't going to ask," said Lisa.

"Maybe not, but I would rather tell you."

"What about more recently?"

"We probably met up every two or three weeks. Sometimes, he would stay over; often we would just go for a drink. It wasn't always about, you know what."

"When did you last see him?"

"A couple of weeks ago. We were going to meet up when he had his week off but I never heard from him. Now I know why."

"Did he say anything about work when you last saw him?"

"He told me about the counterfeit goods if that's what you mean?" Lisa nodded to confirm that she wanted Chloe to continue. "He wanted out."

"Out?" frowned Lisa.

"He said he didn't want to have any part of it any more and was going to stop. I told him he was stupid for getting involved. He said he would sort it. I don't know what he intended to do. Is that why he was killed?"

"We don't know," admitted Lisa. "That's what we're trying to find out. Do you know what counterfeit goods were being brought in?"

"He didn't say. I would guess designer clothes and perfumes. There's loads of that going on around here. You only need to go into one of the local pubs to find some of it."

"Who else did he say was involved?"

"He didn't. He just said that he helps the goods come in and then makes sure they're moved on before any checks are done."

"Did he say how much he got paid for it?"

"No. The first I knew about it was when he told me he was fed up with it. He should never have got involved."

"What dealings have you had with Keith Elton?"

"Not a lot. To be honest, I don't think much of him. He pretends to be nice but he's a bully. Even when he phoned to tell me about Shane, he told me to keep my mouth shut if anyone came asking about him."

"What did you say?"

"I was too shocked to say anything. I put the phone down and cried."

"Have you heard from Keith since?"

"No. Someone popped around the following night and knocked on the door. When I answered, all they said was to forget about Shane if I knew what was good for me. I slammed the door shut and have kept it locked since."

"Was it Keith who came around?"

"I don't know who it was. It wasn't Keith. I would recognise him."

"Did you call the police?"

"I'm not stupid. I know when to let things lie."

Jack looked across at Lisa and nodded. There was no need to put Chloe Adams at any more risk.

***

They drove away while being watched by the youths on their bikes. When Lisa started the car, it caught their attention. They stared across as if contemplating whether to make a move. Each youth held his position as Lisa pulled away. Neither Jack nor Lisa looked across at them. There was nothing to be gained from a confrontation.

Once out of the town, Lisa followed the directions towards the Humber Bridge. She swung up onto the main road and then crossed the expanse of water. With Jack yet to say anything, she concentrated on driving. The thoughts going through their heads would be similar. Chloe Adams was not an airhead. She could see Keith Elton for what he was.

"Have you got any change?" asked Lisa when she approached the toll booth.

Jack reached into his pocket and felt around. He found a two-pound coin tucked away in the corner.

"Here, try this."

She slowed the car and cursed. The sign beside the unmanned booth told her it was card only. She looked at Jack who shrugged his shoulders towards her. Unable to decipher what he meant, she looked down at her bag.

"Don't just sit there; grab my card."

"What card?"

"Any of them."

Jack picked up Lisa's bag and began to rifle through it. A sense of discomfort went through her as his clumsy hands rummaged around her private things. It was made no easier when the vehicle behind offered an impatient toot of its horn. A look back confirmed her suspicions. A van had pulled up within inches of her and was revving its engine loudly.

"Just give it here," scowled Lisa.

She snatched the bag away and took out her purse, which Jack had pushed to the bottom. Another sound of the horn was more demanding. It blared out and came with a shake of a fist. By the time Lisa had her card in her hand, Jack had got out of the car.

She watched him march across to the van with his warrant card held out in front of him. Lisa saw the ashen face of the driver in her mirror. In an elaborate charade, Jack made the man offer up his details. While everything was written onto a piece of paper, Jack performed an impromptu walk around the van. Only when he had looked at all four sides and had examined the documents carefully did he hand the paperwork back to the relieved driver.

He returned to Lisa's car with a piece of paper clutched in his hand. Jack got in and smiled at her. A glance back saw a hand of apology go up in Lisa's direction. She nodded and offered a stern look of her own.

"He says sorry," confirmed Jack. "And here's his name, address and phone number. I'll put it in your bag along with all your other valuables."

"What do I want that for? Am I now on traffic duty?"

"I just thought you might want another option when you get fed up with me," grinned Jack.

"That could be sooner than you think if you do that to my bag again."

Lisa paid the toll and set off towards York. On the way, Jack phoned Nathan Lewis. He instructed him to speak to Olly Hakings and Liam Nicholls. He also needed to search under Keith

Elton's patio. When Nathan sounded confused, Jack told him to find out whether Keith's wife was still alive. If she was, that line of enquiry could be put to bed. Until it was confirmed, he would not be taking anything for granted.

By the time Jack was finished, Lisa was well on the way to York. Already, it felt like it had been a long day. Most of it had been spent in traffic.

"Do you know what I'm thinking?" asked Jack.

"Go on."

"I'm thinking I must be due that coffee by now."

"You had one. Chloe Adams made you a coffee."

"I'm ready for another."

"Did you behave yourself?" frowned Lisa.

"I certainly did. I only went on the furniture when I was told to," grinned Jack.

"In that case, you might get a coffee. Or we could just go back to mine for one."

"Why don't we do both?" smiled Jack.

Lisa looked across and failed to come up with a response. It was a plan she could not find fault with.

Chapter 11

ANOTHER EARLY MORNING MEETING with DCI Louth was the last thing Jack and Lisa wanted. It was exactly what they got when a message was sent to them both at seven-thirty. They were sitting at Lisa's table when it came, their phones pinging successively. Lisa picked hers up and groaned, forcing Jack to offer the same response. Neither felt much joy at what awaited them in the station.

"Does he have nothing better to do?" sighed Jack.

"At least it's an eight-thirty meeting and not eight o'clock."

"Trust you to find some positives. I always knew you were the class swot."

"I just look keen compared to you. Face it, Jack, that's a low threshold to aim for."

"I guess so. At least we have time to finish our breakfast. We wouldn't want to miss out on all this tasty fruit."

Lisa smiled when she saw Jack staring down at the bowl in front of him. The fresh fruit she had chopped into it had only been pushed around the perimeter. It was the same every time she tried to introduce anything healthy. Jack would poke it and then leave most of it uneaten.

The coffee in his hand was going down far better. Once finished, Jack accepted Lisa's offer of a second cup. By the time she returned with the refill, most of the fruit was gone. The only mystery was where Jack had put it. She expected to find pieces of melon and grapefruit hidden around her flat for weeks.

Once they had finished, Lisa drove them to the station. Their early arrival meant she could park beside the front door. On the way in, she saw a small group of officers approaching. A smile in the direction of Kelly Knox was returned. The young PC waved eagerly towards them. She had the look of someone who was enjoying her job.

"Do you think we'll see her out of uniform again?" asked Jack.

"I think there are plenty who would like to," admitted Lisa. "Sorry, that didn't sound right. I meant…oh, forget it. I'll stick with what I said."

Jack laughed. It provided a moment of entertainment before they met with the DCI. Once they were in his office, the day could only get worse.

For once, Jack won the battle to use the lift. He pressed the button before Lisa reached the stairs. When the doors opened, she wandered in without much thought. It was only when they began to move upwards that she realised what she had done.

"Why are we using the lift?" she frowned.

"It was here, so we might as well get in it. Anyway, we've had our healthy moment for the day."

"Eating fruit for breakfast does not give you a free pass to be an unhealthy slob all day."

"Doesn't it?" groaned Jack as they reached the top. "What's the point of eating it then?"

"Because it tastes good and is nutritious," said Lisa.

"Keep reminding me," insisted Jack. "I find it so easy to forget."

From the lift, they walked to Louth's office. The DCI was sitting behind his desk with two empty cups in front of him. It signalled an early start and plenty of time to come up with an impressive list of tasks to delegate. Jack allowed Lisa to enter first, which meant taking the seat directly opposite Louth. Jack sat alongside her, hoping that his day was not about to be ruined.

"Good morning," beamed Louth.

"Morning, sir," they both replied.

"How was your jolly to Immingham yesterday?"

"All beachwear and ice cream," said Jack. "I'm surprised we found time to do any work."

"It might surprise you, Jack, but it certainly doesn't surprise me," growled Louth. "How about you give me an update and I'll decide whether the time was wasted?"

Jack recounted the meeting with Keith Elton. He talked through the dock manager's refusal to believe that anything was going on. His surly manner was noted as was his dismissive view of Chloe Adams. Louth nodded, particularly when they spoke about their suspicions. The disruption to the flow of counterfeit goods would be enough to put Shane Keyson at risk.

"What do you think the counterfeit goods are?"

"Chloe Adams believes they're designer clothes and perfumes. She reckons they're freely available in the local pubs."

"Do you?"

"I don't know. It would tie in neatly with that site we looked at in Hull. I still think it's more likely that yard is handling stolen goods."

"Could the antiques be counterfeit?" asked Louth.

"I can't see how. They're passing through an auction house and some pretty high-end dealers. They would recognise fakes from a mile off."

"Jack's right," nodded Lisa. "They're going through too many sets of hands."

"Which would make it more likely the items are stolen," confirmed Louth.

"That's what we need to find out," insisted Jack. "Let's chase up our expert and see where he's got to on the trunk."

"And in the meantime?" shrugged Louth.

"I think another trip to see Simon Hayton is in order," grinned Jack.

"What for? You've already been to two of his auctions."

"I think it might be time to rattle his cage. How about I go there and tell him he's handling stolen goods?"

"We don't know that," stated Louth. "It might be a red herring."

"It might be," agreed Jack. "Or we might see somebody do something stupid."

"I'm not sure I like the sound of that," said Lisa. "We're dealing with an individual who chops people up and puts them in trunks."

"That's a very good point," nodded Louth. "Jack, I think you should go on your own. We can spare you if anything goes wrong."

The grin on Louth's face was not one Jack was going to respond to. He had suffered enough already with Lisa's early morning bowl of fruit.

***

Jack left Lisa to organise a meeting with the antiques expert. The trunk had been with Alistair Howarth long enough to investigate its provenance and determine what it might be worth. Unchased, the man would take an eternity to respond. They wanted answers and a face-to-face meeting was the best way to get them.

Jack took one of the cars from the station's fleet. He had left Louth's office before he realised that Lisa's keys were in her bag. Rather than go back, he signed out one of the pool cars. He made sure it was not the same one he had driven to Simon Hayton's house. The feeling of that boat wallowing over the speed humps was not something he wanted to repeat.

A Peugeot 308 provided a suitable option. Jack had driven it once before and had found it tolerable. He was not going to be in it for long. The commuter traffic had already subsided, allowing him to navigate through the city with ease.

He arrived at the auction house within minutes. He pulled into the car park and gazed around at the lack of cars. Away from auction day, there was no demand for spaces. Jack picked an area where he could drive straight through from one bay to the next. None of the skilled manoeuvring that Lisa had displayed was required.

He locked the car and did a quick count of the vehicles around him. Only one car stood out, which he recognised as Simon Hayton's. The others were older contraptions, to signal the gap in wealth between the auctioneer and his team. As he gazed across, he saw a battered Ford Fiesta. It looked like it was being held together with rust, with the only value being the retro-fitted oversized exhaust. Jack wandered over to it. Its stupidity was matched by an equally large sound system in the back.

The car had to belong to Billy Ellis. It was something to impress the type of person he associated with. With bald tyres and lowered suspension, the car would be a death trap. Jack flexed his mouth and nodded. If Billy offered him one word of difficulty, the car would get towed to the police compound.

Jack walked to the front door and tried to enter. Its locked state confirmed the lack of activity. He moved around the building and saw a van being unloaded. Weighed down by a large piece of furniture were two men who were trying to carry it into the building.

"Morning," offered Jack.

The grunt from the two lads was enough to recognise them. On the far end was Finn Mann, with Billy Ellis on the side nearest Jack. Neither offered much under the strain of the weight. In front of him, two lifters and shifters were going about their work.

"You can give us a hand if you want," said Billy.

"Not with my back," replied Jack. "I'll leave it to you youngsters."

Jack stood out of the way while the item was taken into the building. It looked like the base of a large dresser. Made with no shortage of wood, the piece had to be heavy. Neither man offered any sense they were finding it easy.

A glance into the back of the van told Jack there were bigger pieces to come. A wardrobe looked particularly cumbersome. Jack eyed it for a few seconds and then followed the men inside. Once they were around the corner, the item was eased down onto a set of trolleys. It allowed them to wheel it into the auction room.

"Is Simon in?" asked Jack.

"I don't know," said Billy with a shrug.

"What about you, Finn? Do you know?"

"No," he muttered quietly.

"Which auction is this lot for?"

"The one next Tuesday," confirmed Billy. "It's going to be a pretty big one. It's a furniture auction followed by fine antiques."

"Has any of this stuff come in from Hull?"

"Not that I know of," shrugged Billy. "We just unload it. You would have to ask the gaffer about that."

"I will, thanks," smiled Jack.

He left the two lads to continue the task of emptying the van. He wandered through the furniture that had been brought in so far. Most of it was solid items from the twentieth century. It would be enough to fill several houses for very little cost.

As Jack weaved his way through, he saw Dean Lucas. The valuer was going about his work at an impressive speed. Nothing was looked at for long. He examined each piece and jotted the details on a notepad. Once each item had been appraised, a sticker was placed on its top.

"Morning," smiled Jack.

"Good morning," nodded Dean. "I would shake your hand but I'm covered in dust. Some of this stuff must have been stored in a barn."

"Is there anything I should have my eye on?"

"Take your pick. It's all solid stuff but it won't go for much. People don't want this sort of furniture any more. They would rather go to the retail parks and buy something trendy that will last for a couple of years."

"What have you got in your house?" asked Jack.

"We're wall-to-wall IKEA," smiled Dean. "I know; it's not a good endorsement for where I work but you try telling my girlfriend that. She wants new and I want a quiet life. You can guess where that compromise leaves us."

"I can," grinned Jack.

"If you're looking for Simon, he's in his office."

"Thanks," said Jack. He left Dean Lucas to go about his work.

Jack went through the door. He saw that Simon Hayton was tucked away in his office and knocked once on the glass panel. A confused-looking Simon peered up from his computer and then offered a moment of recognition. He forced a smile onto his face and beckoned Jack in.

"I wasn't expecting to see you," said Simon.

"It's a live investigation," shrugged Jack.

"It's not that. Normally, it's Dean who wanders in when he needs a second opinion on a piece of furniture. That's not that often these days. He's pretty good at what he does."

"What's he like with stolen antiques?" asked Jack.

"Excuse me?"

"I was just wondering what happens when stolen items get sold through your auctions."

"DI Husker, I can assure you that we do not sell stolen items. We only sell lots from regular dealers or estates where there is paperwork to confirm ownership of the items."

"What if someone had information to the contrary?"

"Then I would ask them to make me aware of it. I would take immediate action to withdraw those items from sale."

"And call the police?"

"I don't think you need me to say that," said Simon Hayton firmly. "We are a highly respected auction house in a prominent city. We do not need to be trading in stolen goods."

"I will remember that when I come back. Something tells me that you and I are going to be seeing a lot more of each other."

Jack looked at Simon and waited for him to react. Simon wiped his brow and took a series of shallow breaths. The auctioneer was showing all the signs that he was beginning to feel some pressure. Jack waited for something to be offered back. When it never came, he walked calmly out of the building.

***

Jack headed back to the station via one of his favourite cafes. He picked up two cups of coffee and muffins to go with it. In the harsh environment of the station, he knew the reaction he would get. Some would bemoan that he had not brought enough for everyone while others would accuse him of being Lisa's servant.

Jack did not care what anybody said. He was past the point where the opinion of others mattered. If anyone was too harsh, he would give them some words of his own. Once others joined in, it would not take much to deflect the attention away from him. Experience had given him a Teflon coating.

Lisa was working with Nathan Lewis when he walked in. Jack deposited the coffee and muffin in front of her. He apologised to Nathan for not bringing him one. Lisa soon made his day when she said that he could have it. She was trying to be good and a chocolate muffin would not qualify in that category.

"Are you sure?" asked Nathan in a manner which suggested it was the first food he had seen in weeks.

"You tuck in. Jack won't ever buy you another one, so make the most of it."

"I will," he grinned.

"Before you do that, can someone tell me where we are with Alistair Howarth?" interrupted Jack.

"I rang him this morning," said Nathan, having been delegated the task by Lisa. "You're booked in to see him at eleven o'clock tomorrow morning."

"Can't he do anything sooner?"

"He's down in London today. He said he could squeeze in a call if you were desperate but he hasn't had a chance to look at the trunk. He said he will go over it in the morning."

"He's had the bloody thing for ages," moaned Jack.

"He was apologetic," said Nathan.

"That's alright then. Sorry, I'm not having a go at you. How are you getting on with the other two lads from the docks?"

"I'm still waiting to be called back. I've just left a second message for both of them. I've had nothing from them so far."

"Keep trying. I'll give them a go as well."

Jack left Lisa and Nathan to continue their work. He headed off to a desk in the corner with his coffee and his muffin. He chose a space away from the others. The last thing he wanted was to waste time on station banter. There were always those looking for ways to avoid doing any work.

By mid-afternoon, Jack had managed to speak to both Olly Hakings and Liam Nicholls. Neither knew Shane Keyson particularly well. Their shifts meant they only saw each other at changeovers. Outside of work, there was no interaction between them.

When Jack raised the subject of the whistleblower report, both sounded genuinely shocked. They had not heard about it and knew nothing about any counterfeit goods coming in through the port. Their job was to move items around. They did not handle the paperwork. Both sounded afraid of what the accusation could mean for their jobs.

Jack assured them that he was only after background information. He needed to cover all angles of Shane's life. Those words did nothing to change their responses. Both lads sounded scared. Jack could not help but wonder whether Keith Elton used that to his advantage.

After briefing Lisa and Nathan, Jack headed out of the station. Lisa was insisting on a night alone, leaving Jack free for the evening. He headed into the city centre to catch up on a couple of errands. By the time he had finished, it was too late to go back to the station. Instead, he walked over to The Cellars.

"You're getting earlier," grinned Alf, whose smile only grew when Jack pushed some money over the counter to square off his kitty.

"It will just be a couple for me and then an early night," insisted Jack.

"I believe you," grinned the barman. "Thousands wouldn't."

Alf poured Jack's pint and pushed it across the bar. A small sip was Jack's instinctive reaction. Satisfied with the taste, he retreated to his corner. With very few people in the pub, he had all the space he wanted.

He was halfway through his beer when the next customer came in. An elderly gentleman approached the bar. He was a regular Jack knew well enough to speak to. They exchanged nods and then Jack's eyes went across to the lady who had walked in behind him. It was Cathy Duggan.

"I thought I would find you in here," she said sharply.

"Have I done something wrong?" he asked.

"You've always done something wrong. We both know that."

"True enough. Can I get you a drink?"

"A white wine would be great."

A nod in the direction of the bar was enough for Alf to respond. Jack did not need to get up from his seat.

"You've been coming in here too much if you get that type of service," laughed Cathy.

"Alf and I have an understanding; that's all."

"And you're on first-name terms. I rest my case."

Alf served the older man and then brought a glass of wine over for Cathy. They exchanged pleasantries before he retreated behind the bar. Cathy eased into the seat alongside Jack and gazed across at him. Her eyes were on him a little too closely to feel comfortable.

"I take it this isn't just a social visit," said Jack.

Cathy allowed her stare to linger. She pursed her lips and took a moment to speak. Jack remembered those mannerisms from their dating days. It always preceded an awkward conversation.

"I'm worried, Jack."

"About Simon?"

"Not just about Simon. It's more than that," she said with a softening voice.

"You know I can't discuss the case," insisted Jack.

"I don't want to. Whatever result comes from it will happen. Neither of us can control that. We can control everything else."

Another stare left Jack feeling troubled. Cathy's eyes were fixed on him. There were all the signs that she was about to make her move.

Behind the bar, Alf was watching. He sensed trouble was coming. With nobody to serve, his eyes studied the exchange taking place. When Cathy Duggan's hand slipped onto Jack's, he felt the need to act. He marched over to the table with purpose.

"Can I get you guys any more drinks?" he asked.

Cathy's hand shot away from Jack's. She looked embarrassed at what she had done. To her side, Jack appeared frozen with fear. He had not been the instigator of the moment and was grateful to Alf for ending it.

"I'll come and grab them," insisted Jack.

"There's no need. I'm going," insisted Cathy. "I shouldn't have come here."

Cathy got up and left the two men alone. Jack's eyes dipped closed for a moment and then he puffed out his cheeks. He had come in for a quiet drink, not to be propositioned by Cathy Duggan. It had been a long time since she had looked at him in that way. It was not something he wanted to repeat.

"You've just saved my life," admitted Jack.

"I wouldn't be too sure of that. If Lisa finds out about it, you might need more than me to save you."

Jack felt a shiver go through his spine. Alf's words left him fearing the confrontation that was coming.

CHAPTER 12

AN EARLY MORNING TEXT from Cathy Duggan came as an apology. She was sorry for going to see Jack in The Cellars and regretted putting him in a difficult position. Jack exchanged messages with her and left things with the understanding they would meet for a drink to talk things over. Jack hoped that would soon be forgotten by both of them. It was bad enough when she made her advance. Being reminded about it would be even worse.

With nothing urgent in the station, Jack headed to a cafe. He went to one that had recently been refurbished. The previous owner had allowed things to slip and had lost most of his customers. Now, with a fresh coat of paint and clean curtains, the place had reopened. As Jack entered, he wondered whether anything had changed. The updated decor would require nothing more than one trolley load of shopping from B&Q.

Even the lady serving behind the counter was the same. She had worked there for several years and had been rehired by the new owner. Jack smiled at her familiarity and ordered one of their specials. She frowned and did not accept the order. Not for the first time, Jack did not understand what she meant.

"We don't do specials any more," she explained. "We have a new menu. It's on the table. We offer table service now."

"Does that allow you to charge more?" grinned Jack.

"It certainly does. It also means you can add a tip," she smiled back.

Jack sat down and picked up the menu. It was a single sheet of cheap A4 paper. No expense had been spent on the printing or the design. A line went through some of the text to suggest the cartridge needed replacing.

The lady followed Jack to the table. As the only customer, Jack would get her full attention. The whole performance felt like an elaborate charade. Jack eyed the breakfast options and then looked up towards her with a confused expression.

"How is this different to your specials?" asked Jack. "The breakfast is the same."

"It's all about marketing," she smiled.

"I'll have the full English breakfast and a mug of filter coffee, please," sighed Jack in an attempt to appease her.

"Is that with white or brown toast?"

"White, for heaven's sake. I want something which tastes good, not some fancy calorie offset scheme."

The lady walked away looking amused. In so many ways, the cafe had not changed a bit. The lady was still surly though Jack quite liked that. She was efficient and, more importantly, she served a good breakfast.

Jack picked up a discarded copy of the local paper and skimmed through it while he was waiting. On the front page, there were sensationalist headlines about corruption in the council. The evidence was one expense claim. Tucked away, a picture on an inside page showed it was just an arithmetical error. It was tabloid journalism at its worst and there was only one man to blame. Once again, Andy Hutton, Jack's least respected journalist, was up to his old tricks. He could make a story out of anything and was not afraid to make up details or attribute them to anonymous sources.

The lady returned with his coffee by the time Jack was on page four. His breakfast came when he had got halfway through the paper. The lady carried it carefully to the table and placed it down in front of him.

"One special," she announced as she turned to walk away.

"Hang on!" called Jack. "I didn't order the special. I ordered the full English."

The lady rolled her eyes when she realised her error. She picked up the plate and then put it straight back down on the table. With a smile and a wink to Jack, she stepped back. Jack knew what she was going to say long before she spoke.

"One full English breakfast, sir."

"Fantastic," grinned Jack. "That's a big improvement on the specials you used to serve in here."

"I'll get your toast," she smiled. "You can't eat a full English without toast."

Jack nodded enthusiastically and then sunk his fork into the first sausage. The next few minutes were going to be a time to savour.

***

Jack left the cafe feeling contented. He paid for his breakfast and left the lady the change. She smiled and nodded her gratitude. They had known each other long enough to be well aware of what each other was thinking.

Once outside in the cold air, Jack found a taxi and instructed the driver to take him to see the antiques expert. On the edge of the city, Alistair Howarth had an expensive-looking office. He had made his money offering advice to some of London's most prestigious auction houses. Now in his sixties, he normally worked locally and was a useful source of information.

Jack paid the driver and rang the intercom outside the building. An upper-class voice greeted him and allowed Jack inside. He was told to wait in reception. As he eased through the door, Jack eyed the pictures that adorned the wall. Most were framed photographs of men in expensive-looking suits. In many of them, they were holding awards and smiling proudly at the camera.

Jack soon got bored of looking at the carefully staged gallery. He sat down and waited for Alistair to appear. He wondered what type of man he was about to see. He had spoken to him on the phone but had never met him in person. Jack had already formed a picture of somebody who looked like an out-of-date university lecturer.

When the door opened, he was not disappointed. The grey-haired man who came through was dressed in corduroy trousers and a checked shirt. His hair was swept over his head to hint at a bald spot being covered. On the end of his nose, a pair of rounded glasses were perched.

"Detective Husker?" he queried, leaving Jack wondering who else he was expecting to find in the building.

"Call me Jack, please," he replied while offering up his warrant card.

"I'm Alistair. Please come through. The trunk, if you can call it that, is in the inspection room at the back."

"I take it you don't like it," said Jack.

"Of course, I don't like it. It's fake," said Alistair bluntly.

Jack tried to avoid showing surprise. Though Alistair would not expect him to have much knowledge of antiques, he did not want to appear stupid. If it was as obvious as Alistair was implying, the police should have realised. Jack followed him through to a room where the trunk was up on a table.

"There you are. One trunk," said Alistair.

"One fake trunk," corrected Jack.

"Yes, and not a particularly good one either."

"For the uneducated, could you explain why you think it's a fake?"

"Detective Husker, I think it is a fake because it is a fake."

"Jack, please."

"Sorry, Jack. The point still stands."

"Please could you show me what makes it stand out as a fake?"

"How long have you got?" sighed Alistair.

"Long enough for you to do as I'm asking," muttered Jack under his breath.

"Let's start with the trunk itself. I think the type and age of the wood is wrong for it to be Chinese but I will put that to one side for now. That is the least of its problems. First, there is the lacquer. The condition is too good. It should have some crazing on it, or cracking if you prefer. This lacquer still has moisture in it, so it retains the flexibility to avoid that. I would say the painting has been done in the past year."

"That recently?" queried Jack.

"I think we are looking at a trunk that is thirty to fifty years old, which has been painted in the past twelve months. Then there are the hinges. They are not of the period. Neither is the lock."

"Could it have been replaced?"

"It's possible but unlikely. To change the lock on a trunk like this would normally cause significant damage. The other giveaway is the handles on the side. They are tarnished, which would imply the metal is cheaper."

"What do you think the trunk is worth?"

"Aesthetically, it looks okay, if you like that sort of thing. I would suggest a vintage shop might get a couple of hundred pounds for it, maybe a little more. As for an antiques shop, they would not go anywhere near it."

"That's interesting," nodded Jack.

"Why do you say that?"

"This trunk was bought through a reputable auction. Do you think the auction house would have known it was fake?"

"I would say so. If the valuer didn't spot it, I would certainly be recommending they get themselves a new valuer," smiled Alistair, appreciating the humour in his words.

"That's extremely useful," nodded Jack. "Do you have any thoughts about whether this item is stolen?"

"I can't say. If it was a rare one-off item, I would be able to trace its provenance. For something like this which, let's be honest, has been knocked together in a workshop, there is no way of telling. The chances are a cheap trunk has been acquired and then painted. That could be done anywhere."

"Do you think it could have come in from abroad?"

"Who knows? The painting has been done fairly well but what does that tell us? A semi-talented upcycler could have achieved that look in their garage. I'm sorry. I cannot be more specific."

"You don't need to be. I have got more than enough to go on for now."

Jack thanked Alistair Howarth and headed back out to find a taxi. Once out of the building, he phoned DCI Louth and told him the news. Louth agreed to brief Lisa. It was Jack who insisted that nobody else needed to know. If word got out about the fake, everybody would put distance between themselves and the auction house. That would bring their investigation to a standstill.

"What about Henry Davenport?" asked Louth. "He must know he's bought a fake."

"I'm not sure he does," said Jack. "Let's leave him to stew on it. If he does know, there's every chance he'll do something to incriminate himself."

***

Jack found himself walking back towards the city when he could not find a taxi. He was cold and feeling irritated when he finally saw one come around the corner. He flagged down the driver who looked confused until Jack held out his warrant card. As soon as he saw it, the driver put on his hazard lights and pulled over to the side. He allowed Jack to get into the back of his vehicle.

"Is this official police business?" he asked.

"Yes, I need to go to the auction house."

"That's fine. It's just that I haven't got a licence to do pick-ups."

"This is an emergency," confirmed Jack. "You will get paid for it."

"I like those types of emergencies," laughed the lad.

They drove through the city and pulled up outside the auction house. Jack thrust a ten-pound note into the hand of the driver. They bid each other farewell, leaving Jack outside the building. It felt eerily quiet, with barely a car in sight.

Jack did not bother to check the front door. He walked around the back of the building and marched inside. He saw Billy and Finn in the storage area, still shifting items around the auction house. When Billy saw him, he placed a table down and looked across at Jack.

"You can't keep away from the place, can you?" he laughed.

"It must be your sparkling personality that I keep coming back for. Or your thieving ways. I can never decide between the two."

"I told you; I've gone straight."

"Where's Simon?"

"Have you tried his office?"

"Not yet but I will. If he isn't in there, I'll be back."

"Whatever," sneered Billy. "You don't scare anyone around here."

"Are you sure?" said Jack. He stared the little runt in the eye.

Jack left the lad to contemplate his thoughts. Scrotes like Billy Ellis never went straight. The lad would be up to something, no matter the protests he offered. Sooner or later, he would come unstuck and would be heading off for a life behind bars.

Jack walked through the auction room and went into the office area. Simon was on his phone when he saw Jack through the window. He waved for him to come in and pointed towards a seat. As the conversation continued, Jack waited for the call to reach a natural conclusion. He was not about to hurry Simon Hayton. He would be ruining his day soon enough.

The call sounded like a jovial affair. Conversations about future golf meet-ups were exchanged. Whoever he was speaking to had a good relationship with Simon. In the time Jack was there, work was barely discussed.

After five minutes of continual chatter, Jack began to show his impatience. He caught Simon's attention and tapped at his wrist. Simon nodded enthusiastically and then carried on as if nothing had happened. He was not about to hurry his call even when asked to.

Another five minutes elapsed before Jack intervened again. This time, it was done more forcefully. Jack told Simon to finish the call with a tone which hinted at repercussions. It brought the conversation to an end.

"Is there a problem?" asked Simon before Jack could speak.

"You could say that," confirmed Jack. "That trunk with the body parts in it is counterfeit."

"That's not possible," said Simon. "There must be a mistake."

"There's a mistake, alright. It's a fake and not a particularly good one at that."

"I'm sorry; I don't believe you. That trunk was inspected by Dean. Granted, he couldn't look inside but he would have spotted if there was anything wrong with it."

"Why didn't you spot it?" asked Jack.

"I don't inspect the lots. I sell them."

"You're the auctioneer," insisted Jack. "Are you telling me you don't even look at the lots you sell?"

"I look at the occasional one. On the whole, I leave that side of things to Dean. I concentrate on the commercial side of the business. Anyway, that trunk would also have been looked at by the dealers who bid on it. They can't all have missed something like that."

"No, they can't have," said Jack. "So where does that leave us?"

Simon looked across the desk and played with his beard. After a moment of thought, he picked up his phone.

"We need to speak to Dean."

"Why don't we get him in here?"

"It's his day off."

"I don't care. Get him in here, now," barked Jack.

Simon Hayton phoned Dean Lucas. He put the phone on speaker to prove that he was not hiding anything. The call rang and then diverted to his voicemail. Simon left a message asking Dean to call him straight back. He told him it was an urgent matter.

"I will get in touch as soon as he returns my call. Dean often doesn't answer the phone when he's off. That's his girlfriend's influence. She's a fairly strong character, to say the least."

"If he calls, I want to know," said Jack as he pushed his number across the table. "What time does he start work in the morning?"

"He'll be here by nine."

"Then I'll be here by half-past eight if I haven't heard from you before. Don't tell him or anyone else anything until I get here."

It was not a request Jack was making. It was a direct instruction and it had Simon Hayton looking down at the floor like a scolded child.

***

Lisa was waiting for Jack in the pub after work. Rather than go to The Cellars, Lisa had insisted on visiting one just around the corner from her flat. It was not somewhere Jack was familiar with, which was unusual. Jack's senses told him that something was wrong.

He arrived a few minutes late. Lisa was already inside and had a glass of wine in front of her. When Jack walked in, she smiled. Jack frowned at the lack of a pint awaiting him. He went over to the bar and picked the only hand-pulled ale they had available. It didn't look up to much but would be better than any of the lagers.

He thanked the barman and took his beer over to the table. A kiss on Lisa's cheek felt like it was met with frostiness. Jack sat down and looked across at her. There was none of her usual warmth coming his way.

"Go on, what have I done?" he asked.

"Who says you've done anything?"

"The lack of a beer waiting for me is a clue."

"You're late," said Lisa.

"That doesn't mean you would have cleared away my pint," laughed Jack.

Lisa narrowed her stare as an admission that she had been caught out. It was only a momentary reprieve before she went on the attack.

"I didn't know whether I was buying another one or two."

"What do you mean?"

"You tell me, Jack. Is Cathy Duggan joining us?"

The fear that shot across Jack's face sent alarm bells through Lisa. He did not know which way to look or what he could say in response. All he managed was a meek, "No," and a quick sip of his distinctively average beer. What was he supposed to say?

To be truthful would almost be as bad as pretending the whole incident had not happened.

"Had to think about it, didn't you?"

"Lisa, will you stop it? Cathy and I are not interested in one another. That ship sailed a long time ago."

"For you or her?"

"For both of us," Jack insisted.

"Then tell me this. Why wouldn't she look me in the eye earlier? I'm not stupid, Jack. I can recognise guilt in a woman a mile off even if you can't."

"I suspect the problem she's having with Simon might be a reasonable explanation."

"That's weak even coming from you. I'm warning you, Jack, I will not be messed around. I suggest you think about that," said Lisa. She downed her wine and got up.

"Where are you going?"

"I'm going home on my own. It will give you some time to contemplate what I've just said."

As Lisa marched out of the pub, Jack looked down at his pint. He would be doing some thinking before he saw Lisa again. That would be over a decent pint instead of the one he had just been served.

Chapter 13

An early alarm meant Jack got up at seven o'clock. After his argument with Lisa, he had been in no mood to continue drinking. That had rewarded him with a clear head. He showered quickly and put on some semi-clean clothes before heading out to a cafe for breakfast. A mug of coffee and two slices of toast were all he had any intention of consuming. With Dean Lucas in his sights, he was not going to waste unnecessary time. He wanted to know why the fake trunk had not been spotted.

The choice of cafe was one he remembered as being efficient. Within a few minutes of sitting down, some toast and a cup of coffee were in front of him. Jack read through the notes of his meeting with Alistair Howarth while contemplating what he would say. It was a futile moment of planning. Once he saw Dean, Jack would march straight in and put him under immediate interrogation.

The lady serving his breakfast smiled at him. They had known each other for long enough to exchange a few pleasantries. It was often about her husband. More recently, they were speaking about the puppy she had taken on. It was wrecking her house and chewing through anything it could sink its teeth into. So far, it had consumed two electric cables, a pair of slippers and the remote control when it had slipped off the arm of the sofa.

Their conversations always made Jack smile. It was a reminder of why he had never wanted a pet. The unpredictable hours of a detective's life were another reason. If he ever settled down, maybe he would think differently. He might also need a partner who did not live in a first-floor flat.

Once his breakfast was eaten, Jack paid the bill and set off across the city. He had no intention of doing anything other than walking. Still too early to get into the auction house, he would wait outside. On the way, he sent a text to Lisa as a first step to defrost their relationship.

Jack arrived just after eight o'clock. Predictably, nobody else was there. The car park was empty, leaving Jack to wander around the perimeter. Suddenly, a car pulled in and raised Jack's hopes. He watched it turn around and drive away in the same direction it had come from.

All Jack could do was sit on a low wall and wait. A glance at his phone told him that Lisa had not responded. He began to type out another text and then changed his mind. The phone was pushed back inside his pocket.

At eight-twenty, Simon Hayton arrived. His expensive car pulled off the main road and took the space nearest the front door. He looked surprised when Jack walked over and met him at the side of his car. Simon ignored Jack's instruction to wind down the window. He turned off the engine and got out. Before any formalities could be offered, Jack began to fire a barrage of questions.

"Has Dean Lucas returned your message?"

"No."

"What time is he due in?"

"Just before nine o'clock."

"Can he get here any sooner?"

"Come inside and I will make some coffee. As soon as Dean arrives, I will find you a room where you can talk to him."

Jack went to object and then relented. The proposal was the best he was going to get.

***

Lisa's morning started later than Jack's. She walked into the station at eight-forty-five, having ignored Jack's text. Still fuming about Cathy Duggan, she headed up the stairs and went into the main office. When she got there, Louth was standing by her desk. She allowed a moment of dread to ripple through her body.

"Good morning, sir."

"Morning, Lisa. Have you got a minute?"

"Of course," she smiled, knowing there was no other acceptable answer.

She followed Louth through to his office. He closed the door and waited for her to sit down. Once she was seated, he eased in behind his desk. He had barely got comfortable when he made his announcement.

"We've just had a call from a lady called Sarah Reynolds. She's found the body of her partner. He's been murdered."

"Oh no," sighed Lisa. "Do we know who he is?"

"His name is Dean Lucas. He works at the auction house."

"That's who Jack is supposed to be meeting this morning. He'll be on his way there as we speak."

"I'll ring him. In the meantime, can you get out to see her? Uniforms are already there."

"Give me the address and I'll go straight there. Do you want to tell Jack to meet me over there?"

"No, I want Jack to speak to the auctioneer. Take someone else with you. Who's in so far?"

"Nobody, as far as I know."

"There must be someone," barked Louth who shot up from his chair like an overweight gymnast. He opened the door and peered out. In the corner of the station, he saw a familiar figure approaching. "Frank's in. Take him."

"Frank Campbell?" asked Lisa in horror.

"He's a fully qualified detective sergeant, just like you are."

"We are talking about the same Frank Campbell, aren't we? Couldn't I wait for Nathan to get here?"

"No, you need to get going. Here's the address."

Lisa got up from her seat feeling like there were lead weights in her shoes. As soon as she saw Frank Campbell, her whole body felt queasy. Despite his insistence that he was a gift to the female race, there was nobody more irritating in the station. Physically, he had little in his favour, with his body appearing as wide as it was tall. His personality was worse. His mode of attack was to offer a constant stream of wisecracks at the expense of anyone who was close by.

Frank was somebody Lisa and many others went out of their way to avoid. He was sidelined on most of the major investigations, leaving him to mop up the trivial items in the station. Occasionally, a lack of resources meant he was dragged in. On this occasion, Lisa was the unfortunate recipient who had been forced to accept the burden.

She shuffled out of Louth's office and approached Frank. Dreading what he was going to say, she moved slowly towards him. When he saw her, his chubby face lit up. She could already see him forming his first inappropriate comment of the morning.

"Morning, Frank. For whatever reason, the DCI has paired us up for a trip out to a murder scene."

"It's about time he separated you and Jack. You must get fed up with seeing him twenty-four-seven."

Lisa went to deliver something back in defence and then stopped. For once, Frank's words made sense. It had to be luck. Frank could not have got it right any other way.

"I'll let you tell Jack that. We're heading out to Hull Road."

"Just as long as we don't have to go to Hull. The only good thing to come out of there is the A63."

"Are you ready to go?"

"Born ready; that's me," grinned Frank.

"Follow me. My car's in the car park."

"Are we going right now?" asked Frank, with a frown.

"I thought you were ready."

"I am...as soon as I've had a leak and grabbed a coat."

"Born ready, Frank," laughed Lisa. "I'll see you outside."

***

Jack was sitting opposite Simon Hayton when the news came in about Dean Lucas. Jack answered the call from DCI Louth and immediately shook his head. The one person he wanted to speak to was now dead. With his girlfriend having found the body, it was unlikely to be a case of mistaken identity.

"I'll head over as soon as I've finished here," said Jack.

"No need," insisted Louth. "Lisa's gone."

"On her own?"

"I've sent Frank Campbell with her."

"Frank!" spluttered Jack. He sent coffee spraying across the desk. "You've sent Frank Campbell out with Lisa?"

"What's wrong with that?" asked Louth.

"Tell me they aren't going in Lisa's car," said Jack.

"What's that got to do with anything?"

"Have you seen the size of Lisa's car and the size of Frank?"

"Stop worrying. Finish what you're doing and then come back to the station. I want us to get our heads together and brainstorm some ideas."

Jack shook his head and sighed. In the confined space of Lisa's Golf, there would be more than Lisa's and Frank's heads being put together.

***

Lisa sat patiently in her car, waiting for Frank to arrive. She turned up the heater and put on her choice of music. The volume was increased to avoid the need for conversation. The last thing she wanted was to listen to Frank Campbell's attempts at humour on the way to a murder scene.

She was there for nearly ten minutes before he came out of the station. Waddling along, he moved at his own pace, oblivious to any need for urgency. Just watching him offered a sense of why he was never included in anything that required some energy. The man needed pensioning off and yet he was only in his mid-forties.

A sudden lurch of the car to the passenger side confirmed that Frank was getting in. His oversized frame slumped onto the seat and left Lisa fearful of what damage he would cause to her suspension. Her fury grew when he forced the seat backwards with all the subtlety of a drunk rhinoceros. Frank Campbell was making himself comfortable and Lisa did not like it one bit.

"It's a bit small, isn't it?" he growled. "Is that as far as the seat goes back?"

"You could sit in the car behind," said Lisa.

"Why don't we take one from the fleet?"

"Because I'm going in my car," she scowled.

"Suit yourself. If you like it cosy, that's fine by me."

Those few words were enough to make every inch of her skin itch. Cosy and Frank Campbell were two things Lisa never wanted to hear in the same sentence.

Lisa set off while Frank was still trying to force the seatbelt around his oversized stomach. He complained when it sent him lurching to the side. Lisa froze when the mass of Frank Campbell swung closer. Thankfully, the turn onto the main road sent him the opposite way. With a click, he was secured and no longer at risk of flowing across her.

On the way, Lisa briefed Frank about the little she knew. That was not much, other than it was the potential key witness in the auction investigation. Frank offered nothing in response. He was still fighting to get comfortable in Lisa's car.

"I said we should have gone in one of the larger cars," he grumbled to a lady who had stopped listening a long time ago.

Lisa drove to Hull Road and turned off down the side street she had been given. The location of the house was obvious. Police cars were outside, along with an ambulance, all with their blue lights flashing. A crowd had gathered around the cordon and were trying to get a view. One youth had his phone held high in the air. He was filming the incident taking place.

"Do you want to deal with that kid or shall I?" asked Lisa.

"I'll let you do it," grinned Frank. "I do like to see a stern lady in action." His words were said in an attempt to get Lisa to bite. It did not have the desired effect.

Lisa shook her head and parked her car. She got out and went straight over to the lad. He ignored her at first and then turned the phone towards her. He was eager to film the new arrivals at the scene. Dressed in his tracksuit bottoms and a hoodie, he grinned inanely at Lisa.

"Please can I ask you to turn the video off?" insisted Lisa. "This is a crime scene."

"I don't have to do that," he growled.

"I'm asking you nicely to turn it off. Don't make me arrest you for impeding an investigation."

"You can't do that. It's police harassment."

"You can use that in your defence if you want. Please will you stop filming?"

"Fuck you," he growled.

As Lisa bristled, the phone was snatched out of his hand from behind. It was thrown to the floor where it smashed and was trodden on by a large foot. Lisa looked across to see Frank Campbell standing beside them. He shrugged when he looked at the lad.

"I think you've dropped your phone and I've accidentally stood on it. Sorry."

"You'll pay for that," he growled as his confidence turned to upset.

"Shall we go in?" smiled Frank.

For the first time, Lisa appreciated Frank's support and the impressive weight he had pressed down on that phone. Though she did not approve of what her colleague had done, it had sent a clear message to the lad.

She nodded once to Frank and then led the way under the tape. A senior uniform came over to meet them. Lisa recognised him from the station though was quick to flash her ID. Frank did the same before the officer took them to one side.

"The deceased is a male in his mid-twenties. He has been stabbed in the neck in the alleyway down the side of the house. It appears to be one blow from somebody who has surprised him from behind. I suspect they knew where they were aiming the knife."

"Who found him?"

"His partner found his body this morning. She's in the house. Her name is Sarah Reynolds. As you can imagine, she's not in a good way."

"Who's in there with her?"

"PC Kelly Knox is inside. We thought a feminine touch might help."

"Frank, do you want to check the murder scene? I'll go in and see Sarah?"

"I could come in as well. I'm pretty good with distressed females."

"I think we might be better leaving this one to me," insisted Lisa.

Lisa went into the house tentatively. She knocked and called out to announce her arrival, aware of the distress Sarah would be feeling. As she tiptoed in, Kelly Knox came out to greet her. A smile and a few words were exchanged before Kelly took Lisa into the lounge.

"Sarah, this is DS Lisa Ramsey, a colleague of mine. Are you okay if she talks to you?"

"Yes," sobbed the girl who was curled up on one end of the sofa.

Lisa could feel her heartstrings being pulled. The loss the girl had suffered would stay with her for the rest of her life. Tucked into a ball, she looked so vulnerable. Her frame against the oversized leather sofa made her look like a child. It was not that she was small. The sofa was too large for the room.

Lisa sat down on the only other chair that would fit in the room while Kelly offered to make some drinks. When they were refused, she sat down alongside Sarah. Comforted by the two officers, Sarah eased herself upwards. She was holding a blanket, which she clutched tightly against her face.

"I'm sorry, Sarah, but I'm going to have to ask you to talk me through the events leading up to when you found Dean's body."

Sarah offered a surprisingly coherent response. She had returned from her night shift at the hospital at eight-thirty. Her shift ended at seven though she had been asked to stay on for another hour. When she got back, she saw Dean's car in the drive and wondered whether he was going to be late for work. Once in the house, she had gone into the kitchen and cursed him because the bin had not been put out.

Sarah had made herself a coffee and one for Dean. She was going to take it up to him but then decided to take the bin out first. That was when she saw Dean slumped against the side of the house. She knew it was him and she knew he was dead.

"What is it you do at the hospital?"

"I'm a nurse. I don't think that would have mattered. Anyone would have known he was dead."

"When did you last see him?"

"Yesterday afternoon. We went into town to do some shopping and got back at about five o'clock. I headed off to work at six-thirty and have not been back since."

"Do you know whether Dean was going out last night?"

"He said he might go out for a drink. I don't know whether he did."

"Where would he have gone?"

"It could be anywhere. Dean has mates in every pub around here. You would need to visit them all."

Lisa said nothing. She had someone in mind who would be happy to do exactly that.

"Do you know if Dean was in any trouble?"

"Not Dean, no. Since he got the job at the auction house, he's been as clean as a whistle. He had some problems before that but not once he got himself straight. We were talking about having a baby," she cried, with a piercing distressed wail.

"What sort of trouble was he in when he was younger?"

"The usual. He was in with the wrong crowd. It was all petty stuff for others who were clever enough not to get their hands dirty. He never went to prison or anything like that. He might have had a community order at one point. I don't know," she sobbed.

"That's fine, Sarah. As you said, it was a long time ago."

"We were going to be a family for the rest of our lives," she cried.

"I'm sorry but I also need to ask whether you can think of anyone who would want to cause Dean any harm."

"Nobody. He was a quiet lad. He got on with his job and spent most of his spare time with me."

"Thanks for your time, Sarah. We'll do our best to find whoever did this. I can promise you that," said Lisa as she beckoned Kelly out of the room.

Kelly Knox followed Lisa into the hallway. She closed the door and listened to make sure they were not being followed. Once alone, she turned to the younger PC. Kelly was the one who had been with Sarah since the police arrived. She would be able to offer up any unusual information.

"What do you think, Kelly?"

"I think the tears are genuine. The sense from the others is that Dean has been dead for a few hours. We can soon check whether Sarah was at work for all that time. I reckon the answer will be 'yes'."

"What about the house? Is there anything odd in it?"

"We had a quick look around when we got here. The only thing of note is that they appear to have bought the entire IKEA catalogue. I haven't seen anything that has come from anywhere else."

"That isn't a crime, is it?" smiled Lisa.

"It should be," laughed Kelly.

"It's good to see you back out in the field. I'd better go and see how Frank is getting on."

"Frank?"

"For some reason, the DCI has given me Frank Campbell to partner on this one," sighed Lisa, with a shake of her head.

"Poor you," said Kelly.

"It will be poor him if he makes one more comment about my car," growled Lisa. She patted Kelly on the back and then turned to face the inevitable barrage of inappropriate comments that would come from her partner.

***

Simon Hayton sat at his desk with his head in his hands. Since Jack had broken the news about Dean Lucas, he had barely offered anything coherent. His level of shock was either genuine or an impressive pre-rehearsed act. Jack would be taking nothing for granted. Nor would he be removing Simon from his list of chief suspects.

"Not Dean. I can't believe anyone would do this to Dean. It has to be a mistake."

"His girlfriend found him," insisted Jack.

"But why? What has Dean done to anyone?"

"You tell me," scowled Jack. "You're the one with body parts turning up in your auction. And remember, they came in a fake item."

"This doesn't make sense," insisted Simon.

"Finally, we have something we agree on. I suggest that between us we might like to find an explanation that solves that conundrum."

"How do we do that?"

"We need to find this Paul Colyer."

"I'll ask the girls to track him down."

"No, I'm asking *you* to track him down. It's *your* auction that he's putting things through and *your* staff member who's been killed. Has he got any items in *your* next auction?"

"I don't know."

"Then find out!" growled Jack. He was starting to lose his patience.

CHAPTER 14

AFTER A NIGHT IN The Cellars with Lisa, Jack eased himself out of bed. Though their relationship had thawed a little, she had been in no mood for him to stay over. The case did not help; not with Louth becoming increasingly agitated. He wanted answers and was demanding faster progress.

Jack's priority was to shower and get dressed. His second was the kitchen, where nothing but empty cupboards awaited him. He had used the last of the coffee the day before and there had been no sign of food for weeks. All that greeted him was a half-used pack of aspirin and an empty jar he had put back on the shelf. He pushed the cupboard door closed and put on his jacket. The answer to his ills would not be found at home.

On his way out of the house, Jack sent a message to Gregor Banks. Ever since Dean Lucas had been murdered, something had been nagging away in Jack's mind. Whatever it was would either be answered or put to rest by a man who lived on the periphery of legality. He usually had his finger on the pulse of every dark deed in the city.

His message was returned within a minute. It always was. It left Jack wondering whether Gregor treated him differently from the rest of the police force. For all he knew, there were others in the station who had a similar history with the man. And yet nobody had been through the courts with Gregor like he had. He had been so close to putting him away. Only old-fashioned bribes and menaces had kept Gregor a free man.

Their rendezvous was arranged for a cafe just off Clifford Street. Jack quickened his pace and soon found his leg giving him trouble. That old injury was still causing him problems when he pushed it too hard. He eased back to allow the burning to subside, knowing that his adversary would get there first. Gregor always did. Being prepared was what made the man the top dog in the city.

Jack slowed his approach when he saw the familiar thugs Gregor operated with. The one to fear was the lad called Bench, who was known to have a short fuse. Prone to violence at the drop of a hat, his limited intelligence did not help. You could see the cogs whirring inside his head with the simplest of questions.

Despite those failings, Gregor always used him when he needed some muscle. Just the look of the lad was enough to send most running for the hills. Short and squat, his huge barrel chest made for an impressive appearance. Add to it his ability to bench-press extreme weights and his reputation had been well-earned.

Jack was wary as he approached the cafe. The other person with Gregor was an older man called Harry. More old-school, he had been one of his father's closest allies. When Donald Banks had been sent to prison and the empire was inherited, Harry came with it. Wisely, Gregor continued to use his profile to secure continuity with both his associates and his enemies.

Gregor saw Jack and waved him towards the entrance. Under the watchful eye of the two goons, Jack and Gregor took a table in the corner. Neither man wanted their back to the room, so they settled on a compromise where they could sit adjacent to one another. Harry and Bench sat at a second table, a respectable distance away.

"We must stop going on these dates," smiled Gregor. "People will talk."

"I've dated worse," laughed Jack.

"I know you have. How is the dating front these days? Are you and that Lisa going to start a family soon?"

"I don't think so."

"Please do. I would love to be a godparent."

"Gregor Banks, the godfather, certainly does have a ring to it," grinned Jack.

"Personally, I preferred Goodfellas," shrugged Gregor. "It was a bit more realistic. Shall we order some breakfast?"

When Jack nodded, Gregor called over a waitress. He ordered smoked salmon and scrambled eggs on toast with a pot of tea. Two full breakfasts were added for the goons, which became three when Jack nodded. The only difference was Jack changed his beverage to coffee.

"I don't know where you put all that food," smiled Gregor.

"I'm like a camel. I store it in a hump."

"I don't think they do that. It's fat in there, not food or water."

"There goes my primary education," sighed Jack.

"Maybe they hadn't made that discovery when you went to school," insisted Gregor. "You did go a long time before me."

"I was lucky," nodded Jack. "I had so much less history to learn than you."

The two men continued to spar until the food came. It was as if neither could bring themselves to talk about business until they had landed a few jabs. As always, the contest was even. Gregor's response when put under pressure was to flick his eyes towards his ogres. Just one word from their master would see Jack heading out through a window.

The conversation slowed while both men consumed their breakfast. The meeting appeared civilised even if there was no shortage of distrust. Neither man would offer anything that could be used against them in the future. It was hard enough to remain on top without scoring own goals.

"I can't believe you still eat that stuff at your age, Jack."

"I'm making the most of it before my teeth fall out."

"If they do, stick them under the pillow. You might get a few quid to add to your police pension."

"I might need it," laughed Jack. "I do have a drinking habit to support."

"And a younger lady with far higher standards than you."

Jack smiled. He popped the last piece of sausage into his mouth and sat back to savour the taste. He was finished as was Gregor who had turned his attention to the pot of tea. He lifted the lid, examined the contents carefully and then smiled. It had been prepared just to his liking.

"I do like a proper pot of tea," he confirmed. "While that finishes brewing, I take it you have something for me."

"I might well do. I just need some information to close off the final part of it."

Gregor frowned. He sensed that Jack was playing with him.

"Don't tell me; you need to know who's peddling stuff on the city's streets. Once you have that, you'll be able to tell me."

"I just want some background information on Dean Lucas."

"Dean Lucas?" frowned Gregor. "Do I know him?"

"You tell me. He isn't somebody I've ever come across. I'm told he was a player a few years ago. Probably at the low end by your standards but he did a bit."

"I don't remember him."

"According to his girlfriend, he stepped away from all that and was making a life for himself on the right side of the law."

"I'm pleased for him."

"I wouldn't be. He was stabbed in the neck a day or so ago. He's dead."

"These things do happen," shrugged Gregor.

"They do if grudges are held over. I want to know who Dean Lucas was in his former life. You know, before he got all loved up and went straight."

"I would have to rack my brains, Jack. Tell me, who's paying for breakfast?"

"That depends on whether your memory improves."

Gregor looked around and smiled when he saw that the cafe was empty.

"Dean Lucas was a money launderer for Freddie Sharpe. When Freddie left the city, Dean lost his way in those circles. He fell on hard times and got a job at the auction house. As far as I know, that's where the story ends."

"Except it doesn't. Dean was found in an alleyway by his girlfriend yesterday morning."

"Don't look at me. I've never met the guy."

"What about Freddie? Where's he these days?"

"Still on the continent, I suspect. The last I heard, he was in Belgium."

"Is it possible he's back?"

A flicker of tension went through Gregor's face when Jack said it. He took a moment to reply after an instinctive check towards his goons.

"Freddie and I came to an agreement between gentlemen. He won't be coming back."

"You mean you ran him out of the city."

"As I said, we came to an agreement. That's all there is to it."

"I don't think it is. I think someone is going over old ground and your counterfeit goods and drugs are just the start of it. Think about it. Your comfortable world could be coming to an end."

"Nice try," smiled Gregor. "It will take more than a dead money launderer to get me looking over my shoulder.

Gregor summoned his goons and walked out of the cafe. There was a telltale glance back towards Jack as he left.

***

Jack settled the bill for the four breakfasts and headed into the station. He declined the offer of a receipt, knowing he would not be putting in a claim. He could imagine Louth's face when he tried to seek reimbursement for the meeting. Attendees would be one gangster and two oversized pets, which didn't have a category for tax purposes.

Wrapping his jacket around him, Jack noticed the cold. His slower pace of walking did nothing to warm him. It was not his leg on this occasion. His stomach was full of a cooked breakfast. It had been a good one in a cafe he would return to. If Lisa ever allowed him to stay over, he might even take her there as an apology.

As he walked, he thought about what Gregor had said. Freddie Sharpe was not someone he had heard about for a long time. Descended from a Newcastle crime family, Freddie had moved south to make his name. The feud between the Banks and the Sharpe families had seen a series of vicious battles. Eventually, Gregor and his father prevailed. Freddie Sharpe had been forced to run to the nearest ferry.

The revelation that Dean Lucas used to work for him had come as a surprise. Dean was not somebody Jack had crossed paths with in his years on the force. That was often the way with money launderers. They were shadowy characters who kept out of the limelight. Few were known about and they were protected as if they were the gangster's offspring. Without a good money man, high levels of corrupt business were difficult to maintain.

Once at the station, Jack went up in the lift. Without Lisa's presence, he did not need to justify using it. Like Jack, she was on a day off, though both of them would be working. Lisa would be doing so from the comfort of her flat. Jack preferred to go into the station.

He grabbed a coffee from the vending machine on the way. When he saw the disappointment flowing into the plastic cup, he wished he had brought one in from outside. No matter how many times he complained, the standard never got better. If you were unlucky, the machine was recently cleaned and the first few victims would taste the soapy liquid. Whether that was any worse than the coffee was up for debate.

He took the cup over to the desk by the window. Jack powered up a computer and began to search through the records they had for Dean Lucas. There was little on file other than the early crimes he knew about. The community order that had been spoken about was mentioned along with some other minor offences. Nowhere did it say that he was a money launderer for Freddie Sharpe.

He was just about to look up Freddie when Cathy Duggan came over. She had come into the station to catch up on some outstanding autopsy reports. When she saw Jack working, she offered a smile. She sat on the desk alongside him and bit her lip nervously.

"We must be a right pair of saddos to be in here on a Saturday."

"You're probably right," smiled Jack.

"I'm sorry about the other night," she said with a grimace. "I wasn't thinking."

"There was no harm done."

"Are you sure?"

"What do you mean?"

"Are things okay with you and Lisa?"

"I think so. Why?"

"Let's just say that I can sense frostiness when it comes to other ladies. I have seen enough dead ones in my time to be able to detect coldness from a mile away."

"She'll be fine," Jack assured her.

"And will you be fine?"

"What do you mean?"

"You know exactly what I mean, Jack."

"You know me, Cathy. I'll do what I always do."

"I know you will," she nodded, with a roll of her eyes. "Why aren't you with her today?"

"I've got a few errands to sort out."

"Like what?"

"The first one is Freddie Sharpe. Do you remember him?"

"It's hard to forget him. He gave me half of my customers back in the day. Wasn't he the one who used to nail people to things to stop them running away?"

"That's him. He reckoned it was easier than chasing after them."

"It takes a certain type of individual to do something like that."

"Normally someone good with a hammer," smiled Jack.

"I don't think that's what I meant. Anyway, why do you need to look him up? I thought he left years ago."

"He did. The name came up in a conversation I was having."

"About the auction house case?"

"Cathy, you know..."

"Enough, Jack. Stop messing around and let me help."

Jack looked Cathy in the eye and felt his resolve being weakened.

"Fine, but it's done my way."

"That's not a problem."

"And not a word of it goes back to Simon."

"I'm not sure we're speaking about much at the moment, let alone anything to do with the case."

"That's probably for the best."

"Do you think he's involved?"

"I'm not answering that. I just wouldn't get too close if I were you. I think there may be a fair bit of muck flying around by the time we've finished with this one."

"I get the hint," said Cathy. "What do you need me to do?"

"Find me some evidence that Freddie Sharpe has returned."

***

Several hours of investigation turned up nothing. Any traces of Freddie Sharpe took them over to mainland Europe. The man had not set foot in the UK since Gregor Banks had hounded him out. Maybe through fear or his own choice, Freddie had never returned.

The last known address that Jack found was in Belgium. Cathy came to the same conclusion and offered up her matching location. Neither of them could pin anything on Freddie or provide any evidence it was him. Whoever had committed the crimes was in the UK. Whether it was the same person responsible for both was far harder to establish.

"It has to be someone here," sighed Jack.

"Have you considered that it might not have anything to do with the auction house?"

"What do you mean?"

"We know the auction house has handled the trunk containing the body. We also know that Dean worked there. Think about it. What has anyone at the auction house got to gain from this?"

"Nothing," shrugged Jack.

"Exactly. They could be innocent victims in this while the real crimes are happening elsewhere."

Jack thought for a moment and nodded. Though Cathy might be right, he had a nasty feeling that her association with Simon Hayton was clouding her judgement.

"I think we should call it a day. Let's sleep on it and then see where we are on Monday."

"Aren't you working tomorrow?" asked Cathy.

"No, I'm going to have a day off."

"Lucky you," sighed Cathy. "I've still got those reports to do. I'll see what I can get done now and then finish the rest in the morning. You don't fancy helping me write them, do you?"

"It's probably best that I don't. The expression 'he doesn't know his arse from his elbow' might be a problem in your game," laughed Jack.

"That wouldn't be ideal," admitted Cathy. "Oh, what the heck, I'll do them all tomorrow. Do you fancy a drink? I'm buying."

"I'd better not," said Jack. "I think I might just have a quiet night in."

Cathy did not put up a fight. She knew the difficulty she had put Jack in. Even a drink between colleagues would leave him with some explaining to do. She shrugged off his refusal with a smile and watched Jack head out of the station.

Jack was halfway down the stairs when a text came from Lisa. It was an offer to meet him at The Cellars. With the case still fresh in his mind, Jack sent a message back. It was a polite refusal. He wanted a night alone to contemplate the case. He also had no desire to explain to Lisa why he had been in the station with Cathy Duggan.

Chapter 15

An evening going through all the case notes had made it a late night. Jack read them into the early hours, with copious amounts of instant black coffee bought on his way back from the station. He had also picked up some discounted sausage rolls that were close to their sell-by date. From the taste, Jack wondered whether that date was this year or last.

The late finish meant he did not surface until eleven o'clock. He got up and had a shave, which was a rare treat on a weekend. A shower to wake his tired body was a must. Once refreshed under the semi-warm water, Jack dried himself and went in search of clothes.

The pile on his chair told him that a washing day was in order. Most of what he owned was piled up or discarded around it. Somewhere under the mess would be some clothes that were not too dirty. Jack searched and then gave up. The whole lot was beyond redemption.

The lack of available options forced him into his wardrobe. An old pair of trousers were stuffed down the back. Unworn for many years, he could not remember why. Jack pulled them out and slipped his foot cautiously into the leg. With each inch it went in, he was expecting an unpleasant surprise.

Nothing came; nor did it when he pulled on the other leg. He dragged them up and fought to button them around his waist. He was surprised when they fitted though could see why they had been abandoned. The turn-ups at the bottom ended a couple of inches above his ankles. Even without pulling them up, they looked ridiculously short.

Jack stared down and shrugged. A brief thought to cut the stitching around each turn-up was quickly put to one side. If anyone was looking at his ankles, they were welcome to enjoy the show. Just to make sure they had something to stare at, he selected his least matching socks. One was light grey; the other was dark blue with red spots.

Jack pulled out an old shirt to complete his look. A pin-striped offering was a slight clash with the grey trousers. He picked up some of the clothes from his chair and carried them downstairs. It would take several loads to deal with a mountain that resembled a European quota surplus.

A search through his cupboards offered a moment of surprise. The large box of detergent was an unwelcome find. Without it, Jack could have left the washing and gone out to do something better. A laundrette would save the day when things got truly desperate.

Faced with everything he needed, he stuffed the machine full to the last inch. He kicked at the clothes left protruding to force the last bits of fabric in. Like a pusher on a Japanese train, he made sure nothing did not make it through the door. Everything he could get in was one less item to wash.

The machine began to groan from the moment it was brought to life. Overburdened by an excess of clothes, it fought with the weight. Even with the amount he had fitted in, it would still require another three loads. With time to kill, the pub was calling his name.

He slipped on his jacket and headed out. A glance at his watch told him he had an hour to fill. That was time for a couple of pints in a comfortable seat. He could grab a bacon butty on the way. It would give him something to battle the unpleasant memory of those sausage rolls.

A brisk walk was the perfect antidote to his late night. Jack marched to The Cellars with thoughts of that first pint going through his head. He contemplated texting Lisa but decided not to. She would still be miffed with him for refusing her invitation the night before. Plus, he had washing to do, which would drag him away just as she arrived.

Jack bought a bacon butty at the cafe around the corner from the pub. Rather than take it in and have Alf moan at him, he settled down on the bench outside. In the open air, the smell of the bacon was divine. Jack savoured it and then sunk his teeth into the juicy offering. Just as he expected, the taste was from heaven.

His only regret was that he had only bought one. It was finished within a couple of minutes and left Jack wanting more. He vowed to stick to one pint and then grab another on the way back. If he kept up the pace with the four loads of washing, there was no reason why he couldn't have eight bacon butties by the time the day was over.

He wiped away the grease with the napkin he had been given. The whole lot was scrunched up and thrown in the bin outside the pub. Once the evidence was disposed of, Jack went inside. From behind the bar, Alf looked at his watch and shook his head.

"This is becoming a habit, Jack."

"So is me paying my tab," he grinned. "I better make this one on credit."

"You're well ahead, so I would do if I were you."

Jack waited for Alf to go about his work. While he poured, Jack gazed around to see who else was in the pub. Two older guys were in the far corner, enjoying a quiet chat. They both had halves which looked like they had been untouched since Alf opened up.

Across from them was a younger man playing on one of the machines. Its flashing lights and noises seemed to have him mesmerised. Occasionally, there was a chugging sound to confirm he had won something. From the lack of emotion, it was hard to know whether there was more going in or coming out. The cynic in Jack could guess which it would be.

Alf finished off Jack's pint and pushed it across the bar. It was lifted and examined ahead of the first sip. That moment when it hit his lips was always to be savoured. After a salty bacon butty, the glory of it was even better.

"Your very good health, Alf."

"Yours too, Jack."

Jack savoured the taste and then eased himself onto a stool. For once, he intended to remain by the bar rather than skulk away to his corner. It would help him keep to one or at least force him to down the second quickly when the time came to return home.

The vibration of his phone changed his thinking. Jack reached into his pocket and pulled out the handset. On the screen was DCI Louth's name, which came with a feeling of dread. On a rare day off, the last thing he wanted was a call from his boss.

"Jack speaking," he offered as he took the phone to his ear.

"Jack, it's Eddie. Where are you?"

"I'm doing my washing. Why?"

"Can you come into the station?"

"What for?"

"We've just arrested Billy Ellis. I thought you might want to be the one to speak to him."

"What's he done?"

"You'll find out when you get here. That's if your washing can wait."

"I'm on my way," confirmed Jack. He put the phone down and took another sip of his beer. "Alf, look after this for me, will you? I'll be back as soon as I can."

"Seriously, Jack?"

"Duty calls," he grinned.

Alf took the pint and put it under the bar next to Jack's kitty. It would be stale by the time Jack returned. What did that matter? Alf knew his best customer would still drink it.

***

Jack left The Cellars and walked in the direction of the station. A passing taxi was stopped with a firm display of his hand and a warrant card. The driver pulled over and allowed Jack to get in. He smiled at the lady who was driving. In her mid-thirties, her brown bobbed hair, square glasses and freckles made her look like Velma from Scooby Doo. Not that Jack was going to say anything. The uncanny resemblance meant she would have shared that conversation on hundreds of occasions.

The offer of a free ride was refused. The journey would only be a matter of minutes and yet it made no sense to walk. The sooner he could get to Billy Ellis, the sooner he could start applying some pressure. Jack was going to enjoy interviewing him, particularly when he reminded him about going straight.

Velma dropped Jack off in the police station car park. She smiled when he paid the fare and told her to keep the change. As he went inside, he was already thinking about Billy. In the olden days, a gnarly officer would have slapped him around before he was interviewed. No longer an option, Jack would have to be more cunning.

Louth was waiting for Jack outside the interview room. Inside was Billy Ellis, along with the duty solicitor. There was no expectation of an expensive private lawyer for the lad. If one did turn up, it would only raise questions. Who was paying the bill and why were they prepared to help someone like Billy?

"I hope I didn't drag you away from your washing," grinned Louth who took a second look at what Jack was wearing.

"It will keep," said Jack. A good soak won't do it any harm."

"I thought you would have more exciting things to do on a Sunday."

"I love doing some washing," grinned Jack. "And anyway; what could be more exciting than coming in here to interview Billy Ellis? What's the story?"

"He was caught inside a country house near Poppleton. The owners were supposed to be away. They came back early and found him in the house."

"How did they catch him?"

"The silly sod cracked his head on a low beam and nearly knocked himself out."

"Did it knock any sense into him?" asked Jack.

"None whatsoever. He is playing the amnesia card though."

"How convenient. Are we doing this one together?"

"Why not?" grinned Louth. "It'll give me a chance to see the legendary DI Jack Husker in action."

"I hope you aren't going to be disappointed, sir."

"No more than usual," laughed Louth.

"Come on; let's get it done. Then you can tell me what you're doing here on a Sunday. Even a DCI is allowed a day off once in a while."

"That's easy, Jack. I'm married and the mother-in-law has popped over. Isn't that reason enough to be here?"

"It bloody well is," laughed Jack.

The two detectives went into the interview room together. Jack smiled at Billy Ellis who remained impassive. Both Louth and Jack offered up their ID. It meant nothing to the young lad. With a bright red mark on his forehead, he was looking utterly vacant.

"I must say this is a surprise, Billy," said Jack. "There was I thinking you had gone straight."

"I have," came his reply.

"Then we must have made a mistake."

"I guess."

"Right, let's get this mistake cleared up and then we can all go home. Some of us do have things to do on a Sunday." Jack flicked a glance at Louth, daring him to say something about his washing.

The tape was turned on to allow the formal interview to begin. The introductions were brief and then Jack asked the obvious question. He knew there would be no confession but was unsure what story Billy would offer up. When his answer came, it was surprisingly simple.

"I went there to pick up an item for Tuesday's auction," said Billy.

"What were you picking up?" asked Jack.

"I can't remember."

"You can't remember? You'll have to do better than that."

"I had a bump on the head. It's all a bit of a blur. I probably need to get it checked out."

"I thought you declined a visit to the hospital," confirmed Jack for the benefit of the tape.

"Did I? I don't remember."

"Just so we are clear, do you need some medical attention?"

"I don't know. What happened?"

"Interview terminated at one-twenty," barked Jack. "We will recommence tomorrow, once the suspect has been checked out by a doctor."

"Why do I need a doctor?" asked Billy.

"Don't waste your breath," snarled Jack. "The tape is off. You can say what you like now."

"About what?" shrugged Billy.

"See you tomorrow, Billy," said Jack.

"Where are you going?"

"I'm going outside to enjoy some fresh air and freedom. I'll let you know what it's like because you won't be finding out for yourself any time soon."

"We'll see," he smiled as Jack and DCI Louth left the room.

Louth went to the coffee machine and waited for two cups of something murky to appear. He handed one to Jack and then took the other through to his office. Jack followed him and sat down on the opposite side of the desk. On a weekend, Louth appeared far more relaxed. His usual abrasive energy was missing.

"You did the right thing there," he nodded. "If we'd continued, we would have been hit with that throughout the trial."

"I just hope we have enough to make it stick. Was the lad caught with anything?"

"No. We think the owners got there before he had time to take whatever he was after."

"What do you think he was looking for?"

"I don't know. He'll have a fair idea of what the good stuff is, so I would imagine he was targeting that."

"Did he have a van with him?"

"He was in his car. It was found parked about half a mile away," said Louth.

"Which means he was looking for smaller items he can carry," stated Jack. "They're also easier to get rid of."

"Surely he wouldn't be stupid enough to put them through the auction house?" frowned Louth.

"He'll have somewhere else to fence it. I would imagine one of the dealers he knows will take it. That's for tomorrow. I've got washing to do today."

"Not drinking?"

"Sir, I am capable of multi-tasking. Washing and drinking go hand-in-hand if you do it right."

Louth smiled. He could imagine Jack doing just that.

Chapter 16

Jack was back at the station at eight o'clock the following morning. Having spent a night in the cells, he was hopeful that Billy Ellis would talk. He would need a better answer than amnesia, particularly after the medics had confirmed he was okay. He might have a mild concussion but there was nothing that would cause his memory to fail.

Jack had no intention of going to interview him early. The lad would be expecting to be seen as soon as the duty solicitor arrived. He would be left disappointed. Only when he had stewed in the cells for an extra hour would Jack find the time to see him.

His first task of the morning was to brief Lisa. She arrived at eight-thirty and looked full of energy. There was no mention of Jack's failure to meet her for a drink. Nor was the argument about Cathy Duggan fuelling any obvious resentment. She smiled at Jack and joined him in Louth's office. Belatedly, Frank Campbell was called in as a rare show of trust.

The meeting took over twenty minutes. First, they exchanged accounts of what they had learned about Dean Lucas. For once, Frank kept to the facts. His only involvement had been to see the body. With a knife plunged into Dean's neck, his death would have been quick. Frank spared everyone further details. Even his thick skin would prefer to forget what he had seen.

The lack of information from Dean's girlfriend was soon overtaken by the revelation from Jack. There were puzzled looks when he offered up the information about Freddie Sharpe. The name was unknown to DCI Louth and Lisa, two newcomers to the city. Frank knew Freddie only too well. He had spent half his career mopping up crimes the man had left in his wake.

"Are you saying Freddie Sharpe did this?" asked Louth.

"No," confirmed Jack. "I'm just saying that Dean had a pretty murky past as does Billy Ellis. That starts to fall into the realms of coincidence, which we don't like."

"It doesn't link us to the body in the trunk," said Lisa.

"We don't know that," insisted Jack. "Remember, Shane Keyson had a criminal past as well."

"That was for assault, wasn't it?"

"That's what we know about. Who's to say he wasn't wrapped up in something more sinister?"

There were general nods before the team were briefed about Billy Ellis. They spoke about the crime and what had led to him being detained overnight. Nobody seemed surprised that a lad with his history had fallen back into his old ways.

"Where does Billy fit into this?" demanded Louth.

"My gut feeling is he was in that house to steal something specific," said Jack. "The place is too remote to be an opportunist crime. He wouldn't even know the estate was there."

"Unless it was somewhere they've been before," said Lisa.

"Exactly. Remind me; where was the estate they were heading to today?" asked Jack.

"That was over at Crayke," insisted Lisa. "It doesn't mean they haven't visited this one as well."

A series of nods went around the room. They were ended when the phone on DCI Louth's desk rang. He picked it up and listened to what was being said before putting the call on hold.

"Simon Hayton is in reception. He wants to see you, Jack."

"That's a shame. I'm going to interview Billy Ellis," shrugged Jack.

"Do you want me to go down?" asked Lisa.

"No, I think you should go in with Jack," said Louth. "Why don't we make Simon wait? Let's see how he is once he's had time to think through whatever is on his mind."

Jack smiled. By the time he was finished with Billy Ellis, he would have a lot more questions to ask Simon Hayton.

***

As soon as they left Louth's office, Jack and Lisa went down to meet Billy Ellis. The lad had been locked in a holding cell overnight and would have had time to reflect on his offence. Jack grabbed a coffee and handed it to Lisa. By the time he had waited for a second one, Billy Ellis was being transferred to the interview room.

"Is there one for me?" he sneered when he passed the detectives in the corridor.

"No, you have to go to Starbucks," smiled Jack. "I recommend the lemon drizzle cake as a perfect accompaniment. Sorry, I forgot. They don't have Starbucks in prisons."

"Fuck you," growled Billy.

"Are you sure about that?" whispered Lisa. "These prisons have a lot more than they used to."

Lisa led the way into the interview room. The duty solicitor was already inside as was PC Mark Langton who had accompanied Billy. With his rosy round face, he grinned at Jack like a Cheshire cat. They had known each other for a long time and often sparred verbally in the station. Mark was one of the few who could keep Jack on his toes.

"Have you softened him up as I asked?" grinned Jack.

"DI Husker, I do not think that is appropriate even if it is a joke," said the duty solicitor solemnly.

"I don't think Billy will mind," assured Jack. "With his amnesia, he's likely to forget about it pretty quickly."

A stern look from the solicitor came as a warning. Jack winked at Mark Langton and then took his seat at the table. With Lisa alongside him, they stared across towards Billy. The lad looked just as he had the day before.

"Did you sleep well?" asked Jack, only to be met by silence. He turned to the duty solicitor and smiled. "Am I allowed to ask that?"

"DI Husker, you know the rules and limits all too well. I suggest we start the tape and get on with the meeting."

Lisa conducted the formalities. She switched on the tape and introduced those in the room. At Jack's request, Mark Langton stepped outside and waited at the door. He would remain there until the interview was over.

"Mr Ellis, would you care to explain why you were caught on someone else's property?"

"I went there to pick up an item for Tuesday's auction," said Billy.

Jack shook his head. He had not expected anything else.

"May I ask what you were there to pick up?"

"I can't remember."

"How about you take us through what you can remember?"

"I remember being sent over there to collect something. When I got there, the front door was closed, so I went around the back, I think. That's pretty much it."

"Do you remember who sent you there?"

"Not really," Billy sighed, with a puff of his cheeks.

"Care to hazard a guess?" asked Jack.

"It was probably Dean. He must have asked me to go over there."

"Why would Dean do that? He was the valuer."

"I don't know. You would have to ask him."

"I bet we would," growled Jack, to a smug look from Billy.

"Did he give you the address?" asked Lisa in an attempt to assist her colleague.

"I guess so."

"Where's the piece of paper with it on?"

"What piece of paper?" shrugged Billy. "He would have just told me and I would have remembered it."

"How did you get into the house?" interrupted Jack.

"I can't remember. I must have gone through the back door."

"It was locked."

"Was it?"

"The sash window had been forced open."

"Not by me, it wasn't. I don't go climbing in through windows. I'm too old for all that."

"You didn't go through the door," insisted Jack.

"Somebody must have let me in. As I said, I can't remember."

"Why did you run away when you were seen?"

"I can't remember that either. That bump must have done more damage than we first thought."

"Mr Ellis, I will remind you that you were checked over by a doctor. He concluded that you would have, at the most, a mild concussion and no memory loss. So, I will ask you again, why did you run away?"

"I can't remember," repeated Billy.

Jack sat back and finished his coffee. His patience had long since gone. Either they would have to charge Billy Ellis or let him go. The lad was going to tell them nothing. He was too well-schooled to be helpful.

"Okay, I think we're at a dead end," concluded Jack. "At the end of the day, we have the links we need. The one person who could corroborate your story has been murdered. You can make what you like of that. You have also handled a trunk with body parts in it. Again, you can draw your own conclusions on that one. Between the two of those and the interview that will follow this one, I'm confident we'll be charging you in the next hour."

"Charging me? What for?"

"For the murder of Dean Lucas," confirmed Jack. "You'll be going down for life."

"I thought I'd been arrested for breaking and entering?" he queried.

"Oh, that. We probably don't have enough to make that stick, so we'll just go with the one we can pin on you. Are we done, DS Ramsey?"

"I think so, DI Husker." Lisa turned the tape off.

Jack got up, leaving a puzzled expression on Billy Ellis's face. He looked across towards the duty solicitor who appeared confused. Billy had seen that look before. He would be getting no help from his solicitor. Whatever he needed to do, he would be doing by himself.

"Who's your next interview with?" asked Billy.

"The man you were stealing items for," confirmed Jack as he moved confidently towards the door. "He'll be trying his best to cut you adrift to save his own skin."

"I didn't kill Dean!" blurted out Billy. "I only went to that bloody house to get some silver for Daniel."

"Daniel?" frowned Lisa.

"Daniel Voss, the man you're going to interview."

"Are you saying you didn't kill Dean?" queried Lisa innocently.

"Why would I kill Dean?"

"To hide the evidence of the address you were given," she shrugged.

"He didn't give me the address. That came from Daniel."

"Now I'm very confused," said Lisa. "Shall we sit back down and sort this out? If you didn't kill Dean Lucas, we don't want to charge you for a murder you didn't commit. DI Husker, have you got enough time to do this now?"

Jack looked up at the clock and sighed. He edged further towards the door. An imploring look came from both Billy and Lisa. He shook his head and glanced back at the clock with impatience.

"Fine, but it will have to be quick. No messing around," stated Jack.

"No messing around," confirmed Billy.

***

The confession from Billy Ellis was surprisingly detailed. Daniel Voss had given him the address after visiting the property to do an appraisal. The house was dripping with silver and had a lot of boxed-up items in the cellar. Anything Billy took would not be missed.

It was not the first time that Billy had stolen items for Daniel. They had met at the auction house and had discussed the difficulty of getting hold of good pieces. Daniel had bemoaned the large estates, which were hoarding it and doing nothing more than keeping it in storage. When Billy had mentioned his past, a plan had been formed between them. Daniel had agreed to pay him for any items he could secure.

At first, it had only been some easy pickings. Some unsold lots had gone missing at the auction house. Too small to claim on insurance, Simon Hayton had taken the hit. It was not an act that could be repeated. He needed a better source, which Daniel Voss had been quick to provide.

His online sales were the perfect place to sell such items. Without the public records of a shop or an auction, any stolen silver could soon disappear. They were always careful not to take one-off items or anything that would be overly memorable. Table pieces were the most suitable. Their commonality allowed them to be traded without consequence.

Jack and Lisa allowed Billy Ellis to speak freely. There was no need to ask questions or press him on any details when he was offering up so much. In fear of Daniel Voss using him as a scapegoat, he did his best to help. His duty solicitor remained silent alongside him.

Billy ended by providing the names of three other houses he had been into. All three had been fruitful, with several pieces taken from each. For every item, Daniel had given Billy thirty percent of the sales value. It was hundreds of pounds for a modest amount of risk.

"Thank you, Mr Ellis. You have been very helpful," said Jack.

"In light of Mr Ellis's cooperation, I would like to think that he might be charged with a lesser offence and be released on bail," insisted the duty solicitor.

"That will depend on whether he continues to cooperate," said Jack.

"I will," confirmed Billy.

"Let me conduct my next interview and we'll complete the formalities soon after," replied Jack. He was not about to confirm who that interview was with. If Billy was happy to think it was Daniel Voss, Jack was not going to correct him.

"Will I go down for this?" asked Billy, with a forlorn look in his eyes.

"It's too early to say. Any willingness to assist will certainly offer some mitigation."

Billy Ellis sat back and let out a deep sigh as Jack and Lisa left the room. Despite what Jack had said, he knew he was heading to prison.

They were halfway towards the reception desk when Lisa stopped and pulled Jack to one side. In a quiet corner, she checked that nobody was in earshot before speaking.

"That Daniel Voss revelation was a turn-up, wasn't it?" she said with a shake of her head.

"I'm struggling to know what to believe," admitted Jack.

"Do you think he has anything to do with the murder of Dean Lucas?"

"It's possible. If Dean found out what Daniel and Billy were doing, it would solve a problem, wouldn't it?"

"But murder?" questioned Lisa.

"I know. I would have thought some old-fashioned threats would have been the order of the day."

"What are we going to say to Simon? We can't tell him about Daniel."

"We'll tell him what he probably already knows. We've arrested Billy for breaking and entering. Why make it more complicated than that?"

"I guess you're right," nodded Lisa.

"And remember, Simon Hayton has come to see us, not the other way around."

Lisa was left to mull over those words as Jack led the way to the meeting. They went through to the reception where they saw their visitor waiting. He was playing with his phone and looking bored. Jack was still struggling to reconcile that Simon was the same person Cathy Duggan was sharing her bed with.

Jack went over and apologised for their lateness. He offered his conciliatory words as he took Simon into a side room. In the drab surroundings of the reception meeting room, he offered Simon a coffee. It was declined by a man who was keen to talk.

"What can we do for you?" asked Jack. "I thought you were supposed to be doing a house call over in Crayke."

"I cancelled it. Without Dean, I don't have a valuer to go with me. Then there is this matter with Billy. Everything feels a bit difficult at the moment. Are you able to confirm what Billy has done?"

"He was caught inside a property near Poppleton. We'll be charging him shortly," said Jack.

"The stupid idiot. He told me he'd gone straight."

"Don't they all?" shrugged Jack.

"I guess," he sighed. "Sometimes, you just want to see the best in people. Please tell me Billy is not involved with Dean's death."

"We don't think so."

"What about the body in the trunk?"

"We haven't got anything that would suggest he is. The key to that is finding out who this mysterious Paul Colyer is."

"I might be able to help you with that. We have some of his items in tomorrow's auction. I didn't realise they had come in until I looked at the catalogue."

"Is the auction still going ahead?" asked Lisa, with a frown.

"I think so. Everything is ready to go. Dean finished the valuations before he was killed. I think the best thing would be to use the auction to empty the building and then close for a few weeks."

"What about manpower?"

"I need to find a second porter. I'll run the auction. I've checked with the girls in the office and they've said they'll be there. I just need someone to help Finn behind the scenes."

"We'll probably be releasing Billy on bail later today, so it's up to you whether you think it's appropriate to use him."

"I'll think about it. If I can get somebody else, I will. If not, I'll use Billy but keep him out of sight. Finn can do the onstage work."

"Have you got a list of the items Paul Colyer has sent in?"

"Not with me but I can send it across."

"I've got a better idea," said Jack. "I'll come over to view the lots."

"Viewing was last Friday," frowned Simon.

"Not for me, it isn't. I'll be conducting a private viewing this afternoon."

***

Jack and Lisa headed back to Louth's office for a debrief. There was no attempt to involve Frank Campbell in their discussions. He had reverted to type and was doing his best to offend those around him in the open office. As Jack walked past, he was recounting one of his supposed conquests. Nobody was impressed.

Louth was on a call when Jack walked in. Not bothering to knock, he sat down and was met with a frown. Lisa offered a half-knock to create the pretence of politeness. It was a token effort to absolve herself of any blame. Gazing around, Jack had the look of a kid intent on mischief. If he was not given something to do in the next few seconds, he would find trouble.

When Louth continued his call, Jack began to fidget. He was soon up on his feet and heading out of the door, only for the DCI to summon him back. It forced Louth to end his conversation. He looked irritated at the interruption, leaving Lisa to diffuse the situation.

"We've made some progress, sir."

"I'll be the judge of that," scowled Louth.

Lisa offered a full account of the facts. She spoke about Billy Ellis's confession and the involvement of Daniel Voss. Like the others, Louth was surprised that the auction was going ahead. He expected the building to be closed down for months.

"Simon Hayton reckons it would be best to clear the place."

"He's got a point, I suppose," admitted Louth.

"It gets better," insisted Jack. "They've got items in there from Paul Colyer."

"Our mystery man in Hull?"

"That's him," confirmed Jack.

"Are the items fake?"

"I'm going to find out this afternoon. I've told Simon I want a private viewing."

"Since when did you become an antiques expert?"

"I'm not. I'm going to take Alistair Howarth with me."

"Alistair's time gets booked up weeks in advance."

"That's where you come in."

"What do you mean?"

"I need your eloquent charms."

"Don't push it, Jack," warned Louth. "What do you need?"

"I need Alistair Howarth to meet me at the auction house at two o'clock. Tell him I need him for the full afternoon."

"I will ask him. I won't be able to tell him."

"Whatever you think best, sir. Just make sure he's there at two o'clock."

"And then what?"

"If the items are what I'm expecting, I will need plenty of uniforms ready for a big day out at tomorrow's auction."

"I think we might take one step at a time. Perish the thought, Jack, but one of your hunches has been wrong before."

Jack grinned. He was pretty sure he would not be proven wrong this time.

***

Jack drove to the auction house at one-thirty. On the way, he picked up a sandwich and a coffee. He needed something to keep him going, especially after his session with Louth. It had taken some time to persuade the DCI not to arrest Daniel Voss. It was Lisa who finally managed to convince him. For now, Daniel was more useful being left to provoke the others at the auction.

Jack pulled into the car park and ate his lunch. From his vantage point in the corner, he could survey the scene. There was only one car there, which was Simon Hayton's. Everybody else was either dead, arrested or on a day off.

Alistair Howarth arrived at five minutes past two. Just those few minutes of lateness irritated Jack. It felt like the man had better things to do than waste time on police matters. Who could blame him? The man had rubbed shoulders with the very best in the trade.

Jack walked over to Alistair's car. The older man eased out and shook Jack's hand. Dressed as he was when he last saw him, Jack wondered whether they shared the same attitude towards clothes. Alistair's were more expensive though looked like they had been worn for just as long.

"Thank you for coming to assist us," said Jack.

"How long do you think this will take?" asked Alistair.

"Hopefully, not too long. It's only the finer pieces I want to look at."

"How many of them are there?"

"I don't know."

"What do you mean, you don't know?" asked Alistair. His lack of a briefing from Louth was obvious.

It forced Jack to explain the purpose of their visit. The importance of confidentiality was stressed. If a piece was fake, he did not want Alistair to tell Simon. It was crucial to the investigation.

"He must know," insisted Alistair.

"He says he normally leaves that side to his valuer."

"Quite frankly, I find that preposterous."

"So do I," said Jack even though he had no idea what the word meant.

"How is this going to work?" asked Alistair. "When he sees me looking at an item, he will know that I think it is a fake."

"I will request a catalogue and then ask Simon to leave us to go around on our own."

"Please don't ask me to lie. I will not do so, no matter what is at stake."

"I won't," assured Jack.

They went inside and were met by Simon Hayton. The biggest surprise was that Simon did not recognise Alistair. When Jack introduced him as a colleague, Simon smiled and took it at face value. It left Jack wondering whether the auctioneer knew anything about the trade.

Simon took them into his office and handed over a catalogue. A list of numbers was stuck to it, showing those lots brought in by Paul Colyer. Simon seemed keen to understand whether he needed to withdraw the lots from the auction.

"You don't need to withdraw them. I just want to know what he normally sends in. Of course, when he collects his money, I want to speak to him."

"I will tell the girls not to release any funds until you give the all-clear. Are you sure you don't want his lots pulled from the auction?"

"That would be the worst thing you could do. If the items are sold and he doesn't get his money, it will force him to contact us."

"Okay, I see your thinking. Now, do you need me?" asked Simon. "I've got several calls to make."

"We'll be okay on our own. Once we're done, we'll pop back in to see you," said Jack.

The lack of any argument was pleasing. Jack and Alistair left the office and headed towards the auction room. Simon had already reached for his phone. He was uninterested in what they were looking at. It allowed Jack to lead the way, with the catalogue clutched in his hand. When he turned to Alistair, his expert was staring down at a piece of furniture with a frown. It was a pine chest of drawers, which had endured a tough life.

"Please tell me we haven't come here to look at pieces like this," he groaned.

"No, that's for the furniture auction, which comes first. Fine antiques follow straight after."

"Thank heavens for that," sighed Alistair.

They moved past the modern furniture towards the better items. Jack went slowly in case anything caught Alistair's eye. The older man scanned the lots though did not move from the path. He was not about to scramble through the jungle of cheaper items.

"That looks more interesting," announced Alistair. "If I am not mistaken, that is a campaign chest."

Jack scanned the catalogue and confirmed the expert was correct. He did not tell him it was a piece from Paul Colyer's list.

"You're right. Could you give me your insight into it?"

"It's probably easier if you tell me what the catalogue says first," noted the expert.

Jack scanned the booklet in his hands and read out the listing to Alistair.

"Early nineteenth-century teak campaign chest, stamped SW Silver & Co. Comprising two sections, with two short over three long drawers. Brass-mounted corners and stamped inset handles. Raised on turned feet."

"And the guide price?"

"Between fifteen hundred and two thousand pounds."

"That seems reasonable," said Alistair, without blinking. "That depends on the condition, of course."

"And whether it's fake," muttered Jack under his breath.

"What was that?"

"Nothing," confirmed Jack.

Alistair went to work on the piece. He took his time to look at every detail. Handles, hinges and corners were examined closely. Then he focused on the drawers. Every one of them was opened and the joints were studied. Finally, he asked Jack to tip the item up. It allowed him to show his surprising sprightliness by sliding under it. It resembled a mechanic going under a car on a trolley.

When he emerged, he went back inside it. He slid out the top drawer and felt underneath. He ran his hand under the top and frowned. When he had finished, he put everything back in place and turned towards Jack.

"No," was all he said.

"What does that mean?"

"It's a fake. A very good fake, but still a fake."

"How can you tell?"

"The feet are incorrect by about twenty years. Also, the feel of the wood is wrong. It's hard to describe to a layman. If you've been in the game as long as I have, you tend to know."

"How obvious is it?"

"I would say only a handful of people in the country would be able to spot it."

"Do you reckon the dealers around here would know?"

"I doubt it. Most of the campaign furniture goes through the London auction houses. They wouldn't get much of it up here."

Jack took Alistair to the next item. He didn't spend long on a Victorian side table. It was exactly what the catalogue stated and was worth its one hundred and fifty pounds estimate. Next to it, a similar conclusion was reached about a console table.

They were a third of the way through the room when Alistair spotted another fake. A French gilt mirror was not genuine. Again, the item was an impressive copy and would not be spotted by most. Only a fleck in the gilding gave it away. Alistair nodded towards Jack knowingly.

"Is this another item you were expecting to find?" asked Alistair.

"What do you mean?" asked Jack.

"I get a sense that the list of numbers you were given will all prove to be fake."

"You tell me," grinned Jack to a man who was staring intently at him.

"Challenge accepted," smiled Alistair. "I think we have an old-fashioned wager on our hands. Shall we make it for a nice bottle of malt?"

"Why not?" smiled Jack.

The next hour saw Alistair invigorated. He moved around the auction room like a man who had been re-energised. His enthusiasm was infectious as was his speed of working. Within half the time, six more fakes had been uncovered.

By the time he was finished, twelve fake items had been noted. They were the same twelve that were on Jack's list. Every one of them was being sold by Paul Colyer. It had cost Jack a bottle of malt but it was worth every penny. Alistair Howarth had given him exactly what he needed. He had also confirmed that the quality of the fakes was outstanding.

"I'm impressed," nodded Jack.

"I will take that as the ultimate compliment," smiled Alistair. "Something tells me you do not impress easily."

"You could be right again," laughed Jack. "I will send you a bottle of malt next week."

"You are a gentleman. Now, what are we telling our auctioneer? He is on his way."

Jack looked over his shoulder and saw Simon Hayton. The man was not about to be informed of anything.

"Nothing. As far as he's concerned, every lot is just as it should be."

"I will leave you to say that, DI Husker. I have my integrity to consider."

"That's fine. I don't mind selling my soul to the devil for a good cause."

CHAPTER 17

DCI LOUTH TOLD EVERYONE to be at the station by eight o'clock. The auction was due to start at eleven, giving enough time to get ready. Jack and Lisa would be in the auction house while the supporting team would wait outside. There would be plenty of them to ensure they had the manpower to perform multiple arrests.

Resources had been dragged in from all corners of the station. At Louth's insistence, none of them had been briefed the day before. He did not want to risk anything leaking out. They would be issued with their instructions just before they left. Eyes would be on those who went straight to their phones. They would be the ones he would watch closely.

Frank Campbell was being surprisingly helpful. He had volunteered to coordinate their efforts in the station. Jack knew what his motive was. It would allow him to sit on his backside and do nothing. For Frank, it was better to be out of sight than a set of boots on the ground.

"I think we should insist Frank comes with us," said Louth.

"Why bother?" asked Jack. "He won't be of any use when we're there. Leave him to sort out anything that crops up in the station."

Reluctantly, Louth agreed. He had too much to contend with to offer much resistance. Jack was right. Frank would be worse than useless and was better kept out of the way.

Louth's briefing took place an hour before the auction. Questions were asked as to who they were going to arrest. It was Jack who provided the intelligence even though he could not appease the sceptics. Further instructions would come throughout the auction, depending on who purchased Paul Colyer's counterfeit items.

If that proved unsatisfactory, the next stage was worse. Nobody would be storming the building or conducting a raid. The support teams were to remain outside and would be parked around the corner. They were only to approach if instructed. That brought looks of consternation and a general sense of frustration to the room.

"So you just want us to sit in the vans?" confirmed PC Mark Langton.

"That's right," nodded Jack.

"And then what?"

"As we decide who to arrest, we'll call in a van for a pick-up."

"How many people are we expecting to arrest?"

"I don't know," shrugged Jack. "One, maybe two."

"One or two?" frowned PC Langton. "There's an army in here."

"It's best to be prepared," said Louth. "The truth is, we won't know until it's too late to change our plans."

"With all due respect, sir, I don't think we're going to encounter a militia at an antiques auction. The most likely crime will be a stolen cardigan."

Laughter rippled through the room.

"As I said, it's best to be prepared. We'll take our positions in ten minutes. Make sure you're ready."

"Primed to react...slowly," muttered PC Langton.

As the meeting dispersed, Louth's eyes scanned for any potential rats. When nothing caught his attention, he offered a supportive nod to Jack and Lisa. They had their plan and were ready to call in support when needed. First, they had to win their greatest battle of all. They had to secure a seat at the auction. If there was cheap furniture on offer, it was likely to be another day out for the oldies.

***

Lisa drove Jack to the auction. Though in good time, she was forced to take one of the last spaces in the car park. That meant reversing into the tightest of corners, after allowing Jack to get out. With skill, she eased the car straight in. She made sure there was plenty of room for her to alight on the driver's side.

"I don't know how you do that," said Jack. "I couldn't have got in there or got out."

"Practice is the answer. I used to park in Newcastle. The smaller the gap, the less chance you had of your car being nicked. Joyriders aren't very good at getting out of tight parking spaces," she grinned.

They went inside and found themselves a seat at the back of the auction room. Out of sight, they tried to remain anonymous. Jack had a copy of the auction catalogue in his hand, with the counterfeit antiques marked clearly. He was eager to see who would buy them. If the fakes were as good as Alistair had described, there was likely to be plenty of bidders.

The only surprise was the lack of serious dealers in attendance. Not one of Henry Davenport, Charles Rickton or Daniel Voss came into the room. Even when the time ticked on to eleven o'clock and Simon Hayton came on stage, they were not there. It left Jack and Lisa wondering whether they had made a mistake. That was when they remembered the schedule. The furniture auction was first. The fine antiques would follow.

It meant they had to sit through lot upon lot of drudgery. The cheap pieces of furniture only went for a few pounds each. There was a lack of interest in the room when each of them was brought out. Jack and Lisa stared at the stage. There was no Billy Ellis. Finn had a new friend who was helping him with the heavier pieces.

It felt strange for the auction to be proceeding. Simon had lost two of his team, one in gruesome circumstances. And yet his approach was to carry on as if nothing had happened. Either he didn't care or the reality was yet to hit him. It all pointed towards some form of sinister involvement.

When the time was approaching noon, an impatient Louth messaged Jack. He wanted an update on who they were going to arrest. Jack had to explain that the furniture auction came first. They had another fifty lots to get through. It did not impress Louth who had men sitting idle. If he had known the order, he would have asked them all to come later.

Jack ignored his rantings and waited. It was no easier to endure inside the building. The auction was tedious, with so much fuss being made about so little money. At one impasse, Jack wanted to reach into his pocket to give the old lady the extra two pounds she needed. If she had thought about her bid for any longer, she was in danger of passing away through old age. So was Jack. It was just as likely he would throw himself off the highest wardrobe.

When the furniture auction came towards the end, there was a notable change in the room. The bargain hunters began to slip away. They were replaced by more serious dealers. Daniel Voss was one of the first to enter and took a seat at the side of the room. Freshly vacated by an older gentleman, it would have been warm for him to sit on.

Henry Davenport and Charles Rickton arrived five minutes later. They appeared at the same time and offered spiteful expressions towards one another. Robbie eased between them and guided Henry to his seat. He was there to look after his man and play protector when needed.

To Jack's dismay, Simon advised there would be a fifteen-minute break between the auctions. It cleared the room of nearly half the people and left him rueing their mistake. A glance at Lisa told him she was thinking the same thing.

"We should have come later," she sighed.

"We're here now," said Jack. "I just hope the next stage is quicker."

"How many lots are there?"

"Less than half of the furniture auction."

"Thank goodness for that."

Henry Davenport saw Jack and Lisa when he settled into his seat. He nudged Robbie and pointed towards them. A forced smile was offered to which the detectives nodded back. There was little warmth coming their way from a man who saw them as no better than dirt on the sole of his shoe.

When Simon Hayton returned to the stage, it took the attention away from them. All eyes were focused on the front of the room. Charles was in position while Daniel had mischief written across his face. It was obvious what he had come to do. He was not going to hold back. He would enjoy his hour of fun and then Jack would have him arrested.

The early skirmishes were notably quiet, with the smaller dealers picking up the low-value items. Then came the first of Paul Colyer's lots. The campaign chest was a standout piece. It had everybody easing forward on their seats. With no obvious signs of it being a fake, there would be plenty of action.

The intensity of the bidding surprised Jack and Lisa. Bids came in from all corners of the room. Alistair had noted that few such items came up outside London. It meant provincial dealers were seizing their opportunity and it took the bidding well past the guide price. The hammer finally fell at two thousand seven hundred pounds, with Charles Rickton declared the winner. His smug expression told everyone he was extremely pleased with his lot.

A response came from Henry Davenport on the next lot. He made sure he won it, despite some aggressive counter-bidding from Daniel Voss. Charles offered one bid and quickly stepped aside. The table was won by Henry, though he had to overpay to secure it.

Henry also took the next item, with little competition. It was another table, which he got below the catalogue price. That seemed to settle him down, making him happy to remain out of the action for a few minutes. It allowed others to do their business while he waited for the next item he had circled in his catalogue. Daniel bought one item. Across the room, Charles was surprisingly quiet.

That changed with the French gilt mirror. Battling with Henry, he secured it at the upper end of the estimate. He followed it with a chair, another item being sold by Paul Colyer. A pattern was emerging and it had Jack whispering in Lisa's ear.

"I think we have our man," said Jack. "Every item from Paul Colyer has been bought by Charles."

"That doesn't make sense," she said.

"Why not?"

"Why didn't he buy the Chinese trunk?"

"I don't know. We'll have to ask him when we arrest him. Let's see who buys the remaining items."

They watched the rest of the auction take place. Nothing changed in the way it was conducted. Henry bought the occasional piece while Daniel was there to cause trouble. He got involved when the mood took him and brought anger to the other dealers. Some of the looks he was given suggested he was putting himself at physical risk.

Charles Rickton was far more selective about what he went after. Other than some token bids, the only decisive moves he made were for the twelve pieces on Jack's list. He was not afraid to overbid for them or pay whatever was needed. They were secured against plenty of head-shaking from his competitors. By the time the auction was over, he had bought every one of Paul Colyer's items. It left Jack to send a message to the waiting support team outside.

Two to arrest and take to the station – Charles Rickton and Daniel Voss.

Once the message was sent, Jack and Lisa got up and made their way to the front of the building. They would wait for their men to come out and arrest them when they set foot outside.

***

Daniel Voss was the first to emerge. Jack intercepted him on the way to his car. He performed the arrest and bundled him into a van. There was barely a protest offered. It was all in a day's work for a man confident enough to look after himself.

Charles Rickton was different. He exploded with rage when Jack put him under arrest. He demanded his lawyer and accused Jack of harassment. He was being victimised when all he was doing was going about his lawful business. There were threats to sue Jack personally for deformation and the impact of any reputational damage.

"Just get in the van," growled Jack as he pointed to the vehicle behind the one Daniel Voss had got into.

"I will not!" shouted Charles.

"Let me put this another way. Either you get in voluntarily or we'll put you in there."

"If you touch me, there will be hell to pay," snarled Charles, his reddened face threatening to explode with rage.

"Lads, stick him in there," demanded Jack to the uniforms accompanying him.

Jack walked back to the car with Lisa. Behind him, he could hear the tussle between Charles and the officers. Despite the outbursts, Charles Rickton was dragged to the van and put inside the back. A final volley of threats was offered just before the door slammed shut.

"That went well," smiled Jack.

"Do you think we've got everyone involved in whatever is going on?"

"No chance," admitted Jack. "Daniel Voss is just a chancer who takes whatever opportunities come his way. Charles Rickton didn't kill Dean Lucas and I can't imagine he chopped up Shane Keyson either. What he might do is help us get to the man who did."

***

Jack asked Lisa to pull over at a coffee shop on the way back to the station. They were in for a long afternoon with the two men they had arrested. Both would be made to wait before they were interviewed. Jack had already decided that Charles would be afforded no concessions. Any opportunity to antagonise the pompous man would be taken.

Lisa knew better than to argue. She pulled onto the pavement outside a coffee shop. Her hazard lights went on and her warrant card was placed in the window. It was a desperate act to ward away any traffic wardens. When her inconsiderate parking was met by shaking heads from pedestrians, she put her ID away. It was better to risk a fine than have her car plastered over social media.

Jack returned with a smile on his face. He balanced the coffee on a cardboard tray and clipped on his seatbelt. Lisa looked across at him and then eased her car back onto the road with care.

"What's got into you?" she asked.

"What do you mean?"

"You look happy. You never smile like that."

"I'm always happy when I'm with you."

"Now I know you're lying. What happened in there?"

"I think I just got propositioned."

"Trust me; you would know if you did."

"Not with this one."

"Go on. Tell me the story," she sighed.

"I think the woman was talking to me," smiled Jack.

"You mean she chatted someone up," corrected Lisa. "Who was she looking at?"

"That's the thing. I don't know. She was cross-eyed. There were two of us at the counter when she made her move. Her eyes were on both of us."

"Maybe she was casting her net wide and seeing who she caught."

"She did use the term 'young man' when she spoke. Mind you, she was at least sixty."

"And you think that means you?"

"The other guy looked about eighty."

"I would still say that's a fifty-fifty shout," laughed Lisa. "Come on, let's get to the station before any more of these boggle-eyed pensioners come after you."

Lisa swung her car into the line of traffic. An angry blaring of a horn from behind was the response to the move she made. She held up a hand and was met with a scowl from the driver. She ignored it and eased along behind the vehicle in front.

When they got to the station, the van containing Daniel Voss had just arrived. He was being led into the building where he would be put inside one of the holding cells. Lisa drove past it and parked in the main car park. They got out and headed to the front entrance.

"Are we going to see Daniel straight away?" she asked.

"Let's see what Louth wants us to do. My preference is to have an initial chat with both of them. I'm keen to know what approach they're going to take."

"Do you think either will talk?"

"I reckon Daniel will have a good story. I don't suppose Charles Rickton will have moved beyond outrage."

Jack led the way to the lift. Lisa accepted the compromise to allow for the coffee he was carrying. He still had both of them in the cardboard tray. They went up to the main office and straight to Louth's office. That was when Jack realised he hadn't got one for the DCI. Either he gave him one of theirs or he would have to go without.

"Quick, take a sip from your coffee," instructed Jack.

"Why?" frowned Lisa.

"It'll stop Louth from pinching it."

They walked in while making sure their lips went to their cups. Louth looked up from his desk and allowed the furrowed lines to form on his brow. He glanced at Jack's hand and saw there was nothing for him. Jack smiled as he slipped into a chair.

"I guess it's too much to expect you to bring me one," he sighed.

"Sorry, I didn't think," said Jack. "Here, have mine. I better warn you, I've got a chest infection at the moment. I don't think it's contagious."

DCI Louth looked at Jack and then across to Lisa. Just a smile from her was enough to change his priorities.

"I will pass, thanks."

"You're not missing much. It's not the best coffee."

"I wouldn't know," sighed Louth. He stared at a scrunched-up cup from the vending machine, which had been discarded on the side of his desk.

"Lisa and I would like to interview the two men once they've settled into their holding cells," stated Jack.

"Can I suggest we do Charles Rickton first?" said Louth.

"Why?" asked Jack.

"He isn't going to tell us anything until he calms down. We might as well start leaning on him early."

"Do you want to be there for that one?" asked Lisa.

"No, you guys can handle it. I'll be on standby if needed. I have a funny feeling we might not have finished making arrests."

Both Jack and Lisa nodded. They suspected Louth might be right.

***

The interview with Charles Rickton served little purpose. The anger of the man had not subsided in any way. He spent most of his time threatening Jack and Lisa about the repercussions of his arrest. With an expensive lawyer beside him, there was no shortage of verbal diarrhoea leaving his mouth.

Even the lawyer appeared embarrassed by some of the outbursts. On multiple occasions, he tried to calm Charles down. Some threats were retracted by him, only to be repeated by Charles straight after. It was an uncomfortable experience for everyone in the room.

Jack and Lisa left Charles to rant in the hope that he would exhaust himself. Despite their patience, the energy of the man was surprising. He offered no signs of slowing. Even an arm across him by his lawyer changed nothing. All they could do was wait for Charles to finish.

Twenty-five minutes of continuous noise was the result. They were the longest minutes of Jack's life. Nobody else got a word in, even a lawyer who was trying to control his client. For most of that time, Jack and Lisa sat impassively, ignoring everything Charles hurled at them. When silence finally came, the lawyer attempted to intervene.

"You will understand my client's frustration at his wrongful arrest," he insisted.

"Wrongful?" queried Charles. "Unlawful is the word you are looking for."

Charles erupted again. This time, Jack interrupted his flow. He informed Charles that he either needed to cooperate or he would be heading back to his cell. With the man in no mood to make concessions, the interview was terminated. Jack had spent long enough listening to him. He was not prepared to waste any more time. He and Lisa got up and left the room, leaving Charles Rickton's lawyer to deal with the anger.

"Let's try Daniel Voss," said Jack, once they were outside. "He might be more reasonable."

They went into another interview room and waited for Daniel Voss to be brought in. When he appeared, he smiled at the detectives and sat down calmly. He declined the offer of a solicitor and was happy to answer their questions. Nothing about the day seemed to be troubling him.

"I must say you're taking this very well, Mr Voss," said Jack.

"Call me Daniel, please. I'm happy to help. If I've done something wrong, I'll accept what's coming to me."

"In that case, tell us about Billy Ellis."

"He's a porter at the auction house," shrugged Daniel.

"What's your relationship with him?"

"Relationship?" frowned Daniel. "I'm not having a relationship with Billy Ellis or any other man for that matter."

"Your dealings with him," confirmed Jack.

"Oh, right, okay. I thought…you know what I thought you meant. Let's forget that conversation happened. Billy and I have known each other for a couple of years. We do a bit of business together."

"What sort of business?"

"You know about the purchases I make at the auction house. Apart from that, I occasionally buy items from him privately. Billy is a keen collector in his spare time."

"Collector?"

"Yes, he acquires interesting pieces. He shares my taste in silver."

"You mean stolen silver," corrected Jack.

"I mean silver that is purchased through legitimate means. Billy has a knack for tracking down high-quality pieces."

"Did you know that Billy Ellis was caught breaking into a country house near Poppleton?"

"I've heard, yes."

"Have you also heard that he was there at your request to steal items that you told him to?"

"That isn't correct. I've never told Billy Ellis to steal anything. I'm a reputable dealer who would never knowingly touch anything stolen."

"What about unknowingly?" asked Lisa.

"As in all businesses, we make all the possible checks that we can. If something slips through the net, then we have to accept the consequences for that."

"Has anything slipped through the net with you?"

"Not that I know of."

"Would you like to explain why Billy was found in a house that you had previously been to for an appraisal?"

"Coincidence. There are only a finite number of houses around here. Paths will naturally cross."

"And how do you explain the fact that Billy told us that you gave him the list of items he was going to steal?"

"I can only presume he's trying to deflect the blame from himself."

"But you do admit to buying items from him in the past."

"Of course, I do. You would be able to see that in my records, as you would with any dealer."

"We will request those records, Mr Voss."

"Please do. I would be delighted to prove my innocence. I've got nothing to hide."

"Even buying knocked-down items from Billy Ellis?"

"I can assure you that Billy does not do cut-price deals for me. That lad knows how to charge top-dollar."

"Then more fool you because he's taking you for a ride," barked Jack.

"That may be the case but it isn't illegal to overpay for good items. There are only so many of them to go around."

Chapter 18

After a night in The Cellars, Jack and Lisa headed to the station together. Lisa had allowed Jack to stay over. That meant fruit and yoghurt for breakfast and a lot of complaints. Jack had visibly grimaced with each piece he pushed into his mouth. At times, it felt like Lisa was feeding a child. All that was missing were the train noises to signal each piece was coming.

He was still complaining when he was sitting in the car. She had refused his request to stop off at a cafe on the way in. Jack had insisted that he needed to buy the DCI a bacon butty to make up for forgetting to take him a coffee. Lisa just laughed and continued to drive to the station.

An update with DCI Louth was completed quickly. With the initial interviews offering little, he did not keep them for long. He wanted Charles Rickton interviewed again as soon as his expensive lawyer arrived. Daniel Voss could be released unless they could make a case for charging him with handling stolen goods. That would require some additional work. It also meant persuading Billy Ellis to appear as a witness.

"If you're satisfied that Daniel Voss has got nothing to do with the murders, get Frank Campbell to do the follow-up work on him. I want you two to concentrate on Charles Rickton and whether he killed those two men."

"Will do, sir," confirmed Lisa. She looked across towards Jack who had already got up to leave.

She followed him out of Louth's office and headed back to her desk. Until they got the call to confirm the lawyer had arrived, Charles Rickton would be left in his cell. Jack went over to the desk by the window while Lisa took the one opposite. As they settled into their seats, Nathan Lewis arrived.

"Morning, Nathan," smiled Lisa. A grunt came from Jack.

"Morning. What's the plan for today?"

Lisa thought for a moment and then ruined the young lad's day.

"You and Frank will need to follow up on Daniel Voss. We need to establish a case to charge him with handling stolen goods as a minimum. If we can support a case for him being an accessory to the burglary, we should go for that as well."

"With Frank?" sighed the lad in disappointment.

"I'm afraid so, Nathan. I think they call it a rite of passage."

Lisa watched all the life drain from Nathan's body. It looked more like a death sentence than something that would toughen him up.

***

The call to confirm that Charles Rickton's lawyer had arrived came at nine-thirty. Lisa got up and grabbed her papers. Jack remained seated and continued typing on his computer. She moved around and stood alongside him. When he didn't move, she felt the urge to say something.

"The lawyer is here."

"That's fine. We'll go down when we're ready."

"I am ready."

"Let's give it a bit longer," smiled Jack.

"Why?"

"Because Charles Rickton is being charged by the hour."

Lisa returned to her seat and filled another twenty minutes by clearing some emails. Jack finally announced he was ready when the time was approaching ten o'clock. He got up and walked slowly towards the lift. Lisa logged out of her computer and followed him.

Once in the holding area, they were met by the lawyer. In his expensive suit, he was pacing up and down impatiently. His client had already been taken into the interview room. When he saw Jack and Lisa coming, he went on the attack.

"I must say I find the delay intolerable," he noted. It was an early and unsuccessful attempt to gain the upper hand.

"We could have closed this matter off last night if your client had been cooperative," noted Jack.

Jack's easy victory ended the conversation. The lawyer had nothing to offer back. Forced to accept the point, he accompanied Jack and Lisa into the room. Sitting on his own, with just a uniformed PC standing guard in the corner, Charles Rickton had the appearance of a man who had spent an uncomfortable night in a cell.

"And about time too," snarled Charles.

The detectives said nothing as they took their place at the table. With battle lines drawn, Lisa completed the formalities. She got as far as starting the tape before Charles erupted. Re-energised, he continued his previous rant.

"Mr Rickton, please will you allow us to interview you?" said Jack, with a stern look towards his lawyer.

The request made no difference. Charles was into his stride and would not be backing down for anyone. Jack terminated the interview, not that his words would be heard on the tape. He and Lisa got up and began to walk out of the room.

"Where are you going?" demanded Charles.

"There's no point in us continuing this interview if you're not going to cooperate."

"Good; then I suggest we bring this ridiculous charade to an end. All I have done is buy some items at an auction as have many other dealers. If you are going to arrest me for that, you will need to arrest all the others as well, starting with Henry Davenport."

"DS Ramsey, I suggest we finish this off upstairs. We'll need to decide whether to charge Mr Rickton with handling counterfeit goods as well as murder."

"Murder!" barked Charles. "I have done nothing of the sort."

"We'll have to judge that ourselves," shrugged Jack. "You won't let us ask you about it." He ushered Lisa out of the room.

Charles Rickton's lawyer went after them. He caught up with the detectives in the corridor. He stepped into their path to stop them from walking away. Jack offered one of his irritated looks to suggest that the lawyer had better be quick.

"DI Husker, my client is uncooperative and hardly a saint but he is not a murderer."

"Tell that to the court," growled Jack. "We're done."

"DI Husker, please allow me to speak to my client."

"Why? We've wasted enough time being shouted at. Your client needs to understand that we will be charging him. The only question is with what."

"Give me ten minutes. If he is still uncooperative, then I will respect your position."

"You've got five minutes and that's it. He will only get one chance. If he's not going to help us then we cannot help him."

A nod from the lawyer confirmed that an accord had been struck.

"Nice work," nodded Lisa as soon as the lawyer had disappeared back into the room.

***

Charles Rickton was a very different man when they returned. He looked deflated, having been worn down by his lawyer. From their position outside the room, Jack and Lisa had heard the angry exchange. The winning volley had come when the lawyer threatened to resign and leave him to face the music alone.

Forced to compromise, Charles was sitting contritely. The lawyer nodded when the detectives sat down and completed the formalities. Once the interview started, the lawyer read out a statement. It had been constructed in the few minutes they had together.

"My client is a victim in this matter. He has been coerced into buying pre-arranged items at the auction. Though unwilling, direct threats to his and his family's safety left him with no choice. He wishes to be cooperative but would like the police to understand the personal risk that puts him at. He is frightened of the repercussions that will come from speaking out."

"Is that the best you can come up with?" asked Jack.

"It is the truth, DI Husker," said the lawyer.

"Then I suggest Mr Rickton starts filling in some of the details."

Charles Rickton reluctantly offered his account. The fake antiques were being shipped in with other counterfeit goods through Immingham. They were being transferred across to the auction where he was being made to buy them. He would sell them on to unsuspecting members of the public. So far, none of them had been spotted as fakes.

"Who's shipping them in?" asked Jack.

"I don't know," he shrugged. "I think he's based in Belgium."

"Mr Rickton, if you want us to believe you're being cooperative, we'll need more than that."

A nod from his lawyer confirmed that he needed to answer.

"I don't know a name. It was somebody Dean Lucas knew. Dean was crucial in this because he was the one who inspected the items."

"Could it be Freddie Sharpe?" asked Jack.

"I don't know. That's not a name I've heard of."

"Who's your contact?"

Charles allowed his head to bow down and then muttered the name that Jack was expecting.

"Paul Colyer."

"Have you ever met this Paul Colyer?" asked Lisa.

"Never. Dean gave me his number. Since then, he just messages me."

"Have you spoken to him?"

"No."

"So who threatens you?"

"Paul does. I get regular WhatsApp messages from him."

"We'll need to see them."

"I delete them as soon as I've read them. I don't want them on my phone."

"Just so we are all clear on this, let me go through it again," said Jack. "Somebody in Belgium is shipping the goods through Immingham. They are being sent by Paul Colyer to the auction. Dean passes them through for you to buy. You then sell them to the public."

"That's about right," admitted Charles. "Remember, I only do it because I'm being threatened."

"Naturally," acknowledged Jack. "If you don't mind me saying so, it all feels a bit convoluted. Why don't the antiques just get sent directly to you to sell?"

Charles Rickton smiled. "In our world, provenance is everything. Once they have passed through an auction, they are legitimised. I can then sell them on with a history."

"But you have to pay auction prices for them?" frowned Lisa.

"Yes, to Paul. It only costs us the auction premium."

"What do you get out of it?"

"My safety," insisted Charles.

"You'll have to do better than that," said Jack.

"Okay, I get a kickback. Half of the cost is reimbursed to me. If I pay six hundred, I get three hundred back."

"Which is why you can pay top-end prices," interrupted Lisa.

Charles nodded reluctantly.

"I suppose there's one thing which troubles me," said Jack. "How does this tie into that Chinese trunk that Henry Davenport bought?"

Charles Rickton looked at his lawyer in desperation. The lawyer stared back with an expression that advised his client to answer.

"I was meant to buy it. Things got out of hand in the auction room. Henry bought it to prove a point. He hadn't even looked at it. Even if he had, he wouldn't have known it was a fake. He doesn't deal in Oriental items."

"Why did you let him buy it?"

Once it went for more than double its value, I stepped away. I didn't know what was in it."

"But I'm guessing you know why the body parts were in there."

Charles Rickton nodded and took a series of deep breaths.

"It was sent as a warning. I told Paul it was going to be the last shipment I was prepared to take. I guess that was his response. I should have known something was wrong. The trunk was nowhere near as well put together as the other fakes."

"What do you mean?"

"The items coming in are top-notch. Only an expert would be able to tell them apart from a genuine antique. On the most recent batch, I could only spot three of them."

"And the trunk?"

"Everything about it was wrong. Others might not have noticed but I did. I spent some time studying Chinese antiques, which gives you an eye for the details. I'm guessing Paul Colyer wanted to get my attention."

"Did you know the man inside it?"

"No. The whole thing operates on a need-to-know basis. I don't need to know anything about the import chain."

"What about Paul Colyer? Do you know who he is?"

"I've no idea. I believe he is someone high up in the antiques trade. He does have a fair bit of knowledge."

"Are you sure it's not your man in Belgium?"

"No, it's someone over here. I'm certain."

"How?"

"When I first told him I wanted to stop, he knew too much about my family. It was as if he was watching me."

The look of fear on Charles Rickton's face was genuine. It sent a shiver through the detectives' spines.

***

DCI's Louth's meeting followed the interviews. He called his team into a room and insisted that all the facts were shared. For the first time, it felt like significant progress had been made. A chain had been established that had brought the crime to York. And yet there were still plenty of gaps in a case that was only just starting to come together.

A whiteboard was brought into the room. Lisa drew a series of arrows to show where they believed the goods had travelled. Names were offered alongside each of the points, with question marks placed alongside those that remained unconfirmed.

Freddie Sharpe was noted as the possible man on the continent. Charles Rickton had said it was somebody Dean Lucas knew. His previous association made him the chief suspect. It was also a city he knew well. That made it easier to flood the market with goods.

Keith Elton and Shane Keyson were the obvious names for Immingham. If Shane wanted out and had reported the crime, he had paid the ultimate price. It was unlikely for him to be operating alone. With an overbearing boss, he had to be acting under instruction.

Paul Colyer was the brains in the UK. He was the one with the link between Hull and York. He arranged the transfer of the goods to the auction house where Dean Lucas processed them. Dean would put a value in the catalogue and make sure the items were hard to examine. As the police closed in on him, he had been disposed of.

The final piece of the jigsaw was Charles Rickton who bought and sold the items. Or he did until Henry Davenport got involved and found himself wrapped up in the crime. Charles's insistence that he was an unwilling partner was going to prove difficult to substantiate. In court, his aggressive nature would make it hard to win any friends.

"We need to find this Paul Colyer," insisted Louth to nods from everyone in the room.

"I don't think he exists," said Jack.

"What do you mean?" barked Louth. "Who's going around killing people if he doesn't exist?"

"He exists, but not in the form we're expecting," corrected Jack.

"Jack, can you keep this on planet Earth for the rest of us?"

"Paul Colyer is an alias."

"For who?"

"I don't know," shrugged Jack.

"Well that's a step forward," sighed Louth.

"Someone is operating with him as a pseudonym. Think about it. Nobody has ever spoken to him. He only communicates by email and messaging. That's the work of someone whose voice would be recognised."

"Okay, I'll go with it," nodded Louth. "Give me the options."

"There's only one," said Jack. "Simon Hayton."

"What about Keith Elton?" asked Nathan.

"He wouldn't know the antiques game," said Jack. "Don't get me wrong. He might be guilty of Shane Keyson's murder but he isn't Paul Colyer."

"What about Daniel Voss?" asked Lisa.

"Or Henry Davenport?" asked Louth.

"Or even Dean Lucas," said Lisa. "We need to find out whether Charles has received any messages since Dean's death."

"In other words, everyone is a bloody suspect," growled Louth.

Jack wanted to object to the barrage of suggestions. He couldn't. It was difficult to put up much fight when he knew his colleagues were right.

***

The afternoon was spent trying to agree on the next steps. They were reaching the point where they had to decide what to do with Charles Rickton. They either needed to charge him or release him. Louth seemed to flip-flop between the two, unsure what was for the best. They couldn't hold him indefinitely and yet they had no evidence to link him to the murders.

Under pressure from Charles Rickton's lawyer, the decision was made to release him. Once he had confirmed the messages had continued after Dean Lucas's death, Louth agreed to provide protection. An officer would be stationed outside his house for the next forty-eight hours. For once, Charles did not put up much opposition.

The more he thought about it, the less Jack was convinced that Simon Hayton was the killer. He was not the type to go around stabbing people or stuffing them into boxes. Even if he was the brains behind the counterfeit antiques, it was more likely that Keith Elton was the murderer. Nobody who had met him would need much convincing of his guilt.

Louth wanted to leave any arrests until the following morning. Both men would need to be brought in and questioned under caution before any decisions were made. The DCI instructed everyone to go home and get some rest. Those who were not detailed to collect the two men were told to be back in the station by seven o'clock. Amidst the groans, Jack got up and headed out of the door. An early start would mean leaving the pub in good time. That meant getting to The Cellars quickly to avoid missing out on valuable drinking time.

Lisa hurried after Jack and caught up with him on the stairs. She offered him a lift back to her flat, which was eagerly accepted. She said she would swing past his house to pick up a change of clothes. Jack was unsure why he needed them. The ones he was wearing were good for another day.

"We are going to eat something tonight," she informed him as a condition of the hospitality she was offering.

"That's fine. Do you want cheese and onion or salt and vinegar?" grinned Jack.

"In a minute, it will be battered detective," she scowled.

Jack laughed even though the warning was clear. There was no point fighting it. If Lisa wanted to go out for dinner, he would not argue. So long as the restaurant offered some unhealthy options, he was happy to go. He had to find a way to counteract the inevitable fruit and yoghurt that would be inflicted upon him in the morning.

Chapter 19

Jack was on his way to Hull when the message was relayed to him that Keith Elton had been arrested by the local police. Under DCI Louth's instruction, they had made their move on his arrival to work. He was being taken to the police station in Immingham where he would be held until Jack's arrival.

It vindicated Jack's decision to leave early. He had told Lisa that a dawn raid was being conducted to bring Keith in. And yet the truth was far simpler. Jack wanted time to pick up some breakfast on his way over to meet him. He had gone to the station to collect one of their cars and had stopped for a bacon butty and a coffee on his way out of York.

His last-minute decision not to ask Lisa to borrow her car was something he was pleased about. While they had enjoyed their pasta the night before, he had been close to doing so. A glance across at the greasy mark his bacon butty had left on the passenger seat told Jack it had been a narrow escape. If he handed Lisa's Golf back to her in that state, she would have been likely to punch him.

With the taste of the butty still fresh in his mouth, Jack applied his foot to the accelerator. He was keen to hear what Keith Elton was going to say. Was he a murderer or just somebody operating a fraudulent enterprise? Or was he Paul Colyer as a growing number in the station were beginning to believe?

***

Lisa was given the task of going with the team to the auction house. She was waiting with a police van and a car when Simon Hayton pulled into the car park. The look of shock on his face told her he was fearing the worst. They weren't there for a chat when there were that many police vehicles in attendance.

He pulled his car over to the side of the building. Parking up, he looked across in the hope there might be a sensible explanation. When he saw Lisa flanked by uniformed officers, his head bowed. They had come for him. Nothing was going to change that.

"There has been a terrible mistake," he insisted.

Lisa performed the formalities and ushered Simon Hayton over to the van. Offering no resistance, he climbed in and allowed his head to sink into his hands. There had been no need to cuff him when the man had lost the energy to fight. It was hard not to feel sorry for him even though it might be an act. Someone was guilty of murder. Until proven otherwise, he remained their number one suspect.

***

Jack arrived at Immingham police station at nine o'clock. He had battled through the traffic to get there. He parked outside and went into a station that was unfamiliar. Not once had his career taken him anywhere near it.

"Hi, I'm DI Jack Husker from York. I've been told to ask for a DS Norris."

"Do you mean Ron?" asked the young officer behind the desk.

"I guess so," shrugged Jack.

"Wait here; I'll find him," instructed the lad. "Help yourself to a coffee if you want one."

Jack looked across at the tatty offering and decided he would wait for Ron. If nothing else, a bit of local knowledge might offer something drinkable.

He was not kept waiting for long. A man in his mid-fifties came through a side door and approached him. He held out a hand enthusiastically and then looked Jack up and down. Jack's instinct was to do the same. He soon realised the significance. They were both wearing the same style of clothes from a scruffy jacket to crumpled trousers.

"It's good to see someone who knows how to dress. I'm DS Ron Norris. Call me Ron, please."

"Jack Husker. It takes dedication to look like we do," grinned Jack.

"If you come through, we have Keith Elton in one of the holding cells. Do you want to interview him or get a coffee first?"

"You know the answer to that," grinned Jack.

"Coffee it is. The boss isn't in today. We'll meet in his room."

"I take it he's got a good machine."

"The best in the station," laughed Ron. "We can't have it being wasted on those that don't appreciate it."

Ron led Jack through the offices. It was similar to York, with little having been spent on the decor in years. A tatty mixture of desks had been formed into a variety of shapes. There appeared to be no logic to the layout.

"This way," said Ron as he continued to weave through the path that had been left.

Jack was forced to hurry along behind Ron. The man seemed to have the ability to swerve his hips like a slalom skier. Jack lost sight of him when he swung around behind a wall. Fortunately, it was in a quiet corner of the station. Jack soon caught up and was only yards behind when they entered a grand office.

Ron pointed to a sofa at the side. Jack sat down while Ron went to work at the coffee machine. Pushing a cartridge into a slot, he produced a cup which had the right aroma. He reached into a fridge beneath it and took out some milk.

"Extras?"

"Just a splash of milk for me, please."

"Right you are," nodded Ron who performed the necessary duties.

Once Jack had a coffee in his hand, Ron made one for himself. He took it over to a chair and sat down alongside Jack. They toasted each other and took a moment to relax. It was just what Jack needed after his early start.

"How was Keith Elton when he was arrested?" asked Jack.

"Pretty abrasive," replied Ron. "He had to be cuffed for our protection."

"Was he violent?"

"Not particularly, though I don't think it would have taken much for him to lash out. Have you met him before?"

Jack nodded. He took Ron through his previous dealings with Keith. From being pleasant in their early exchanges, he had begun to show a more aggressive side when the level of questioning increased.

"Is it murder that you're investigating him for?"

"We're not sure. He's certainly involved in the import of counterfeit goods. I would say there's a fair chance he'll be linked to the murder as well."

"Are you okay if I come in with you?" asked Ron.

"Absolutely. I would like two of us to have a go at him," confirmed Jack.

"There is one thing you need to be aware of. The lawyer for Keith Elton has just turned up."

"Is that a problem?"

"Let's just say that he's a pretty impressive lawyer for a dock worker."

"Do you think someone else is paying for this guy?"

"Either that or our humble dock worker has a sideline that is making him an awful lot of money."

"That's all the more reason to keep him waiting," grinned Jack. "Nice coffee, by the way."

"Nothing but the best for the boss in this station," smiled Ron.

The two men took their time to go through the information they had. Jack talked through his meetings with Keith Elton while Ron concentrated on the arrest. It was a cordial meeting between two men with a similar outlook. Jack could imagine Ron being his equivalent in the Humberside police force, with just as much appetite for conflict.

Messages were passed into their meeting on two occasions. They were from Keith Elton's lawyer who was getting frustrated at being kept waiting. The second came with a threatening tone. Jack glanced at the time. He saw that it had only been thirty minutes. Another ten would not do any harm.

Once they were ready, Ron took Jack downstairs. They were met by a man who could only be Keith's lawyer. In an expensive tailored suit, his cuffs protruded to offer up gold embossed cufflinks. He was in his late thirties, with slicked-back hair and a smile that needed punching. Everything about the man reeked of money and smarm.

"Finally, we get some action from this so-called police force."

"Sorry to keep you waiting," said Jack. "The charge sheet took a while to pull together."

"Not for my client, it didn't."

"I'm DI Jack Husker and this is DS Ron Norris."

"Edward Coles. I won't shake your hand if you don't mind."

Jack didn't mind. It would either be a limp wet handshake or a hand crusher. Neither would improve how he felt about the man. He allowed Ron to take them inside the room where Keith Elton was sitting with his arms folded. His aggressive stare was directed across the table to the chairs that Jack and Ron would sit on.

Ron performed the formalities for the tape. As soon as he was finished, Edward Coles launched into his speech. It registered his concerns for the amount of time they had been kept waiting and for the behaviour of the officers who had performed the arrest. It was a predictable marker being laid down for the future.

"I can only apologise for the thirty minutes you were kept waiting," offered Jack. "If Mr Elton would like to put in a formal complaint about his treatment while being arrested, we can deal with that promptly. Mr Elton, would you like to put in a formal complaint?"

Keith Elton sat impassively. A glance towards his lawyer was met with stony silence.

"I will take that as a 'no'," confirmed Jack. "In which case, let us move on to the matter at hand."

"Which is a case of harassment," interjected the lawyer.

"Which is a case of murder and handling stolen goods. I suggest we start with the lesser charge before Mr Elton talks us through his role in the murder of Shane Keyson."

"DI Husker, you are making wild assertions," warned the lawyer.

"These wild assertions are going to put Mr Elton in prison."

The two men locked stares. Neither Jack nor Edward blinked. It was a test of wills which ended when Edward turned to Keith Elton to see how his client wished to proceed. All he got was a nod of the head from Keith.

"My client is prepared to admit that he had knowledge of, not undertook, the import of counterfeit goods. He will admit that on the understanding that he had no part in, or knowledge of, the murder."

"Let's keep things simple and put it in language that we can all understand," said Jack. "What did you know about the import of counterfeit goods?"

"I knew it was happening," confirmed Keith. "When I found out, I told Shane to knock it on the head. It would only lead to trouble. I thought he had but I was wrong."

"So you weren't involved in it?" asked Ron.

"Correct."

"Where were the goods coming in from?" asked Jack.

"I don't know."

"What about any dealings with Paul Colyer?"

"I don't know the guy."

"Let me get this straight," said Jack. "Counterfeit goods were being brought in through your port and you're claiming to know very little about it."

"I said I was aware of it," corrected Keith.

"How did you become aware of it?"

"I caught Shane acting evasive at the end of one of his shifts. He was hanging around as if he was waiting for something to come in. He denied it at first. When the container was landed, he had no choice but to tell me."

"What did you say to him?"

"I was furious."

"Did you hit him?"

"No, I didn't hit him. Twenty years ago, I would have done. I guess times have changed on that score."

"Why didn't you stop him from doing it?"

"I thought I had."

"What about the whistleblower report that Shane put in?"

"I don't know what the lad was thinking. That was always going to cause trouble. I guess he couldn't find another way to stop it."

"Do you think it got him killed?"

"I would guess so," shrugged Keith.

"Clearly, my client is speculating on this point," added Edward Coles. "He had no involvement and has no information relating to the murder of Shane Keyson."

"You made that clear," confirmed Jack.

"Then I think we are done," said Edward.

"We are for now," said Jack.

"What is that supposed to mean?" barked Edward.

"It means that we have some more information to gather and then we'll be sitting down with Mr Elton again. Until then, I suggest he makes himself comfortable in one of our cells."

"You cannot detain him without good reason," stated Edward.

"He will be here until I say otherwise," said Jack as he left the room with Ron. Behind him, there was a sense of outrage from a lawyer that Keith Elton would be paying extortionate rates for.

***

The York part of the operation was not going well. Lisa and Frank were in the interview room with Simon Hayton. Alongside him was the duty solicitor who was yet to speak. It was hard for him, or anyone else, to say anything when all Simon Hayton had done was sob. It had started when he was alone in the cell and had only got worse when he was brought in to be interviewed.

Lisa tried her best to calm him down. With Frank offering nothing but impatience, she tried to divert Simon away from his sorrow. Some idle conversation did nothing to change his behaviour. Everything about the man offered a look of genuine distress.

"Mr Hayton, we're happy to break for a few minutes if that would help you," advised Lisa.

The response she got was more tears. In the absence of an acceptance of the offer, she decided to continue. He would need to answer their questions eventually. She had seen criminals offer up their tears before and then plead guilty at a trial. It was unusual to see it go on for so long. Either he was the best actor in the world or Simon Hayton was truly upset.

"Mr Hayton, we need to ask you some questions," insisted Lisa.

"I know," he sobbed loudly.

Lisa asked the uniformed officer to bring in some more tissues. He was quick to oblige and eagerly left the room. The sound of Simon's continual distress was hard to listen to. Nobody was going to stay in there willingly and watch a man on the verge of a breakdown.

"What will happen to me?" wailed Simon.

"That depends on what you've done," grinned Frank, offering nothing to suggest that he cared.

"I haven't done anything; I promise," insisted Simon.

Lisa allowed him a moment to dab away his tears with a tissue. When he looked for a bin, she told him to leave it on the side of the table. He scrunched up the tissue and stared at Lisa through his sodden eyes. For a moment, there was quiet in the room. It was unlikely to continue for long.

"Mr Hayton..."

"Simon, please."

"Mr Hayton," continued Lisa. "I would like to start with the matter of the counterfeit items that have passed through your auction. Would you care to explain how they got there?"

"They were brought in as lots for an auction."

"What I am struggling to understand is how they were not spotted. After all, you're a high-end auction house. You must have experts who check these things."

"We do...we did. Dean was our expert. He should have noticed."

"Why didn't he?"

"I don't know. I can only think he was in on it."

"Why didn't you notice, Mr Hayton?"

"I don't look at the lots. I leave that to Dean."

"Is that wise? It's your business to know what's happening."

"I have been busy with the commercial side. We get so much these days. We struggle to cope." A flicker of his tone suggested the tears were close to returning.

"Why didn't you take on more staff?"

"I was going to. I haven't got around to it."

"Let's go with your theory of Dean being in on it. Is that why you killed him?"

"Oh my goodness!" gasped Simon. "You don't think…" With those few words, the distress returned in an instant.

Lisa paused the interview and beckoned for Frank to accompany her out of the room. They left Simon to cry his tears under the watchful eye of the solicitor. Once they were outside, she closed the door to seal off the noise. Beside her, Frank offered the look of someone who had seen it all before.

"What do you think, Frank?"

"Guilty as sin. Those waterworks don't fool me for a second."

"You're all heart," smiled Lisa.

"Well, he's just a bit soft, isn't he?" he laughed.

***

Jack's parting argument with Edward Coles was still fresh in his mind when he pulled out of the car park of Immingham police station. The expensive lawyer was outraged that his client was being detained until the following day. No good reason had been provided, which only fuelled his annoyance. Jack had shrugged off his protests and then offered his explanation. That was not good enough for Edward Coles who was out for blood.

His threats had filled the room. Jack had brushed them away and told him to fill in a complaint form. That had only made him more irate. People like Edward Coles did not fill in forms. They won their battles in the courtroom.

Jack had left Ron to deal with him. His colleague appeared to relish the confrontation as much as he would. He was just like Jack and would not back down in the face of aggression. Pompous arseholes were the people he dealt with best. He would take Edward Coles to the limit of his frustration and then hold him there for as long as his blood pressure allowed.

The decision on whether to charge Keith Elton would come later. First, Jack needed to know how the interview with Simon Hayton had gone. Like Keith, he was likely to be blaming deceased men for the counterfeit goods. It was harder to make that same case for the murders. Parts of Shane Keyson did not put themselves inside the trunk and Dean Lucas did not plunge a knife through his own neck.

The murders remained the most intriguing part of the case. They were so different and yet had to be related. Could two different men have committed the acts of brutality or was it somebody prepared to travel? For Shane Keyson's death, there were logistics to consider. That narrowed things down and made Keith Elton a key suspect. Not only could he get close to Shane but he would also have access to the trunk.

Jack was deep in thought when a message popped up on his phone. Slowing the car, he glanced down to see it was from Gregor Banks. He wanted an update and was suggesting they meet up. Jack looked at the sign ahead. He was only twenty minutes away from York.

He pulled over and sent a quick message to Gregor. A drink was proposed at a pub on the way into York. It was slightly out of the city but would be easy for Jack to get to on his way back to the station. He knew Gregor would accept. The gangster never missed the opportunity to speak to him.

The instant response confirmed that Gregor would be there. Jack eased back onto the road and pressed his foot down. It was not to beat Gregor to the pub. He would never be able to do that. He was thinking about The Cellars. Once he was done with Gregor and had returned the car, his long day had earned him a few pints.

Jack rehearsed the words he would say when he got there. It was pointless because Gregor would soon take control of the conversation. Until he had an answer to his question, he would not rest. The gangster wanted to know who was putting goods onto the streets and what York police were going to do about it.

It made Jack smile to think about how concerned Gregor was. He would expect Jack and his team to act swiftly when somebody else was committing the crimes. When it was his men, he expected a different approach. He demanded that the two sides operate hand-in-hand.

When Jack reached the pub, he saw that Gregor was already there. An expensive Mercedes with darkened windows was parked in the corner of the car park. A suited man was standing beside it with a phone clutched to his ear. He would not be the only one keeping watch over Gregor. At least one other goon would be inside, positioned a few paces from his master.

A smile and a nod was offered by Jack when he parked the car. He deliberately put it as close as he could to the Mercedes. He reversed in and left the car inches from its side. Nobody would be getting in until he drove away. The goon looked at him and scowled. Jack winked back. He knew the man would not strike unless he was told to do so.

"Good afternoon," said Jack as he got out. "Is your owner inside?"

A venomous look came with real menace. Jack ignored it and walked towards the entrance of the pub. He would only be having a coffee. His hard-earned drinking time would come later.

Gregor was waiting for Jack. He was sitting by the window and had watched him arrive. One of his larger ogres got up and beckoned for Jack to take his place. Jack nodded and waited for him to move away from the chair, which he was holding like a butler.

"Sorry, but I get nervous with him standing behind me. He blocks out the light."

At Gregor's request, the ogre moved away and allowed Jack to take his seat.

"Let me get you a pint," said Gregor.

"Coffee for me," said Jack. "I'm driving."

"Is that what you call it? I thought you were going to get into the car with me with that piece of parking," laughed Gregor as he pointed to his view of the car park. "That all looked a bit intimate from here."

"I was just making sure we could keep an eye on each other."

"Rest assured, I always do that."

Gregor sent the goon to get some drinks. Jack's coffee and a glass of sparkling water was all that was wanted. It left the two men alone and created a rare moment of vulnerability for the gangster. Not that Jack would try anything. Their relationship had moved beyond the violent stage.

"I'm after information, Jack. Please don't tell me you have nothing."

"I've got something but you're not going to like it."

"Go on."

"Freddie Sharpe."

"I told you before. That chapter was closed off a long time ago."

"I think a sequel is about to be written. We think Dean Lucas was back in contact with him. That's before he was killed."

"You're wrong. Freddie Sharpe is still in Belgium. I checked."

"Then he's got somebody over here. Those goods are coming from him. We're sure of it."

Gregor Banks went to object but didn't. He appeared troubled by the suggestion Jack had made. He flexed his face and looked across towards the bar. His bodyguard felt an uncomfortable distance away. If Freddie Sharpe was thinking about making a return, he would need his manpower around him. Any slight slip might prove fatal. It put a bad feeling inside him. It would only get worse if Jack's words proved to be true.

Chapter 20

THE DECISION TO REARREST Charles Rickton had been made by DCI Louth late the previous evening. He had brought Charles in at nine o'clock, having collected him from his house. Jack was on his third pint when the news came through. Even Lisa was surprised when she heard about it. Sitting opposite Jack in The Cellars, she struggled to understand what Louth was thinking.

They were no clearer to knowing when they made their way to the station for an eight o'clock briefing. Jack contemplated skipping it, only to be told by Lisa he was going. If Louth said everybody had to attend, Jack was not going to be excused.

As a compromise, she agreed to grab some breakfast on the way in. She waited outside a cafe while Jack collected some bacon butties and coffee. He emerged quickly, with a box held in both hands. He got into the car, weighed down by his purchases.

"Are you feeding the five thousand?"

"Just you, me and Louth."

"You got Louth a bacon butty?" frowned Lisa.

"I thought it might put me in his good books."

"Creep," she grinned. "I don't blame you though."

"It also means I can charge it to expenses," laughed Jack.

Lisa drove quickly to the station. The smell of the bacon was permeating through her car. It would linger and offer a reminder when she drove home that evening. She didn't care. The smell was so good it could be savoured for a second time.

She parked in her favourite space and saw that the DCI's car was already there. He seemed to be spending an increasing amount of time in the station. Whether that was an indication of the state of his marriage was hard to say. He had referenced the health kick his wife had put him on. Maybe that was enough to drive them apart. The more she thought about it, the more she wondered whether there were similarities to her relationship with Jack.

Jack led the way into the station. He went straight up to Louth's office with the box clutched in his hands. Like a child delivering an apple for the teacher, he unloaded the items in front of the suspicious DCI. First, the coffee and then the bacon butty were placed down in front of him. As the smell began to assault his nostrils, Louth looked up towards Jack.

"Okay, what have you done?" he growled.

"Nothing. I just thought you might like one," shrugged Jack.

"Now I am worried," said Louth.

"I could take it away again."

"Not a chance. I would rather be worried while enjoying a bacon butty than not be worried," laughed Louth. "I still want you in the briefing at eight o'clock."

"I'll be there," confirmed Jack as he headed back out of Louth's office.

It gave them all fifteen minutes to eat their breakfast. Back at their desks, there were plenty of complaints coming Jack's way. Each person who passed him offered the same comment. They wanted to know where their butty was. Jack ignored them and sunk his teeth into the juicy bacon while Lisa hid away in the corner. She was enjoying the change from fruit and yoghurt and did not need others to see how eagerly she was devouring it.

At eight o'clock, they all made their way to the briefing room. Feeling content, Jack took his usual seat near the corner. Lisa sat on the opposite side, something she had always done since she and Jack started dating. It was better to remain apart than offer constant reminders they were a couple.

Between them, Frank Campbell slumped down, with Nathan by his side. They were close to finishing the case relating to Daniel Voss, who would be getting charged with handling stolen goods. There was not enough evidence to prove he had any knowledge of the burglary. That would rest firmly with Billy Ellis. He would go to prison for his crime.

DCI Louth made his way to the front of the room, still dabbing at his mouth with a pristine white handkerchief. The bacon butty had been just as good as he expected. It was so much better than the rabbit food he was getting served at home. He was still unsure what Jack's motives were but was not about to dwell on it for long. Hopefully, his most troublesome detective would find a reason to provide another offering soon.

As he gazed across the room, he saw that most of the team had gathered. Any stragglers would have to catch up after getting a few wise words when they entered. A subtle cough forced heads to turn to the front. Everybody was ready, which was unusual at such an early hour.

"Thanks for coming in promptly. I know some of you find great difficulty in these early meetings," he began, with a glance over towards Jack. "Overnight, some of you will have become aware that we have rearrested Charles Rickton. That means we have three men in custody; Charles Rickton, Simon Hayton and Keith Elton over in Immingham. Jack, can you give everyone a quick overview of your meeting with Keith Elton."

Jack stood up and provided a summation of the events. He kept it brief and soon returned to his seat.

"After consulting with my superiors overnight, we have decided to charge both Charles Rickton and Keith Elton with the import, possession and sale of counterfeit goods. They will be released on bail. Simon Hayton will not be charged at the moment. That may change as further investigations take place."

"What about the murders?" asked Frank Campbell.

"I'm afraid we have drawn a blank on that one. Unless anyone has anything fresh to offer, we are still at square one. Does anyone have any information that would counter that view?"

There was silence across the room. Eyes flicked around until there was a general acceptance that nobody had anything to say.

"In that case, I want us to refocus. Starting Monday, I want everyone back in here with a clear head. I want every detail relooked at and every person reinterviewed. I want us to follow our nose with proper old-fashioned police work. If that means blood, sweat and tears, I want us to accept that. Something has been missed and I want to know what it is. One way or the other, at least one murderer is still out there. I want them found."

With a slam of his papers on the desk in front of him, Louth had set out his demands. It brought a groan. He was not going to rest until he got the result he wanted.

***

Those that were gathered left the room together. Everyone seemed to accept the result even if nobody was happy. Even the most cynical of officers had to admit that Louth was right. They did not have enough to charge anyone with the murders. They had suspicions and plenty of circumstantial evidence. None of it would take either crime to court.

As the team dispersed, Lisa headed back to her desk. She had promised herself she would get out of the station early to allow her time to tidy up her flat. Her parents were coming down from Newcastle and would be staying over. That meant a night on her sofa while they took the bedroom.

Common sense told her to stay at Jack's house. And yet she was not quite ready to have that conversation with her parents. She had spoken about Jack and told them they were close. She did not need a discussion about their sleeping arrangements.

Jack had already been warned that she would not be able to see him. Her absence would allow him to spend his Friday night in The Cellars. They had agreed to meet up the following day. That would probably be for some food and another evening in the pub.

***

Jack spent an hour at his desk and then headed down to see whether Charles Rickton and Simon Hayton had been released. By the time he got there, both men were gone. Jack was left to talk to the uniform who had dealt with them. Charles Rickton was in the process of being taken home on the proviso that he surrendered his passport. Over in Hull, Keith Elton would have the same condition imposed.

Simon Hayton had got into a taxi. He had left with the appearance of a broken man. Still with tears running down his face, the whole situation had left him distressed. It only confirmed what Jack thought. Simon was not their murderer. He was just someone in the wrong place at the wrong time.

Once he was finished downstairs, Jack headed out of the station. He wanted some fresh air ahead of spending the afternoon filling in reports. The whole case still troubled him, particularly the clues that had been missed. How could two men be killed in such gruesome circumstances without anyone knowing who did it?

Jack wandered through the streets, oblivious to what was around him. Nothing about the case made any sense. Without any specific place to aim for, he went where his feet took him.

If it was later in the day, that would be a pub. Approaching mid-morning, it could only be a coffee shop.

Jack walked into an old favourite near the Barbican Theatre. The tired-looking offering was one he knew well from the past. Danny, one of his informers, had used it as their meeting place. Now, it was just a usefully-located cafe. Jack went in, ordered a coffee, and headed over to a seat at one side.

Without being seen, a lady walked in behind him. She beckoned to the server to add another coffee to the order. She moved towards Jack, closing the space with her stealthy footsteps. Just as Jack was about to sit down, she struck from behind.

"Got you!" she announced, forcing Jack to spin with alarm.

He was met by the weathered face of Cathy Duggan. The sudden moment of surprise sent Jack's heart racing. His hand went to his chest as he stumbled forward. His instinct was to sit down on the nearest chair. "Sit down before you fall down," was something many a barman had said to him. That instruction had never been more appropriate.

"Don't do that to me," said Jack. "You'll finish me off."

"Sorry, I couldn't resist," grinned Cathy.

"Where did you come from?"

"I followed you from the station. I was going to call after you but then I began to wonder where you were going. Sneaking off like that, I thought you might have a fancy woman on the go."

"I struggle to keep up with one, let alone two."

"That's because..."

"That's because I'm old and knackered," interrupted Jack. "I might as well say it before you do."

"I've heard about getting your insults in first. Normally, they're directed at the other person," smiled Cathy.

"I'm saving you a job."

Cathy sat down opposite Jack. It coincided with two cups of coffee being brought across by the waitress. They smiled at the young lass and then waited for her to leave. Once she was finished, their conversation resumed.

"I wanted to speak to you," said Cathy. "It's nothing to worry about."

"I worry about everything," shrugged Jack.

"You don't need to worry about me," she smiled.

"Why do you say that?"

"Simon and I are finished. It's not a question of whether I think he's guilty, which I don't. It's just made me realise that we're not going to grow old together. We might as well face that fact now. I know we've just bought a house and all that but I don't love him. I thought I did but you know how it is."

"Why are you telling me this?" asked Jack.

"I don't know. I thought you should know. Don't worry, I'm not expecting anything from you. You've got Lisa and I'm happy for you. I don't want to be the one to ruin that. It's the first time I've ever seen you relax in the company of a woman. That should tell you something."

"It tells me that she's worn me down."

"You can joke all you like, Jack. Everyone can see it even if you can't."

"Where does this leave you?"

"It leaves me where I always was. I've got a job I love in a city I feel comfortable in. I'll rent somewhere for now and then buy myself something once Simon and I have sorted out the finances. He'll probably want to buy me out of the house in Fulford. It's a nice place."

"I wouldn't count on that."

"That's if you don't lock him up, of course."

"It's not that. I don't think the Simon you moved in with is the same one you'll see now. I can't see him continuing with the auction house. Not after everything that's gone on."

"He'll find something else. He's got more about him than you give him credit for."

"He must have," laughed Jack. "He tamed you."

"Who said he tamed me?" growled Cathy.

"You were happy to walk around in just a towel in front of him."

"Who said I only had a towel on? You've got no idea what I was wearing under it." With a wicked grin, Cathy Duggan finished her coffee and stood up from her chair. "Look after yourself, Jack. After all, you'll be seeing a lot more of me unless you start catching some of these murderers."

Jack forced a smile and felt a shiver go down his spine. He had no idea whether that was a promise or a threat.

***

Charles Rickton waited for the cover of darkness. He peered carefully through his front window and then hurried out the back door with his bag clutched in his hand. Inside were the clothes and the small amount of possessions he would need. He smiled. Did the police think he was stupid? Taking his passport was not going to do anything to control him. He had plenty of cash. His phone had been left in the kitchen. Without it, nobody was going to trace him.

Once he was clear of his house, he made the short walk to the car. The taxi was waiting where he had instructed. He threw the bag inside and eased onto the back seat. A middle-aged man looked over his shoulder without offering a smile.

"It was Hull, wasn't it, mate?"

"That's right. Hull docks."

"Which one?"

"The fishing dock."

"That's going to cost a fair bit. How are you paying for it?"

"Cash, and plenty of it, as long as you say nothing," replied Charles. He eased open his jacket and showed the man a stuffed bundle of notes.

"You're talking my language, sir."

Charles Rickton sat back and felt the warmth of the heaters blow on him. He slumped down and watched the city go past. He would not be returning for a long time. Maybe he would never return. His reputation was in tatters and a spell inside would do nothing to change that. There were other places he could go where he would feel welcome.

The driver headed out of the city past Tang Hall. With the traffic easing after the Friday rush, they made quick progress. It would be the largest fare the driver had taken in weeks. Only the occasional airport run was further though they were on the books. This was a cash fare that nobody would ever know about.

As Charles began to relax, his eyes drifted closed. Nodding off, it was hard to fight the tiredness that had accumulated in his body. Locked in that cell, he had been unable to sleep. He was not a man built for incarceration. They would not have dared do that to Henry Davenport. They should never have done it to him. They had taken liberties and it would not happen again.

The constant humming of the tyres on the road sent Charles into a deep sleep. His body had long since given up the fight to keep him awake. As the countryside slipped by, the driver maintained his silence. There was no need to wake him. His sole job was to deliver the man to his destination.

Through the early evening darkness, he maintained a constant speed until the outskirts of Hull came into view. The driver slowed, his eyes watchful for any police. The last thing he needed was a ticket to prove where he had been. He had picked one up just a week ago. Another would threaten his licence.

That need to avoid a penalty put him on edge. Bus lanes and yellow boxes became his mortal enemy. He observed them all, aware that his passenger was sleeping. He had made no mention of a deadline or what time whoever he was meeting would be expecting him.

The driver picked his way through the city's streets until the docks were staring at him. The greyness was illuminated by the lights from two boats. He slowed to a crawling speed and jolted the car to wake his passenger. Charles sat upright with a splutter and a cough. He stared out of the window and tried to acclimatise his eyes.

"Where are we?" he said in panic.

"Hull docks. Where do you want me to drop you off?"

"I'm looking for the Shirley Princess."

"What does it look like?"

"It looks like a fucking boat! What do you think it looks like?"

"Easy, mate. I was only wanting to know the type. Is it a small fishing boat or one of the large trawlers?"

"It's that one," said Charles as his hand shot towards a boat moored on the end. To his relief, it was one of the larger vessels.

The driver pulled up alongside it. Charles reached into his pocket and pulled out a wad of notes. He gave the man the agreed amount and then took out another two hundred pounds. It was pushed across and held firmly when the driver tried to take it.

"You never saw me, okay?"

"You got it. Safe travels," nodded the driver as the notes were released.

Charles Rickton grabbed his bag and got out. He hurried over to the Shirley Princess, checking in all directions as he walked. A man in a thick sweater and jeans came over to meet him. He looked like a gnarly old sea-dog who had seen years of service on the water. A withered rolled-up cigarette was held between his narrow lips.

"Brendan?"

"That's me."

"I'm Charles. Paul told me to come here."

The man smiled and nodded. He beckoned towards the boat.

"Get yourself tucked down below deck. There's a bunk down there you can sleep on and a change of clothes if you want something warmer. The crossing shouldn't be too rough if we get going straight away."

"I'm ready when you are."

"Then make yourself comfortable. We should be in Belgium by mid-afternoon tomorrow."

"Aye aye, skipper," grinned Charles Rickton. The man was the ticket to his new life of freedom.

Chapter 21

Jack rose early. He stared at the pile of clothes that was still filling his chair. His washing day had barely made a dent in it. It had not helped that his previous attempt to catch up had been left in the machine long after the cycle had finished. Everything had needed to be rewashed. Nobody wanted to smell of stale water even someone as unfashionable as Jack.

A late-night text exchange with Lisa had been the highlight of his evening. He had gone out and had two pints in the company of Alf. After that, the pub had got busy. Unable to face the noise, Jack had retreated to the sanctuary of his home. He had fallen asleep in his chair and had only made it to bed in the early hours.

Lisa had enjoyed a good night out with her parents. They had gone for a meal in a French restaurant close to her flat. It was fairly new and not somewhere Jack had been. Maybe they would break from their normal visits to an Italian and go there as a couple.

With her parents taking her bedroom, she had been left to sleep on the sofa. They had exchanged messages from their makeshift beds in their lounges. Jack was curled up in his chair while Lisa was under a duvet. Neither had much to say. It was just idle messaging and a promise to meet up once her parents were on their way back home. If it was before lunch, then it might be for food. If not, the pub would be calling their names.

Jack ignored the pile of clothes and went through to the bathroom. He shaved and then immersed himself in the shower. The water felt much needed to soothe the aches in his body. He was too old to sleep in a chair. And yet he never seemed to learn.

He stayed under the heat until he felt a shiver go through him. It forced Jack to get out before the cold overwhelmed him. He cursed when he looked at the empty rail. It meant a wet-footed march to the linen cupboard. Cursing his stupidity, he dragged at the pile and sent everything tumbling towards his feet. He picked a towel off the floor and carried it through to the bedroom.

Jack dried the remaining moisture from his body. He dressed quickly in the clothes he had worn the day before. Another armful was grabbed from the pile and taken down to the kitchen. He thrust everything into the machine and set it for the quickest wash. With the morning at his disposal, he would find it hard to shy away from some domestic chores.

The lack of food in the house forced him to go out to a cafe. Feeling hungry, he chose the nearest one. He ordered the full works and two cups of coffee to wash it down. A breakfast as good as the one they served would need more than one cup.

While he waited, Jack sent a text to Lisa. She responded quickly. Her parents would be staying for lunch, which would delay their meet-up until the afternoon. Jack thought for a moment.

Should he offer to go over to say hello? Common sense told him that was a treat to save for another day.

Instead, he agreed to meet Lisa in town once her parents were gone. It would give them the rest of Saturday and all of Sunday together. Louth had been clear that he wanted nobody working over the weekend. On Monday, they would be starting again from the beginning. He expected a fresh approach from his team.

"One full English and two cups of coffee," announced the waitress.

Jack thanked the lady and stared at the plate that had been put in front of him. It was packed with all the unhealthy treats he liked. The rest of the weekend would compensate with healthy offerings. It was a time for his palette to savour the taste of proper food.

He swept up a sausage and bit into the end of it. The feeling it gave him could not be replaced by anything without calories. He allowed the flavour to work its way through his taste buds. For the next few minutes, it would just be him and a plate of breakfast.

***

It was two-thirty by the time Jack walked into town. All his washing had been hung up and left to dry. In his hand, Jack clutched an overnight bag with a few essentials in it. He would be staying over for at least one night. The time for dancing around that issue was long gone even after the complications that Cathy Duggan had caused.

He felt for her and her realisation that Simon was not the man for her. She had been so happy when they had bought the house together. If it wasn't for the case, it could have worked for them. Jack was sure of it even if Cathy was not.

Jack met Lisa on the corner of Parliament Street. A quick hug followed the smiles they exchanged. In a display of public affection, they both looked comfortable. Neither had anything to hide from those around them. Not any more. Those issues were in the past.

"I take it you're staying over," she grinned.

"If I'm allowed to," beamed Jack.

"You're allowed to. You might need to help me do some washing first. I've not been able to do anything with my parents at home."

"As I told Louth, washing is one of my favourite activities."

"Not drinking?"

"That's exactly what he said," laughed Jack. "Careful, or you'll turn into him."

"And you'll get a slap," warned Lisa." Anyway, since when have you worried about what Louth says to you?"

"Since he told us that we had to start from the beginning again."

"What do you mean?"

"If we have to start from the beginning, I need to go to The Cellars."

"Why?"

"That's probably where I was when the first crime was committed."

"How's that going to help the case?"

"I need to interview Alf," grinned Jack. "Are you coming?"

"You know damn well I am," smiled Lisa. She took Jack's hand and curled her fingers around it. On a Saturday afternoon, with no case to think about, there was nowhere else she would rather be.

Chapter 22

The Shirley Princess docked in a small fishing harbour in Belgium at six o'clock on Saturday evening. Brendan had waited until darkness before he approached. It was not a watched port though it was no time to be complacent. His cargo was far too important to make a mistake. There would be consequences if things went wrong. Nobody needed to tell him that.

He tied up the boat with the help of the driver who was waiting. Once secured, he slipped below deck and walked slowly over to the bunk. Charles Rickton was still slouched on it. He had not moved for the entire journey and looked racked with sickness.

"We're here."

"About bloody time," he sighed. "That was horrendous."

"Look on the bright side. You won't be doing that again."

"You're damn right, I won't. I'm done with boats."

Charles grabbed his bag and threw it over his shoulder. He allowed Brendan to lead him out from beneath the deck. A quick check confirmed that it was safe for his onward travel. The two men shook hands. With a quick nod of their heads, Charles walked carefully along the gangplank. A hand from the driver steadied him as he stepped off.

"Welcome to Belgium, sir."

"Are you my driver?"

"I certainly am."

"Where are we going?"

"Paul is waiting for you. He's arranged your onward travel."

"Is he over here?"

"Yes, we had to get him out as well. It's all getting a bit hot in the UK."

"Is it far?"

"No, it's a warehouse around the corner."

"Why a warehouse?"

"That's where we export from. It made sense to use it."

Charles hurried over to the car. The driver opened the rear door for him. A respectful nod acknowledged the act of kindness. He was being treated like the gentleman he was. Not a criminal. He was someone of importance. The man who would take him to Paul Colyer respected that.

The driver got in and told Charles to buckle up. With his seatbelt fastened hastily, they drove slowly away from the dockside. The driver never stopped looking around, his eyes on permanent alert. It was no time to be caught by somebody he had missed. He turned out onto the main road and accelerated gently. It was another step towards Charles Rickton's freedom.

Just when Charles was beginning to get comfortable, the car pulled into an industrial zone on the left-hand side. Taking care not to attract attention, they drove slowly. Another left turn took them into a yard where a barrier opened. The conversation with the security guard sounded like it was in Dutch.

Once inside, they passed a lorry on the right. They went into a building through an open shutter door. As Charles stared out, he saw the warehouse around him. To one side were crates ready for export. On the other, bare breezeblock walls had created a series of rooms.

At the driver's insistence, Charles got out. With his senses on high alert, he clutched his bag and waited for Paul to come. It did not take long. He heard the footsteps approaching and then saw a figure emerge through a door. In the far corner of the building, a tall man was walking towards him. Dressed in a long woollen coat, his silvery hair sat proudly on a cruel-looking face. As he got closer, the scar on his cheek became visible.

"Paul?" queried Charles.

"Paul's on his way," the man grinned.

"Who are you?" asked Charles abruptly.

"I'm Freddie Sharpe. Freddie to you."

"Charles Rickton; pleased to meet you," he offered eagerly. He reached out his hand and was met with a frown.

"I don't shake hands. It spreads germs."

"Oh, right, no problem," insisted Charles.

"I take it you had a pleasant journey," said Freddie.

"I wouldn't describe it as pleasant."

"It got you here, didn't it?"

"I'm not complaining," lied Charles. "It was just what was needed."

"Brendan is very good at what he does."

"Where's Paul? Is he joining us?"

"Your companion will be here in a minute. As soon as he gets here, you two can be on your way."

"Where are we heading?"

"Don't ask me. I'm always the last to know."

"What about my business back home?"

"Stop worrying. We'll put someone in there to run it for you. When things have cooled down, it will be waiting for you."

"That's a relief. I would hate to think that Henry could muscle in."

"Henry?"

"Henry Davenport. He thinks we're rivals. It's laughable. We're miles ahead of his tinpot business."

"Rest assured, we'll make sure Henry is put in his place."

"Good man. That's what I like to hear."

Almost unnoticed, a man approached Charles Rickton from behind. He moved quietly, with his soft feet barely making a noise on the concrete floor. His presence was insignificant as he slipped into position. By the time Charles noticed him, he was within striking distance.

"Evening, Charles," he offered in a quiet voice.

Charles Rickton almost jumped out of his skin. The man behind him was close enough to touch. As he turned, his eyes stared at him. For those few seconds in his life, nothing made sense.

"Finn?"

Finn Mann smiled when he looked towards Charles Rickton. A glance across at Freddie was met with warmth. The older man appeared to have softened. There was a genuine sense of kindness spread across his face.

"It's good to see you made it over in one piece," said Finn.

"I don't understand. I thought I was meeting Paul."

"You are, well, sort of," he shrugged. "That's one of the names I go by. I have many others. Paul seemed to work for this one."

"But...but...what's all this got to do with you? You're just an auction porter."

"I needed someone on the UK side," grinned Freddie. "What's better than keeping it in the family?"

"Family?"

"Finn's my nephew. I'm very proud of him."

"But..."

"Come on, we need to get going," insisted Finn. "We need to get across the border tonight."

"Where are we going?"

"I'll explain on the way."

Charles Rickton's head was scrambled. Finn was somebody he only knew from the auction room. His sole interaction had been to load and unload furniture from his van. At times, there had been some harsh words. He had treated the lad like a servant.

"Happy travels," said Freddie. "Send me a postcard when you get there."

"But..."

Finn ushered Charles through a side door. There was no time to answer the questions that were bouncing around inside Charles's head. Was Finn the murderer of Dean Lucas and Shane Keyson or was that the work of Freddie? It made Charles's head hurt to think about it. He had to get away and yet Finn was his ticket to freedom.

***

Freddie Sharpe waited for the two men to depart. Finn had done well to close down the operation. Once their cover was blown, it was all about damage limitation. He had disposed of Dean and Shane and had got Charles Rickton out of the line of fire. The only anomaly left was Keith Elton. What did that matter? The guy knew nothing more than a delivery address and the code to recognise the crates.

Once he was alone in the warehouse, he walked back to his office. He had work to do if the next part of his plan was to come to fruition. Charles's business would be a nice addition as would the bonus he had offered up with Henry Davenport. With one less rival, the market would become his. York would be flooded with his products. Not just antiques. There would be goods flowing into every corner of the city.

He sat at his desk and allowed himself a moment to dwell on the past. There were historic wrongs that needed to be dealt with. It had been too easy to chase him out of the city and turn him into a pariah. Now the prodigal son would return. He would not be welcomed but what did that matter?

Such thoughts brought a smile to his face. He eased his feet up onto the desk and slunk further into the leather behind him. It would be his time to reclaim a city that was once his. No matter the resistance, York would soon fall under his spell.

A knock on the door interrupted his moment. He called out to summon his visitor in. The door opened slowly to offer up the sound of soft footsteps behind it. It was Finn, his smiling face a welcome sight in his office. In his hands was a towel, which was being used to dry his fingers meticulously.

"Is it done?" asked Freddie.

"It's done. Next time, you might like to get a bigger trunk if you're going to give me a fat bastard like that."

"How much did you get in?"

"Just his head, arms and feet. There was no way I was getting his legs in. They were like tree trunks."

"I can't believe he wanted to shake my hand," sighed Freddie. "Is Brendan coming for the rest of him?"

"He'll be here in twenty minutes. He'll dump everything on his way back."

"Good work, Finn. You and I are going places."

"Not as far as Charles will," he grinned. "Where do you want the trunk sent?"

Freddie thought for a moment. He traced his finger down the scar on his face. It brought a look that was crueller than the devil himself.

"Send it to Gregor Banks. Tell him it's about time he and I had a little chat."

Acknowledgements

Thank you to everyone who helped in the publication of this book. All contributions, no matter how small, were greatly appreciated.

THE KILLING GAME

AVAILABLE NOW

Nervously, he stumbled down the dark narrow corridor. The drink had not helped, the four double vodkas the minimum he needed to calm his nerves. His hands reached up, searching for somewhere that might offer balance. There was nothing. The recently plastered walls were smooth, offering the hint they would wipe clean easily. Maybe he was just one of many who had trodden the very same path.

"What are you doing?" he mumbled to himself. His thoughts turned to his wife and children at home. He had let them down. For too long, he had not been there when they needed him. If it all went wrong, he would never be there for them again.

He had to fight the uncertainty that was in danger of overwhelming him. After all, this was for them. This would allow them to be free of the burden of debt. It was a debt which he had caused.

He moved to the end of the corridor and paused when he felt the metal handle. This was the most important decision of his life. He could turn and leave at any moment. After all, he was in charge. That was what they had told him. It was his choice to do it, not theirs. He stopped and allowed that thought to go through him. A shake of his head confirmed his feelings. Who were they kidding when they said he could walk away?

In one direction, there was the opportunity to have a life. The other meant nothing. The world he was running away from would only hunt him down. With a deep breath, he gripped the handle and closed his fingers around it. He gave it a heavy twist and stumbled forward into the room. Despite his fear, he would confront whatever was awaiting him.

Inside, his opponent sat quietly. On the opposite side of a table, eager hands played with the chips that were set out. They were turned over between confident fingers. There was no mistaking the expertise with which it was done. They were hands that were comfortable with the small plastic discs and the value they represented.

To the right, a symbolic stack of money was piled up on the green felt surface. Not all of it; the full amount would not fit on the table. It was enough to signify its presence as was the gun which lay beside it. No doubt, it was loaded and ready to be used. The barrel was pointed in the direction of the empty chair. The money and the gun offered the two potential outcomes. The reality of it could not be ignored.

"Mr Brand, please take a seat."

The voice was not as harsh as he was expecting. That made it worse. It should have been a threat or at least a barked order. It should have demanded that he sit at the table. To his opponent, he was a piece of dirt on a shoe, a creature barely worthy of being there. The politeness felt unnerving as was the smile. He wanted to hate his opponent. That was difficult when no ill feeling had been offered.

"It's Darren," he replied.

He eased himself onto the simple wooden chair and pulled it up to the table. In front of him was a pile of poker chips, all stacked neatly for the game. A closer inspection confirmed their value. Darren totted them up in his head. There was half a million sitting there. Never before had he played for such high stakes. Whatever the outcome, he never would again.

"It's all there."

"Sorry; force of habit. In my line of work, everyone is out to rip you off."

"What is it you do?"

"I'm in the recovery game. You know, breakdowns. I mainly do trucks."

"That sounds like a lucrative business if you don't mind me saying so."

"Not as much as it used to be."

"I guess that is what brings us here. Have the rules of the game been explained to you?"

"Not really."

"Then let me oblige. We are playing heads-up Texas Hold'em poker. There are two half-million stacks, with starting blinds of five and ten thousand. The blinds will double every ten hands. If you win, you take the million in cash. I guess you don't need me to explain what happens if you lose."

Darren Brand looked directly at the gun. He was shaking. His eyes focused on the trigger which could end his life. He tried to drag his stare across to the money. He was fighting a losing battle against the tide of realism ripping through him.

"Where's the million?"

"In the case over there, minus what you see on the table."

"Can I count it?"

"If you want. The combination is six-six-six on both sides."

"The number of the beast."

"Appropriate, don't you think?"

Darren shrugged. What did he care if they wanted a joke at his expense?

"I won't bother, thanks. I'll trust you."

"Are you sure?"

"Yes; you've got a kind face."

"That's good because it might be the last one you ever see. Do you want to deal or should I?"

"Haven't we got a dealer?"

"It's probably best to keep this game to ourselves, whichever way it turns out. It leaves one less witness to worry about."

"I guess," sighed Darren. "You can deal."

His opponent smiled and picked up the deck. The cards were spread face down around the table. Flat hands moved them before they were brought back to a pile. Darren indicated where he wanted the cut, an act the dealer completed with confidence. A card was discarded and then a brief exchange of looks preceded two cards being placed face-down in front of each player.

Darren flexed his fingers. He bent them backwards until they offered a sickening crack. His opponent grimaced and watched him reach for his cards. The corners were eased upwards, to reveal the identity to eager eyes. All the while, both players scanned the table, hoping for clues. There was nothing; not even a flicker. Instead, two sets of eyes stared down at what had been dealt.

"I'll call you," said his opponent. Five thousand was pushed in to even up the blinds.

Darren processed the information. He had an off-suit ace and a king. It was a hand to back heavily in a one-on-one game. He tried to remain calm to offer no clues to his opponent whose eyes tore into him. He kept the bet simple and pushed thirty thousand across the table.

"I'll raise you," confirmed Darren. As he stared at his opponent, his whole body felt more sober.

"And I'll call you," came the immediate reply. A matching bet was pushed into the middle without a blink.

A card was discarded from the top of the pack before three cards were dealt. The king of diamonds, the jack of hearts and the two of clubs were placed face up in the centre. Neither player offered a hint of what they were thinking and yet it was close to being the perfect scenario for Darren. It gave him the top pair with an over-card to go with it.

Darren took a moment to think and then counted out his chips. It was up to him to make his bet. Seventy thousand was assembled into a pile. Another glance towards his opponent brought no reaction. Nor did the act of pushing the bet into the middle of the table when he announced that he was raising the pot.

There was an initial moment of silence. A hand reached up and was dragged across his opponent's chin. Those steely eyes stared venomously at Darren. They were searching for any fragment of information.

"I'll call."

The ace which followed made Darren's heart race. It was time for him to make his move. His hand pushed a stack of chips into the centre without them being counted out. His excitement didn't allow it. The need to get his chips into the pot had overtaken any requirement to play things cool.

"I'll raise you," confirmed Darren.

"And I'll raise you all in," was the immediate reply.

Darren looked shocked and stared at his opponent. The temperature of the room felt like it had increased by a few degrees. The sweat on his forehead was dabbed away with a hand. He pulled on his shirt. It was clinging to his beating chest.

He watched his opponent's chips being pushed confidently into the middle. He looked down at his own pile and released a loud sigh. He was committed. There was too much in there for him to fold when he had the cards to back up his bet. With a deep breath, his trembling hands pushed everything he had to the centre of the table. It was his life, his family and everything he had ever worked for that was eased away from him.

"I'll call," he said nervously. The tone in his voice gave away his fear.

The cards were flipped over. Darren offered up his two pairs. They were no match for the set of three kings his opponent revealed. He was beaten unless the final card produced one of the remaining two aces.

Across from him, his opponent did not show any emotion. When the last card was dealt, there was still nothing and yet Darren knew it was over. The disappointment at seeing the four of hearts would be taken to his grave. He slumped back into his chair and forced out a nervous smile.

"What happens now?" he asked, the question punctuated by the sound of a soft whimpering groan.

His opponent picked up the gun, cocked back the hammer and fired a single bullet directly between his eyes. Darren Brand's lifeless body slumped back into the chair. His problems were over. His debts would be taken to his grave. Opposite him, a sense of satisfaction spread through his opponent.

Death came with a cruel smile.

Printed in Dunstable, United Kingdom

71654932R00184